Tame the Beast

Book 4 of the Loverly Cave series

Daisy Thorn

Copyright © 2024 by Daisy Thorn

All rights reserved.

The characters and events portrayed in this book are fictitious. Any similarity to real persons, living or dead, is coincidental and not intended by the author.

No part of this book may be reproduced, or stored in a retrieval system, or transmitted in any form or by any means, electronic, mechanical, photocopying, recording, or otherwise, without express written permission of the publisher.

Proofread by Love and Edits.

Contents

Dedication	VI
A Note from the Author	VII
Playlist	VIII
Love Hive Chat Key:	IX
Prologue	1
1. Zoe	12
2. Zoe	24
3. Matteo	31
4. Zoe	35
5. Matteo	39
6. Zoe	46
7. Matteo	53
8. Zoe	60
9. Matteo	70
10. Zoe	79
11. Matteo	82

12.	Matteo	88
13.	Zoe	96
14.	Matteo	100
15.	Never Have I Ever	106
16.	Zoe	107
17.	Matteo	113
18.	Zoe	121
19.	Never Have I Ever	132
20.	Matteo	133
21.	Never Have I Ever	140
22.	Zoe	141
23.	Matteo	145
24.	Matteo	148
25.	Zoe	156
26.	Matteo	164
27.	Never Have I Ever	175
28.	Zoe	176
29.	Never Have I Ever	188
30.	Zoe	189
31.	Matteo	209
32.	Never Have I Ever	214
33.	Zoe	215

34.	Matteo	228
35.	Never Have I Ever	233
36.	Matteo	234
37.	Zoe	241
38.	Zoe	253
39.	Zoe	257
40.	Epilogue	267
Afterword		270
Acknowledgements		271
Also by		272
About the author		273

*For My Cougars
Who said age matters?*

A Note from the Author

Welcome to Loverly Cave Town, where we are expected to go through an interconnected series.

Please note that I cannot promise you won't encounter spoilers if you read the books out of order.

Tame the Beast is book FOUR of the series and drops hints here and there about characters from previous books. But with that being said, this book can be read as a complete STANDALONE.

Additionally, I do not recommend reading this book before you have read at least one of the first two book in the series. Grace and Luke's story is deeply intertwined with the other stories and may be hard to understand without proper context.

P.S. The book features explicit sexual content and is meant for mature audiences only. There are mentions of lactation, postpartum recovery and a lot of meddling from family members. This is a romantic comedy, and I urge you to not take anything you read here seriously. All details and facts have been extremely over exaggerated.

Playlist

Public – Make You Mine
Daniel Santoro – As Long As You Love Me
Patrik Jean – Numb
Meghan Trainor, Mike Sabath – Wave
Eight Waters – To the Moon and Back
Mark Ronson, Miley Cyrus – Nothing Breaks Like a Heart
Adele – Can I Get It
Chase McDaniel – Project
Panic! At the Disco – House of Memories
CYRIL – Stumblin'In
*Find complete playlist on Spotify
https://open.spotify.com/playlist/5zcVitPltrGlpA1hi8nMCB?si=07c00b7c54284eb2

Love Hive Chat Key:

- CookieJ – Jennifer Levine
- Ninasunshine – Nina Colson
- Willoflove – Willa Loverson
- Toughtolove – Fanny Lovesil
- Therunawaybride – Grace Levine-Colson
- Joydontpissmeofflevine – Joy Levine
- Tinyhousebigheart – Jacob Levine (Jacob is a special boy who took his wife's last name in marriage)
- Kevini'mnotNerds – Kevin Holstead
- Peaceforall – Random townie

Prologue

"Honesty is the key to a relationship. If you can fake that, you're in." – Richard Jeni

Zoe

Have you ever woken up in the morning, feeling the teasing rays of a spring sun caressing—or more like mocking—your skin with its false sense of warmth and just knew that everything is about to go to shit?

I have.

Today. This morning. I woke up scowling at the sun, accusing it of lying right to my face since spring in Chicago might as well just be called winter two-point-oh, or better yet an encore, and yet the star around which the earth orbits was glowing like a virgin around her long-lost crush.

So, if the sun was lying, then what could be said of everything and everyone else?

Does it sound like I have some trust issues?

I have. But I prefer to call it intuition derived from years spent honing that ability.

Still, I picked my sore body off the bed and tracked over to get ready for the day. I have no idea why suddenly my muscles decide to cramp up and hurt like tiny whiny assholes because I haven't worked them out anywhere near this level of strain.

I am a scientist, for Pete's sake. My version of work out is running down to the lab and back. But I do like to take care of my body, so I do some light cardio daily. Again, emphasis on the word "light," so, why in the world my back hurts like a mother…I have no idea.

I must've pulled a muscle when I was running around, playing fetch for my boss—the best, most awarded pathologist in the country, Doctor Joy Levine. Also known as the evil witch of the wicked seas in KePah University and really, everywhere else too.

The woman is abso-fucking-lutely brilliant when it comes to science and medicine, but human interactions, empathy or a sense of humor is as foreign of a subject to her as it perhaps is for me. And that is why I am the only assistant who has been able to stick around for longer than one week.

It's been two years since she came into my class as a substitute for one day and hired me on the spot.

Why, yes, maybe I am a little brilliant myself. But trust me, that didn't come naturally. It was rather honed out of me by years and years of hard work—and my mother's pressure on me. But that's just what you have to do if you want to end up in KePah University.

The place is like a Fort Knox of educational institutions. And my mother really wanted me to end up here.

And while it is absolutely *riveting* to dive into my childhood trauma, today is not the day for it.

Or for my back pain and intuition.

And although we are not friends, I respect her, and I want to be her when I grow up. Despite her running me ragged each and every day—hence my strained back. Probably. Most likely.

Because today is too important to feel off.

Tonight is our annual—ridiculous—awards ceremony and dinner at KePah University. It's the biggest thing of the year meant to honor the hard work of our faculty members throughout the year. KePah is very old and takes its traditions to extremes so when I say the awards dinner is not just a mere show to placate the employees, I mean it.

We are talking about a red-carpet—which is blue in our case—style event with high end catering, cameras and cocktail dresses that cost an arm and a leg. The kind you only wear once and then stick to the back of your closet to meet its maker or moths.

Every year, the board selects—supposedly fairly, but not really—a few of the most accomplished professors, deans, and so on, to present them with special awards. Followed by the fancy dinner I don't have to—don't want to—go to. Neither is it expected of me since I've never attended before being a mere assistant, but I will grit my teeth, don the over-priced dress I got and listen to the tedious talks and butt licking because my boyfriend is getting his award tonight.

It is still surreal to say that out loud. Justin Hunt is my boyfriend. The Justin Hunt. The brilliant cardiologist and a professor at our university. He, and my above-mentioned boss, Dr. Levine, worked on a project together for which they are being recognized tonight but that is also essentially how I really met him.

I was there every step of the way, helping and researching alongside them and Justin took notice of me. This god of a man with tall, lean figure, blond luxurious hair, and a dazzling smile, took notice. The most influential man on campus, the heir to the KePah dynasty, asked me out to dinner two weeks after we all started working together.

I had to pinch myself a few hundred times when he slipped into my office after hours, saying he could no longer hold back. Could no longer just watch me from afar and needed to ask me out for a dinner. Even if that was all I'd give him. He would take it.

I am not one of those girls who was ever easily impressed by a guy, but Justin? He took my breath away and I knew I was falling for him even before we made it to that dinner and a few dates later fell into bed together. Because Justin is someone who fits my life plan. He fits so well I still can't believe I found him. He is everything I've wished for since I was young girl—smart, well-established, career-driven—so, when he approached me, there was no way I was going to resist in any way, shape or form.

Sure, our relationship is not conventional. We don't see each other every day and sometimes it's only once a week or two, but we are both busy adults and I understand that. Even though sometimes I wish for more.

And maybe, just maybe, that weird feeling I woke up with has something to do with him taking the next step in our relationship? What if I am getting all these strange feelings because things are about to change and not in that dreadful way I am anticipating?

My brain is just programmed to think of the worst-case scenario. That is what I have been taught from a young age, and being a scientist doesn't help.

Putting away the thought of my childhood and current warning bells inside my head, I get ready and hurry to work, running around the fancy lab and helping Dr. Levine get ready for dinner tonight while pretending she doesn't still slightly terrify me after working together for so long.

I go through the motions of checking up on the bodies we are working on currently, finishing up the reports time on those and making sure her dress arrives on. Yet those warning bells I've tried to put away start blaring louder and brighter as the day goes on.

Especially after yet another unanswered text from Justin.

But I keep shoving them down further and further through the evening and the walk to the auditorium. I shove them down through the flashing lights from cameras that I avoid because that kind of attention was never my thing. I shove them down through some mindless conversations with a few colleges who have also come out tonight.

I shove them down and down until I am so numb and have convinced myself that the world is made up of unicorns and rainbows. I don't realize I've shoved my heart so far down, it is numb to what my brown eyes are seeing. To the shift in the atmosphere.

I don't realize that it is *my* boyfriend in a perfect black tux with a woman on his arm. A gorgeous—even if it's in a fake kind of way—woman clinging onto him with her nose tipped up as if the rest of the world is beneath her. And why wouldn't she feel that way?

That is exactly how Justin Hunt makes me feel. Only naïvely, I didn't realize I wasn't the only one. He has someone else. Somehow in the span of one week I haven't seen him, he found someone else. Someone so important he brought her with him to show the rest of the world. And he looks so damn happy with her there, blessing everyone with that blinding smile of his.

But then what was I?

Justin is shaking hands with everyone around them, accepting congratulations on his award while the woman at his side bristles with pride, and runs her hands all over him as if to make sure there isn't a single soul in here who doesn't realize the claim she has on him.

And what a claim it is...

Forget a simple shift in the atmosphere. It's a full-blown earthquake inside my chest.

I must still be too numb, too crumbled beneath the rubble of my heart, otherwise I am sure my knees would give way when my eyes fall onto her arm, the one she has him in a death grip with. There, just at the end, where the ring finger is, lays a diamond so big I'm not sure she's able to lift her hand up with that on it.

Additionally, there is a platinum band on his ring finger as well. One I've never seen before.

He got married in a week? Or was he seeing her at the same time as me?

Oh, hell...Zoe...stop being a naive fool.

Late night calls. Seeing each other so scarcely. Unanswered texts. Avoidance of showing me his place or to make our relationship public...

No, he didn't just get married. He was married. He *is* married.

I have been in love with a married man for a year.

I have been dating a married man for a year.

Suddenly, all the pieces of our dysfunctional relationship fall into their rightful place. It all makes perfect sense. It all *fucking* makes sense, and despite the PhD I earned I was stupid enough not to see the biggest lie right in front of nose.

I should walk right up to him and claw his face out. I should damage that blinding smile of his and make sure everyone sees him for what he is, but I don't.

Instead, I turn and run as fast as I can, because after an earthquake there is generally a tsunami that follows. And the waves of mine are washing up the shores already. Alongside a healthy dose of nausea.

Fuck you, sun.

You won't fool me twice. Yesterday I might have fallen for your lies and false sense of warmth but not today. Not after I saw through the fuzzy sunrays and revealed the murky skies full of lightning and thunder.

Yes, I might be completely losing it because I am having conversations inside my head with the sun. But since everything else is going to shit why not add insanity into the mix? Obviously, I've been having the symptoms for a while now with all the weird emotions, nausea, and sore back.

It doesn't help that I couldn't get a wink of sleep the whole night—tossing and turning, searching in my head for the answers to questions I've been asking myself far longer than just last night.

Why? What is so wrong with me that I am the one being lied to all the time? What is so wrong with me that I am not deserving of that love I so desperately want. Maybe I should know better...

Jesus, how could I be so naïve?

Me!

A person, who is basically a know-it-all in deceit and lies department since I was born, fell for it blindly. But just because we are parched for some water, doesn't mean the sand will magically become it.

Once again, I feel the stinging sensation crowding the sides of my eyes as my chest tightens and my stomach recoils from pain and agony and I want to—so desperately want to—curl up and let the destruction within me lose once again. I want to just give in to the weakness begging me to give up and admit defeat, but I can't.

I won't.

I won't allow another man to walk all over me again. Those men can go to hell and take those sneaky tears with them while I will keep going. Keep climbing up. Keep living and proving that I am worth it.

Only, my resolve lasts all of one hour before I make my way into the lab in hopes of distracting myself with work, yet as soon as I step inside the chilled building with beautiful architecture, memories of us hit me like a train wreck. The first touch happened just there below that white table where he was explaining his idea to Dr. Levine and me.

It was barely a caress, yet his eyes snapped to mine right that second, and I had to suck in a lungful of pungent, formalin-scented air around us to keep from falling off that stool. I remember telling myself it was nothing and I shouldn't get any ideas but the next day he did it again and this time there was no mistaking his intention. Or shall I say, lie…

The first kiss we shared was right around the corner, in the hallway where anyone could see us, but Justin said he didn't care, actually his exact words were, "Let them see who managed to get the prettiest scientist all to himself."

And I melted like an ice cube in the dessert.

Evaporated straight into him.

When in reality, he chose the time of day when no one but me was in the lab. There would be no one to walk in and see anything.

The memories assault me from each corner and all of a sudden, the only thing I want is to drop to the cold, tiled floor and wail like a baby once again. I am not a crier, so just why the hell am I feeling so much all of a sudden? Why is this pain raging and blasting through me like a serrated knife?

Breathe, Zoe! Time will heal you. And maybe a few cut off penises, even if they come from the corpses in our lab. It will still make me feel better.

I have just managed to put on my lab coat without breaking apart when a voice startles me.

"Zoe?" I whip around—or more like jump out of my skin while clutching my heart—to see my boss frowning at me from the door to her office.

"Oh my God, Dr. Levine," I say in a breathless voice, and I swear I see a small smile tug on the corner of her lips.

What is this? The official apocalypse? In two years, I've never once seen her smile.

"Sorry to spook you. What are you doing here?" she asks me when I should be the one asking her that.

Dr. Levine never shows up on Saturdays, therefore, I thought it would be a safe space for me to hide and distract myself today.

"Um, I-I'm always here on Saturdays. Catching up on work." I stumble on my words slightly because she still frightens me at times. Joy Levine is beyond beautiful with her long, rich dark brown hair, dark, deep eyes that seem to see more that you are willing to show and a lush curvy figure that turns nearly every male eye, however, I haven't seen her give anyone a time of day. Not once.

Dr. Levine is the epitome of a gorgeous workaholic.

"You are?" she asks with surprise because I've never told her I come to catch up on work during the weekends. Because like an idiot I was always alone during them, believing my boyfriend had study groups, conferences or business meetings.

"Y-yes. Um, there is a lot to do, and I can't quite do it all during normal hours," I admit to my inadequacy and cringe, dropping my head down as I await her lashing out that I'm too incompetent to finish the basic tasks she gives me during the week, yet it doesn't come.

Nothing comes out of her mouth for a long, pregnant minute, forcing me to lift up my eyes and only then I see her shoulders drop, the hands she had twisted in front of her chest, loosening and her face morphing into a weird mask of confusion, pain and sympathy?

"Zoe, go home, I'll take care of it today," she finally says with a long exhale and all I can do is blink in return.

"Um, what?"

"Go home; I got this today." She waves me off.

"But you're never here on Saturdays." The words tumble out of my mouth before I can think better of them because who the hell do I think I am talking to her like this but once again she doesn't give me that death glare I expect. No, her eyes are full of some other emotion I can't understand.

"Well, that's no longer true, and I'll be here all the time from now on." Bitterness. That's what I see in her eyes. "So go, live your life. Don't be stuck like I am."

Live my life? No, thank you. I have tried and tried again but living my life is not for me. "Um, if you don't mind, could I stay?"

Dr. Levine pierces me with an assessing gaze, and I wish I would take her offer of leaving because like I said before, my boss seems to see way more than anyone else, and asks me, "What's wrong, Zoe? What happened?"

"N-nothing." My voice shakes, the truth just begging to be allowed to climb out and spill right at her feet. To share this pain with someone else but I don't exactly have any friends and my boss seems to be the last person who I should spill all of my crappy life choices to. I can't. However, Dr. Levine keeps pushing and when she utters my name in that authoritative doctor's voice of hers, I break.

I break into messy, ugly wailing. That beast inside my chest squeezing my insides all too hard. *Why does it hurt so much?*

"Please, let me stay here. I can't go home today. Please," I plead, because even in a room full of memories I feel better than alone in my small apartment where all I have are my own vicious thoughts to be lost in.

But is this any better? What is wrong with me? Why can't I stop crying? And in front of my boss nonetheless. Damn it.

Out of nowhere, I feel Dr. Levine's hand on my shoulders, patting me awkwardly like that action is a foreign gesture for her.

"Zoe, how about you calm down and tell me what happened so I can help you, okay? I don't have solutions for tears; I need real words." Damn it, I am messing up everyone's day today, and now my boss has to deal with my antics which makes me sob even harder, shaking under her touch. "Zoe!" she calls out in a demand, and that right there does the trick.

"I saw him with his wife," I mumble out, the admission to my failure tumbling out of me without my permission and evidently it shocks her just as much as me because all of a sudden, she grows stiff next to me.

"You saw who?" she says almost in a whisper but still wielding it with authority and a dark edge I haven't seen before.

I swallow hard before answering her, but maybe I swallowed too much of my sanity along with that lump because I spill it all. Along with more damn tears. "My boyfriend. My stupid, stupid boyfriend. The one w's been lying to me for the past year. He is fucking married, and he showed up with his wife at the ceremony yesterday."

Instantly, Dr. Levine's naturally golden-toned face pales and she says softly, "Zoe, are you talking about Justin?" My eyes snap up to hers so fast, I felt my irises strain.

"H-how did you know?" Oh, God, please don't tell me she knew this whole time? Knew that I was stupid enough to date a married man and make a fool out of myself. Did she catch us after all?

I am awaiting her to tell me what an idiot I am or at least look at me with disgust when something so unexpected happens, I am lost for words.

She laughs.

Laughs.

A belly-deep, tears-down-your-cheeks kind of laugh but it had a sardonic note. But she keeps laughing and laughing as if some kind of dam broke loose inside her and now, she can't stop. I even forget to be concerned that she might be laughing at my pathetic self in my worry for her.

"Doctor Levine? Are you okay?"

"Oh, Zoe, I think we need to move on to first name basis after this," she says, while wiping the tears underneath her eyes, as she keeps laughing but not as hard anymore and takes a long, assessing look over my whole body, glancing over my ordinary blonde hair, dull brown eyes and an unflattering figure that I tried to work hard on for Justin but could never get to be an extra small in size. I am not as beautifully curvy as Joy is, but I am not skin and bones either. Like I said, unflattering. But the way she watches me makes me want to tug on my coat to hide it all.

Jesus, what is going on?

After a moment, she looks up and says, "I guess he has a type. Shame his wife doesn't really fit the bill, huh?" I feel my brows furrow further into confusion at her comment.

"What are you talking about, Doctor Levine?"

"Joy," she says all of a sudden and before I get a chance to ask why she is telling me her name that I already know, she dumps an atomic bomb on my already shattered heart.

"Women whom I have shared a boyfriend with get to call me Joy."

1

Zoe

"My best birth control now is just to leave the lights on."
– Joan Rivers

Whoever created the saying, "It can't get any worse..." clearly needs to get an MRI and a CT scan, along with a full bloodwork and neuropsychological testing. Hell, let's add a urinalysis, just in case as well. Because I swear, I see two pink lines but also, I shouldn't be trusted with determining anything at this point since clearly my eyesight has left the building ever since I met Justin. No, scratch that. I am simply blind because there is no other explaining for how I got myself into this situation in the first place.

But those are two pink lines, right?

Well, ten of them from the five tests laid out in front of me, but I must be seeing double from so many lines. Yeah, that's it. Those are not really two lines, just my shit eyesight. And the never ending throwing up is simply me still being disgusted with Justin's betrayal two weeks later.

Two weeks. It has been two weeks since the night I swore to never stuff my intuition up my ass. Two weeks of having sleepovers with my toilet bowl and then piling myself up with so much work during the day that I simply didn't have the time to go throw up some more.

But it was also two weeks of eye-opening and clarity that I have never had before. That next morning after the night I—and pretty much everyone else—found out about Justin's *wife*, life turned upside down.

My boss, whom I was slightly scared of, became my best friend and comrade in Justin's betrayals, and I guess the sun does shine up on you when you are below the crap level because I could not be any more grateful for her. If not for Joy, I would probably still be wallowing in misery and participating in self-destructive thoughts like "what's wrong with me?" or "why can't nobody ever love me?" and so on.

But Joy put those to rest real fast.

She's good like that. She knows when to yell at you until your brain cells snap back in place or shake you until you realize it wasn't you. It was always him.

Justin is the issue here. He is the manwhore who could never have enough, and it finally caught up with him when over the last couple of weeks, the students he thought it was a good idea to sleep with, decided to come forward and do a little tell all.

Yeah, Justin Hunt is in deep crap now and it almost makes up for everything he has done. Him losing his precious status *almost* makes up for the fact that I was all but a toy to him. A pretty, willing distraction when he needed one. And not once did he try to contact me or offer a single explanation for anything.

Joy got one, but not me.

Because who am I?

Just some silly, little assistant he could use and forget.

No, I need to snap out of this! I need to remember what Joy said. *"Forget the asshole like dust under your bed. Sweep it and throw it away or else you will keep sneezing."* But it was much easier to keep on track when she was here, working alongside me. However, Joy had to leave a few days ago to go see her father who had been diagnosed with cancer—or that's what she was told at least—and now I am all alone.

Well, it's me, the toilet bowl and…ten pink lines.

See? Things could definitely get much, much worse.

A week later I can no longer pretend. I can no longer play the role of a naïve, in denial girl, hoping that somehow five different brands of in home tests were all faulty because my vomiting doesn't cease its fit. My period is nowhere to be seen, breasts are slightly larger and hurt like a mother… And those ten pink lines turn into elevated hCG levels on the blood test I drew myself late at night when there was no one else around.

When not one soul could see me sliding down the wall as my tears ran down my cheeks. When no one could question why I smashed half of the glass tubes in the laboratory or why I cried out and kept asking the universe, *"WHY? WHY? WHY?"* nonstop.

Through my tear-coated eyes, I look down one more time to the paper clutched tightly in my fist where the simple, English, black letters on white, printing paper state one simple truth…

I am pregnant.

Very pregnant.

Very alone and pregnant.

Very screwed, alone, and pregnant.

I am pretty much every kind of pregnant except the happy and excited one, and I think that kills me more than the fact itself.

Becoming a mother never did make it to my life plan. It never seemed like an option with everything I want to accomplish, yet…

Yet before I even think of jotting down the pros and cons or do any of my regular pragmatic brain crap, my heart has decided to take charge and decide that I will have this baby.

And I will protect her or him with all I've got.

Despite the tears still making their exit, I let out a long shaky breath, look down at my still flat stomach and lay my shaky hand on top of it.

"It's you and me, little one. Just you and me." Strangely, talking to the tiny life growing inside of me—the one I never saw coming—fills my heart with a whole new emotion, one I don't understand, yet it makes me smile. A small, unsure lift to the corners of my lips but a smile, nonetheless.

Gently, I draw the palm of my hand across my stomach. "I hope you are ready for this, bug. Because I am not sure I am."

I don't know what being a mom is, mine never bothered to show me.

But hell, I'll crawl to the finish line, dragging myself there on sheer will if I must, but I will give this baby the best life I can.

After I finally sit down and write *"the plan."*

So, I am giving myself another two minutes to pity little poor me, to pop the last balloons of illusion I've created, to cry and scream in the empty lab until I cut that crap right out. I am giving myself the last two minutes to allow Justin Hunt into my head. The very last two to send him to the lowest pits of hell for making me fall for him. Because he doesn't deserve a second more.

"Deep breath in and out," I instruct myself, and do just that. Then squaring off my shoulders, I step over the pile of broken glass, pull my chair out and get my notebook out.

<u>My Life Plan two point oh</u>

1. Stop crying.

2. Forget the asshole exists.

3. Call my dad.

4. Call Joy.

5. Schedule an appointment with an OB.

6. RESEARCH!!!

7. Live my best life as a single mom.

8. Give my baby the best life.

9. FORGET MEN!!!

There. Now, I can do it.

I know, what an "impressive" list, but I already had one of these made at fifteen years old, and I have crossed off nearly every point I had on there. I graduated high school with honors. I got into the best university in America. I work for the one of the most accomplished pathologists in the world and I even had that picture-perfect man...but look what it got me in the end...

A lab full of broken glass and a positive pregnancy test...

So, it's time to try a different approach.

Call me a coward but it took me a few weeks to call my dad. Even now as my finger is hovering over his name a part of me is terrified of letting it slip and hit dial.

It's not that I think he would yell at me. Not at all. It's that I don't want to be a disappointment to him after all he's done for me. But every day that has gone by without me talking to him, has been killing me.

I take a deep breath and press on his name.

"Hey, Dad."

"Zoe girl!" He greets me with excitement like he always had. "You need to call your old man way more often than this! I haven't heard from you in a few weeks, and I was about to send out a search owl."

I can't help the chuckle that escapes me. "Dad, since when are there search owls?"

"Since my daughter forgot me and I had to train one."

"Mhh." I roll my lips to stop the laugh. "And how is that going for ya?"

"Oh, it's going great. Beth knows your scent and I had her find that shirt you left the last time you were home and she brought it to me. Well, she pointed her beak that way, so you better watch out."

Beth is my dad's twenty-year-old owl who has no interest in flying, let alone chasing his missing daughter across the country, but that is why I love him. Kevin Holsted is ridiculous and hilarious and so loving, this world doesn't deserve him.

And neither did my mother.

Well, that woman didn't deserve anyone, if we are honest here, so it's no wonder both my biological sperm donor left her, and my stepdad—who I consider my father—did too.

No, Kevin is not the man who I share a DNA with, but he is the one who's always been more of a parent to me than anyone else, and I think him seeing how my mother treated me was what made him snap, pack his and my clothes, and leave her when I was sixteen.

I still remember that day and I can still feel the sting of my cheek where she slapped me.

Life with Kelly Jones-Holstead was hard but not in the physically abusive way. No, up until that day, she never touched me like that. It was always her words that did the trick.

My mother is a demanding, cold, overachieving bitch and she never did anything to hide that fact. And everyone in her life was supposed to live up to her standards; if we didn't, she made sure we knew how displeased she was with us.

My biological father left when I was a newborn and apparently, it was my fault because based on her words, I cried too much as a baby and he couldn't listen to it anymore...

Like I said, she wanted everyone to live in her form of perfection and somehow, she was lucky to find Kevin when I was around five years old, and that man took all her shit until that one day.

He helped me with homework so she wouldn't yell at me if I got a bad grade. He covered for me when I wanted to go hang out with friends instead of studying like she preferred I do twenty-four-seven.

Even when I was six years old.

He was the man who taught me how to ride a bike, swim, cook and drive a car. He was the one who signed me up for dance and showed up for the competitions because mom always thought it was a waste of time and I should just do more Spelling Bees.

Don't get me wrong, I enjoyed school, and I was good at it, but not to the manic point she wanted me to.

In all honesty, I think Dad stayed with her for as long as he did because of me. Because he knew she would ride me to death if he wasn't there, but eventually, even his angelic patience ran out and thank God for it. I was legally his daughter by that time, so we finally left and never looked back.

Sucks that same can't be said about all the trauma she left me to deal with.

"I think you should give her a little break in training and all since here I am, calling you."

"Fine, fine, we will stop for now. But stay vigilant. Beth will come for ya." This time I do finally let out a loud laugh and he joins in on the other end.

"Oh God, thank you for this, Dad. I really needed a good laugh right about now," I admit to him, wiping the tears off my eyes.

And just like that all the humor is gone as if he can sense why I am calling. "Zoe? What's going on, honey?"

Shit, I had this whole plan of what to say to him—yes, I wrote out another list or ten in the last two weeks—but now my smile is replaced with those tears I promised not to have anymore, and my words get lost.

Damn it, I keep deviating from my plan. I keep messing it up because I cry way more than I should and I still think about the bastard when I shouldn't at all.

But how could I not when he didn't even bother to say "Hello" to me when we crossed path in the hallway the other day. No, he was just casually walking with a suitcase in his hand—he must've just come back from seeing Joy in Loverly Cave—and all I got from him was a nod.

A nod!

After a year of what I thought was a loving relationship. It has been over a month since the awards ceremony and all I got was a nod.

I almost let it go. I almost kept walking in the other direction when my pathetic heart decided to give him one last chance. I turned around, and looking at his retreating form, I said, "I'm pregnant."

Justin stopped dead in his tracks, freezing right there on the spot before slowly turning to face me. A part of me—that desperate one—wanted to believe he would react somehow, I don't know, positive? Maybe he'd be happy?

But once again, I was proven wrong when the bastard opened his mouth. "And what? Need me to pay for the abortion?"

There. That was that final snip.

"The only thing we will abort are your balls. Want me to pay for that?" I told him with a deep sneer he's never seen on my previously docile face.

"So what do you want from me? Be a daddy? Sorry to break it to you, but I'm not interested," he said with that sweet disgust.

The blood in my veins was reaching a dangerously high level, threatening to claw his lying tongue out but I still managed to say, "The only thing I want from you is a signed document saying you give up any and all rights to my baby."

"I knew you were smart," he answered with a patronizing smile. "I'll send it your way by the end of the day. In return, you'll send one that says your offspring won't come after me at any point in life."

My offspring. *My*.

At least there was one thing already that we shared with my baby. Both of our sperm donors were useless assholes.

I walked away from Justin, sending him the document he wanted, and in return got one I requested that same minute. I told myself it didn't matter, that I could do this alone and keep the job I loved so much without being affected by seeing him day-to-day and I kept selling that delusion to myself because I was a strong, independent woman but damn it, it still hurts so fucking much.

It hurt when he dismissed his child this easily. Discarded her just like me.

Strong women can hurt too. We can feel too much too. We can be in pain and dying on the inside with none-the-wiser, and that's what I am doing right now.

"I-I am okay now."

"What does 'now' mean? When were you not okay and why haven't I heard about it until *now*?"

I take a deep breath and decide to just spit it out. "I'm pregnant."

Silence.

"Dad?" I ask, worried. I should have FaceTimed him. That way I would at least see it if he had a heart attack from my news, but instead, I'm left in the dark and the longer the silence stretches the higher my panic levels are rising. "Daddy, please say something!"

He clears his throat. "You are pregnant." It's not a question, more of an amazed statement like I have just told him the best news ever. "You are not joking right now like I was about the whole owl search rubbish, right? You wouldn't do that to your old man."

"Nope, I am not joking in the slightest."

"Oh, thank the Lord," he exhales loud enough for me to hear it over the phone. "Zoe girl, how dare you tell me that I'm going to be a grandpa over the phone when I can't hug you right now!"

"Um, well frankly I had no idea you would react like...that."

"And how else am I supposed to react when my daughter gives me the best news ever?"

"I don't know, maybe tell her she's an idiot? Or tell me how irresponsible I am or ask what I was thinking...or hell, ask me about the father of the baby? Aren't you mad that I am not married and having a baby?" I fling my arms up and down while pacing around the airport—I'll get back to that—spilling all the insecurities that have been building up in my head over the past few weeks.

"First of all, my daughter could never be called an idiot. And I mean, *ever*!" he deadpans. "Secondly, if you wanted to be yelled at, I can send you your mother's phone number. She was always good at yelling for no reason because there is none here. And finally, I assumed he was not in the picture since you've never told me about him. You tell me about all your boyfriends, and I don't care to know about your one-night stands or whatever it is you kids call it these days."

Great, let's add shame for lying to my dad to the ever-growing list of my fuck ups because I never did tell him about Justin.

That should have also been a warning sign to me. The fact that I didn't want to introduce Justin to him should have made me realize my instincts were telling me something. It was as if my brain was left on an island, lighting up SOS signs with fire and all that stuff and I kept flying over it without notice.

"I was seeing someone for a while, Dad, I just never told you about him since he was my boss. Well, my boss's boss and I didn't know how to explain that."

"I think you did it fine just now," he grumbles, clearly not happy I kept it from him. "So, is he or is he not going to be a father?"

"No. He is not."

"Does he know?"

"Yes."

"And?"

"And he asked if I needed him to pay for the abortion."

Silence echoes through the phone with only dad's harsh breathing on the other end. After a few beats, he says, "He doesn't deserve to be in your life then."

"No. He doesn't."

"But maybe keep the door open if one day he realizes his mistake?"

And I wonder where I got my hopeless heart from. Dad and I might not share any blood, but I certainly do take after him.

"Dad, you know how you wish my mom never happened in my life?" I ask but keep going without his answer. "Well, I wish for this baby to never know that lying piece of garbage. The only good thing he did was show us all his true colors." I'm fuming now, but I'll take anger over tears any day.

"That's not the only good thing," Dad says. "He also contributed his particles to my grandchild."

"Daaaad," I groan because leave it up to him to snap me out of my rant just like that. "You are well over the blushing age. You can use the word *sperm*."

"I prefer particles because I don't like to think about some bastard with my little girl like that, okay? Let me be happily oblivious." Little girl being a twenty-nine-year-old woman. Sure.

"Sorry to disappoint but that's called delusional." Right at that moment, a loud voice speaks, announcing that my flight is about to be boarding.

"Where are you?"

About that...I ended up calling Joy before my dad which was a good thing, seeing as she curbed my panic from seeing that damn paperwork Justin sent me. She could sense something was off and told me to come to her. Not asked. Joy doesn't waste time like that. Nope, it was an order that I gladly took.

I didn't tell her about my pregnancy when she asked what was wrong, but I could hear her loud and clear without having her tell me that we would be discussing whatever this was as soon as I landed.

"In an airport."

"Why?"

"I am going to see my boss. She's in California now."

"Okay, and when are you coming back?"

"In a week."

"Great, then I'll see you in a week."

"What? You're coming for a visit?" I ask, now excited to be coming back to Chicago because I don't see my father enough. He is up in our hometown in Oregon, and unfortunately, it is not as easy for us to make it over to one another with my crazy work schedule.

"No, honey, I'm moving to Chicago."

"What?" I screech.

"I can't be the best grandpa across the whole country now, can I?"

"Dad, you don't need to do that. At least not yet. How about we talk once I'm back, and you wake up on the rational side of the bed?"

"Now who's the delusional one?" I can hear the smirk in his voice. "Rational was never my thing."

We say our goodbyes and he promises me to not make any life-changing decisions without us talking about it first, and for the first time since I read those test results, I feel something change in me. I am still scared but I'm no longer destroyed over what Justin did.

Maybe him severing that last cord between us did the trick. Maybe it was my dad's support.

Or maybe...it's this weird, giddy feeling I've had in my gut ever since I bought this ticket.

The feeling of rightness.

As I hear my boarding group being called up and get into my seat, I feel almost excited for this new chapter in life. Something is calling my name in Loverly Cave, and I can't wait to explore it.

2

Zoe

"Home is people. Not a place." – Robin Hobb, Fool's Fate

Welcome to Loverly Cave Town where love is the answer to any question.
Population three thousand one hundred and four.

I fell in love with this quirky, little town the moment we hit the town limits, and got a glimpse of it from up the hill as the car rode down the curvy roads.

Loverly Cave was nestled in a valley between tall, bulging, lush green mountains protecting it from one side and a vast, powerful, and that kind of cold ocean that was giving me the chills from all those miles away was washing up the shores of the other side. The famous cave—which looked more like an arch—for which the town was named was standing proud and tall, keeping watch of all its residents.

It was rumored that if two people tied the knot under the cave their union would last a lifetime and then some, and I wish I was still the kind of person who believed in superstitions. This seemed awfully romantic.

And something I'd love to do before Justin happened in my life. Now all I wanted was to just get through the next seven months. But still, I could appreciate the beauty and love around me, wrapping me into a warm, fuzzy cocoon.

As we drove into the town the colorful buildings—and I literally mean every color known to mankind—greeted me. Ivy crawling up the sides of some lined every cobbled street. Silly-named stores and cafes like: Sip of Love coffee shop, Love & Peace bar, Fifi's Goods, Tough Love gym, B&B (Bagels and Balance) Cafe, Peace-out Diner and more were scattered all over.

There were also three "therapy" cars driving around, offering their help free of charge. Those were: Love Car, Peace Car and Hug Car and they alone made me smile, not to mention all of the happy locals strolling around the town, smiling, laughing and waving at us like we are good friends.

After living for so long in a busy city amongst cutthroat professionals this type of behavior seemed almost foreign. And that moment was the first time I had asked myself if I wanted to raise my child in a big city surrounded by doom and gloom.

And for the first time I wasn't sure anymore. But it would be crazy to add a move across the country when my life is already insane as it was, so I pushed that thought out my head and just enjoyed the day looking around, smiling, waving back until we arrived at the beach in front of three cottages.

One was blue, the other one yellow and the one I was being led to was the cutest bright pink cottage in the middle of them. This one—surprisingly—was Joy's residence that she along with two of her sisters—Hope and Grace who got the other two – were conned into buying by their mom and her best friend but recently and very much surprisingly Joy's life took a wild turn, one that brought a sexy Viking into it and what left me even more stunned was the fact that she actually moved in with the guy into his tiny house of all places.

What type of magic he wielded over her is a mystery to me but since she no longer uses this cottage she offered me. To keep. Like forever.

Well, she offered me the bare walls of a one-bedroom cottage from the seventies with an unfinished loft, puke-yellow kitchen and camping gear, but still I broke down in tears once again. Apparently, crying was the horrible side effect of my pregnancy.

As if all the vomit, breast pain and back ache wasn't bad enough. *No, Zoe had to be extra sensitive and having her friend show her kindness can drop her over the edge.*

"Jesus Christ, what is it with females surrounding me and their never-ending Niagara Falls?" Joy mutters under her breath and placing her hands around my shoulders, shoves me down into a forest green camping chair.

"W-why? I-is there a-a camping c-chair inside the house?" I manage to get out through the sobs that still haven't ceased.

I hate crying. But I would like some credit for keeping it together since the freaking airport. Because let me tell you, seeing your grumpy boss slash best and only friend waiting for you at the airport, standing there with her arms crossed across her chest, her foot tapping away and her face in a mask full of concern and worry was very cry worthy for me! She even promised not to start the mile long questioner until after I was settled even though she kept watching me with her narrowed eyes as if seeing all the secrets I was harboring anyway.

And then there was meeting Grace—Joy's youngest sister—who came out to pick me up as well was strike number two against those tear ducts because no one else ever showed me so much kindness except my dad. She ran up to me, with a wide smile on her face, wrapping me in a bone-crushing hug even though we've never met before. And then the keep-the-cottage-if-you-want comment.

Yeah, that broke me. Just like that. She offered me her house just like that.

"There is a camping chair because miss 'I-am-not-staying-in-this-town' aka your boss Joy here refuses to get real furniture," Grace answers and smirks at her older sister.

There Levine women were blessed with superior genetics and wit. I haven't met Hope yet, their middle sister, but I could imagine she looked just as beautiful as these two. While I was contemplating suing every pregnancy website and book that has lied to me and told me the weight gain will be noticeable during third trimester, yet I keep growing more and more each day.

I don't even have any pants to wear anymore. Andddd here comes a fresh wave of absolutely ridiculous tears.

Over pants.

"Okay!" Joy snaps and grips me by my shoulders bending over until her face is leveled with mine. "I've patiently endured these tears for a few days now, you're welcome and I'll take my thanks in the form of coffee and chocolate. But this stops now and what I mean is you are going to talk. Right this second."

What do I do? That's right, spill more tears that earn me a groan from Joy.

"I'm p-pregnant," I manage to stutter out and the room grows silent. Yeah, that seems to be the standard reaction to my news.

Grace yelps quietly and slaps the palm of her hand across her mouth but Joy just stares at me without moving. Not one muscle on her face betraying what she's really feeling.

"Are you sure?" Joy's voice carries that deadly kind of calmness in it. It's that kind of calm voice that lets you know there is anything but calmness behind it. But despite the goosebumps, something warms up inside my now very cold chest at her fierce protectiveness of me. Her hands are still on my shoulders but now she's gripping me way stronger. I am not sure for whose sake but I'm grateful she's keeping me from falling over.

"According to the science you and I love so much, yes, I am sure," I answer her, and pull out the paper from my bag. The one with the blood work results. Joy takes the paper from my hands and all I see are her big brown eyes moving rapidly over the numbers and words on there.

"How am I supposed to do this Joy?"

"Fucking bastard!" She curses and folds the paper with extra force and leans over me again. "Okay, so I understand this whole 'woe is me' thing but that shit stops here and now. There is no more woe is me. There is no woe, period. From now on I need you to channel your inner 'I am a cold heart bitch' thing, mhkay? Because the Zoe

I know? She can take on anything. She's got this. You are a rock star Zoe Holsted! This child is lucky to have a mom like you and *not* have that sperm donor in his or her life, you hear me? And you are not alone! You have me and the rest of the Levine clan at your side as well." I nod despite my insides still shaking with fear for the baby's future but that's the Dr. Levine effect for you. Her tone alone leaves no room for argument, and I swear I feel myself relax. Like she just set my world back on the right track that I couldn't find by myself.

"Hell, I guess your baby even has an uncle now," she adds, running her tongue over her teeth. "But the jury is still out on whether it's a good or a bad thing. God knows, Jacob is nothing but bad influence."

"Which Jacob? Your sexy Viking fake fiancé?" Yeah, there's a whole lot more to her moving into the tiny house story.

Grace snickers. "Trust me there's nothing fake about that," she says, and Joy cuts her a look.

"Yeah. That one."

"Um, why is your Jacob my baby's uncle all of a sudden?"

"Didn't I tell you? This duck-loving hippie is apparently Justin's brother," she clicks her tongue while I choke on mine.

"What?" I shriek.

"Mm-hmm. But that's beside the point right now."

Sure it is! But Joy doesn't elaborate anymore.

"Now tell me did you see the doctor yet? How far along are you? Prenatals?" She started throwing questions at me and I was just nodding, shaking my head, or giving quick answers that I am ten weeks along and have been feeling like crap.

"Okay," Joy claps her hands and reaches for her phone. "Jacob," she says after a few seconds of rolling her eyes at the phone, "Cut the crap for one minute," she pinches the bridge of her nose, "Don't you dare get another ducky shirt or I swear I will serve it as breakfast for you tomorrow morning and no, I don't care about the new bet you have going on with Alec, but speaking of him, grab my sister's weirdo of a boyfriend and come to Fifi's store." I presume Jacob is asking why because Joy answers, "We need to get a fucking bed with the best mattress and chairs. Real. Comfortable. And food. Lots of food. So, we need Alec's truck and your muscles."

Joy hangs up and looks at Grace. "Luke better show up in the next five minutes at the store as well," she says to her and Grace nods.

"Way ahead of you sister. He's already on his way. So are mom, dad, and the rest of the Fantastic Four. They are so excited," she claps her hands together looking like I just gave her an early birthday gift.

I have no idea what's going on and who all of these people are – Fantastic Four? – but without any more questions, ten minutes later, what seems like half of Loverly Cave are walking around Fifi's Goods with us, carrying blankets, plates, glasses, pillows and whole bunch of stuff to the register while asking me if I like this or that.

"Joy," I hiss and pull on her arm. "What the hell is going on?"

"Nothing. Just making sure you are comfortable while you are here."

"I am here for a week. I can manage with an air mattress and camping chairs." I fold my arms across my chest because she is being ridiculous right now.

"That will be a big, fat no. Now stop pouting and choose a comforter." She proceeds to lift up the one with cats in sunglasses all over it and the one with freaking rainbows with silly eyes on them.

My eyebrow quirks up all on its own, "You are serious right now?"

"As a heart attack," she deadpans and thrusts two colorful monstrosities at me. "Which one would make you feel happier?"

"Neither." I don't particularly care for happy at the moment.

"Cats it is then," she shoves the other one back and an hour later the inside of the pink cottage is unrecognizable.

By the end of my first day in Loverly Cave, I have met more people than I could remember, was told by a cute but slightly scary grandma in a neon pink Addidas suit that by tomorrow I will have a whole list of best baby names complied for me and was branded as another daughter by Jennifer and Rick Levine—Joy's parents.

I was overwhelmed. That's what I was. I've never had this before and when I went to call my dad at night and told him about it all he said, "Looks like I won't be moving to Chicago after all. Remind me the name of this town?"

I don't know what he meant by that because I definitely wasn't staying here. I wasn't moving.

Right?

3

Matteo

"I almost had a psychic girlfriend but she left me before we met." – Steven Wright

"**M**atty." Mom's voice pulls me away from a stunning brunette with a nice rack who I've never met before. Tourist. Just how I like them.

"Yes, Ma?" I reluctantly turn my head away from the girl but not without sending her a little wink enjoying the pink creeping onto her cheeks.

Although, she's not the first wink of this morning. There is an abundant supply of willing bodies at the bar and it's not even ten AM yet.

And here I thought I wasn't going to make it home for the spring break.

"I can't die in peace," my mom announces all of a sudden, and I stiffen right before furrowing my brows and hurrying her way.

"What do you mean? Why are you dying? Are you sick?"

"I can't die in peace knowing my son is a manwhore."

Ah, it's that kind of morning. Got it.

And here I was just thinking that being home wasn't bad. Apparently, my loving, amazing mother can't get behind my lifestyle which includes sampling as much of the fine bodies offered to me as I can.

I've been away to college for the past four years and every time I come for a visit, it revolves around me settling down. And while she was tame about it before, this time around it's as if someone switched my dear mother—the kind Willa Loverson—with an evil doppelganger.

It also doesn't help that her friends feed the delusions as well and now the three of them are sitting opposite from us, all wearing grave expressions and nodding sympathetically.

Jenny Levine—the most recent addition to the crazy committee—even has tears in her eyes.

Five-star performance.

Sighing, I step away from her and go back to prepping the bar for the busy day ahead.

"Mother, you are not dying."

"But what if I am? Would you want my soul to wander aimlessly through the afterlife? Actually, now that I think about it, it wouldn't wander. No, I'm one hundred percent convinced it would haunt you until you put me out of my misery and found a nice girl or a boy. Really, anyone who is not just looking for a one-night ride!"

A shudder runs through my spine at the image she planted in my mind. Damn, eternity is a long time to be haunted by my mother's ghost because that's the timeline on when I plan to settle down.

Also, I'm pretty sure almost every girl I take to bed has a notion of "more" with me. So, really, she should stop blaming my companions. They are not the problem here. But it will be a dark day when I admit to being the problem.

The answer: my mom and her unrealistic expectations are.

"Don't you have some kind of a meeting to get to?" I ask them all.

"You know what? I think we should reschedule it," Mom says to her friends. "How can I leave him alone in here? Look at this!" She points to the full bar, boldly staring down every girl who walked in here as soon as the doors opened this morning. Which was fifteen minutes ago, and the line was there from about eight AM.

"It's like Americas next top model in here only the cheap knock-off version," Nina Colson very helpfully adds. She comes from the original line of Loverly Cave residents and that means she is as hippie as they come apart from believing in free will.

Nope. To my mom and her crazy friends, free will is apparently nonexistent when it comes to dating.

"They are all looking at him like he is their next meal!" Mom yells out a little too loud.

"And what are you going to do? Step in front of him and guard his penis?" Mrs. Fanny Lovesil—the elderly karate specialist who owns the local gym *Tough Love*, and in all honesty scares the crap out of me—asks Mom as her eyes dart down to my manhood.

"Do you think that will work?" she asks in all seriousness, and I just stare at her in horror.

"You are not bodyguarding my dick, mom."

"Well, someone has to!" She flings her arms back to the full room.

"Oh, they will," I flash her a grin at which her face screws up into a foul grimace.

"Well, you did raise a stud, Willa." Fanny winks at me, and my mom groans some more as I send her my signature grin. She might be scary, but she does have a good taste.

"I knew I liked you, Fanny."

"I think my impending death is a lot closer than y'all think," Mom mutters with a sour expression. "Matty! How hard is it to just choose one and love her forever? Dad and I did it. We fell in love from the first moment we met and look at the life we built."

Yeah, until he did die. Really died. Not the pretend way mom is and that family she's talking about was never the same again.

"Mom, I love what you and Dad had. But it doesn't mean it's out there for everyone."

"Nonsense!" she throws out. "You just need our help to find it."

My head snaps up to the four now very excited faces. "Oh no! Oh, no no no." I shake my head, pointing to them. "There will be no helping me! I don't need it. Don't want it. I like it this way."

My mom comes up to me and with a lethal calmness pats my cheek. "Don't worry, Matty. Mom's got this. Fantastic Four, I'm calling an emergency meeting right now. We can do it while we cook for Joy's friend." And with that, the four of them hurry out the door.

That's it. I'm never coming back home to take over the family bar. But it doesn't mean I won't enjoy my last day in my hometown, so I turn around and wink at that brunette again.

4

Zoe

"When life throws lemons, catch them and make a cocktail." –Unknown

Talking myself out of moving here was a whole lot easier before I discovered that the local bar called Love and Peace—or LPs for short—is up and running at ten AM and that is quickly swaying my opinion to the "big, fat yes" side.

I am not even sure why I came here in the first place since I can't drink, all I knew was that I needed to get away from those happy in love couples.

I've spent the whole day yesterday with the lot, learning all about Hope and Alec's story as he made a bet with her to prove that romance is not dead. And he did, so now, she's wearing his unconventional ring on her finger. Then learning in great detail how far gone my boss is for the Viking guy with the kind smile and shark slides and their plant babies. Seriously, how did she do it? How did she move on from that bastard Justin so fast? But even as I was asking myself those questions, I already knew the answer. The way Jacob watches Joy, the way he seems to know her needs before she has a chance to say them out loud, speak volumes. They speak, undeniable love. The kind that can heal the worst of cracks. And it warms my heart that my baby has an uncle like that.

That was the real shocker for me.

Yeah, Jacob and Justin are brothers. Half-brothers, but still...my mind is still catching up to this news. And apparently, they are so estranged, Jacob doesn't even consider him as one, and after a few minutes of colorful curses he said the only good thing the bastard has done was donate his DNA to his future niece or nephew.

Do you think Joy would be okay if we became sister wives? Because I want my own Jacob.

Even Grace and Luke's story made me envious. To carry their love over years, to hurt and break only to be put back together by fate. Or local crazies—aka their mothers.

It was all too much. And when they invited me to join them at the beach this morning, I already knew I wouldn't last long.

I am very happy for these three sisters. I truly am. But I can't be around them right now.

Every time I see their love, my heart aches for that feeling.

Have I ever been in love like that? So all-consuming? So big it spills over the town limits? So fluffy everyone around you wants to puke?

I thought I loved Justin but that wasn't love. It was a pathetic excuse at affection and sex. No fluff there. No, ma'am.

I open the door and step inside the bar expecting it to be empty, instead it is half full with what seems like half of the female population of LC and the other half is of whole bunch of locals drinking weird looking cocktails, some muddy looking concoctions in to-go cups from Sip of Love coffee shop I saw earlier.

Why are there so many people in the bar at ten AM? And then my lungs register the delicious smelling food they are all eating away, which is a weird thing for me to say by itself because the past month the only thing that has smelled good was water and even then, I managed to puke from the smell of it. And I guess it makes sense it would be a popular place.

Huh, I am really liking this bar already, despite the crowd. I have no idea why Joy was going all crazy in telling me to stay away from here.

Noting the long L-shaped bar on the left side, I make my way over and prop myself up on one of the only free bar stools closer to the corner. Fine by me.

I sit down comfortably and look around. Everything here is in different color and styles. There doesn't seem to be a single piece of furniture that matches in here and somehow it works out quite nicely. The whole bar gives off major hippy, relaxed vibes and I am here for it.

Relax me away, LPs.

Not a second after I decide to relax, my whole body tenses up as my breath gets caught somewhere in my stomach because it couldn't even bother to make its way up as soon as I saw the man standing in front of me. Smiling the most dazzling smile. The one that reflects in his dark, warm eyes.

"Well, hello there, Sunshine," the most beautiful stranger whom I somehow didn't notice as soon as I walked in says in the sexiest raspy voice I've ever heard. I think his appearance coupled with that voice has rendered me speechless and a little bit stupid because I can't for the life of me produce a sound.

I open and close my mouth a few times and watch as his head tips to the side regarding me with curiosity while that dazzling smile turns downright cocky because he definitely knows what he's doing to me right now.

Great, I've stooped down to gawking at sexy bartenders. The ones who have "flirt and have sex" with your customers written down in their contracts. Because he is definitely *that* kind of bartender. I mean, look at him. I almost want to take both of my hands and point at the man standing in front of me.

Long dark hair that is gathered in a messy bun at the back. Dark, mesmerizing eyes, that smile. The short, trimmed beard, the thin silver chain peeking from his half-unbuttoned short sleeved shirt, and don't even get me started on his toned, not-too-buff form. And the damn tattoos. Of course he has a damn tattoo on his arm and one on his chest that is also peeking from beneath his shirt.

And even if I was the kind of girl who was in a position to have a one-night stand, I would sure keep my distance from this one because he has that whole *I-will-rock-your-world-and-destroy-you-for-all-future-men* look written all over his handsome face.

No, thank you. I am still planning to have satisfying orgasms in my life later on. Way later on. So later on that I don't even see it on the horizon. But nevertheless, I don't need anyone messing with my future orgasms.

"Can I get you something or are you just window shopping today?" he asks me with amusement.

"I'll take a water." Because I sure need it to cool down my suddenly burning insides.

"Water?" He lowers his chin and arches one eyebrow at me.

"Yep."

"Okay, one fresh H2O with delicious, crisp ice coming right up." He smiles again and then proceeds to make a cocktail with just one ingredient. Water.

He even uses the shaker, tossing and turning it as if he is putting on a show here for me and despite myself, I feel the corners of my mouth tip up just as my thighs clench because talk about arm porn.

This guy is ridiculous.

But hell, maybe I'll take some window shopping with my water as well. Looking is not a crime, right? Just no touching, Zoe!

With his tongue poking out in the corner of his mouth, he pours it into a martini glass, propping a lemon twist on top and slides it my way with that same dazzling smile but he doesn't retract his fingers from the stem of the glass, and I don't notice it before I go to grab it. Suddenly feeling very parched, my fingers wrap around his, and I swear we must've both got electrocuted right that second because our eyes snap up to each other that same moment. And both are filled with the same question. *What was that?*

5

Matteo

"Age is an issue of mind over matter. If you don't mind, it doesn't matter." – Mark Twain

What was that?

I take my fingers off the glass and rub them against the palm of my hand without breaking eye contact with possibly the most gorgeous blonde I have ever met.

And trust me, I have quite a list to compare her to. But not one of the previous girls who happened on my way of life could hold a candle to her with those magnetic brown eyes, makeup-free face, plush lips, and curves for days.

I mean, have you ever seen tits as magnificent as hers? Because I have never had the pleasure and it has been all I could think about. Especially when she sat down, and I had an obstacle free view of her low-cut cleavage.

Talk about instant hard-on.

I noticed her even before she opened the front door to my bar. She was standing outside, contemplating something when I saw her through the windows and used all of my inner will, that my mother has been preaching about since I was born, to send her mental messages to come in and sit at the bar.

It worked. But don't tell my mom. The woman doesn't need any more encouragement.

Thank God she's not here already, plotting and cooking her life away for some new girl in town who just came here and apparently was taken under the local crazies wing.

My condolences.

Because if she saw me now, saw the way my breath hitched as we touched, there would be no more plotting. Nope, she'd go straight to planning our wedding. Like I said, Willa Loverson is obsessed with finding me the love of my life and apparently the whole town is in on it now too.

What they all seem to forget is that I am not interested in marriage and babies. Only good times.

Yet something happened when she brushed her fingers against mine. Something scary.

Probably chemistry. Yeah, our bodies are just trying to clue us in and I'm all ears.

So, I decided right here and now that I must have her. It's my last night in my hometown before I head back to college and not once during this spring break did I want to take a girl home as badly as I do Sunshine. Not even the brunette I was flirting with a second before she walked in.

And look at that, I even gave her a special nickname already. Something that never happens since usually they are all darlings to me. Why waste my imagination and creativity on someone who won't be there the next morning, yet when I saw this one, she reeked of that pure sunshine. The kind that can get you through the worst days full of lightning and thunder. And that right there is the first time I've ever said anything poetic about a girl.

Fuck...

I am not a poetic kind of a guy. I am the one who is there for the good time. One maybe two nights of wild sex and a kiss goodbye. But something about Sunshine here has me thinking I've been doing this life wrong.

Fuck! Wrong train of thought, Matteo. Abort! I repeat, abort!
Yet…

What was that? I am still rubbing my fingers against the palm of my hand when she breaks our eye contact, clears her throat, and takes a sip of the water cocktail I made for her.

Water fucking cocktail. Yes, I'd do just about anything to drink *her* cocktail later today. And I know she's interested in that too, but this little touch we shared spooked her. I see it in her eyes, so I gotta get to work. Gotta prove it was nothing, right?

"Can I get you anything else?" I ask, and she shakes her head. Sunshine here is clearly dismissing me but what she doesn't know yet is that I don't know how to take a no for an answer.

"Are you visiting our overly loving town or moving here?" I keep asking because I have zero desire to move on to other customers. Someone else can take care of them.

"Visiting."

Look at that, all the stars are aligning already.

"So, a tourist?" I start wiping the glasses that were just washed so I can at least pretend to be busy.

"You can say that."

"Is it living up to your expectations?"

"Not sure yet. What is with all these questions?"

"Just trying to get to know you."

"What if I don't want to get known." She frowns, and for a second I contemplate if I chose the right nickname for her.

"Why?" I ask, genuinely curious and she narrows her eyes at me.

"You're still asking your questions."

"Can't help it, Sunshine. I have a curious nature."

"No, you have a flirting nature," she says, and I throw back my head, laughing.

"That I do, Sunshine." Her eyebrows raise.

"You won't even deny it?"

"Why would I?" I shrug and continue cleaning the glasses. "I don't pretend to be someone I am not."

The mysterious girl lifts her water cocktail to those plump lips and as she takes a sip, I hear her mumble quietly to herself, "Well, there's a unicorn," and I can't help myself but let out a "neigh" king of noise, imitating a horse.

As soon as I do it, the water she was trying to drink comes right out—or more like sprays—as she laughs, and I would gladly continue cleaning the water spills and making an idiot out of myself to hear that laugh again.

"Jesus Christ." She wipes her face with a napkin I give her. "You are ridiculous, you know that?" she asks but there is still a small smile lingering on her lips. "Never have I ever met a guy like you."

"Oh." I snap my fingers, following with pointing my index one at her. "That's an excellent idea. Let's play Never Have I Ever."

She looks at me like I've grown two heads just now.

"Don't you need to make drinks or work or something?"

"Nah, don't worry about that. It's my bar so I can do whatever I want."

"It's your bar?" she asks with raised eyebrows and takes a sip of her water again.

"Well, technically it's my mom's still while I'm finishing up the school." Anddddd there goes that water back on my bar top as she spits it out again.

"Oh my God, how old are you?"

"Twenty-three."

The girl slaps her hand over her face and starts mumbling something about, *Oh my God, that makes me a cougar. Sure, let's add that to list of my ever-growing issues*, and I lick my lips with growing anticipation.

"It happens to be my favorite print." I wink and watch a beautiful blush creep onto her cheeks. "So, I take it you're older?"

"Oh, that I am." She suddenly turns around on her stool eyeing the people, then turns around with a grimace and says, "And I don't see you being into that."

Ah, she wasn't eyeing the people, she was looking at all the girls who've been eye-fucking me and killing her with their eyes and it clearly bothered her.

Why does it make me feel irrationally euphoric about that?

"Well, I am now." I smile, running my tongue over my lips as I let my eyes roam over her body that I can see. And me likes what me sees. Very much.

Sunshine's mouth props open, those plump lips falling apart and my already hard dick, strains against the zipper more and more with every passing second that her cheeks grow pinker and pinker.

Does she even realize how fucking sexy she is? Fuck the number that comes with her age. I couldn't care any less.

After a long beat, she swallows hard and I just about come in my pants, imagining my cum down that throat as it bobs with each swallow.

"Why are you looking at me like that?"

"Because you're hot."

She rolls her lips to hide her smile. "You're very good for my self-esteem right now."

"Then keep me." I lean forward.

"As who or what?"

"Oh, Sunshine, take your pick." I smile and start ticking off my fingers. "Personal wish ball, bestie, speed-dial fun, personal trainer, but I must warn you, my workouts all require naked bodies."

"Of course they do," she sasses back.

"Hmm, I promise they won't disappoint. So? What's it going to be?" I lean closer just as she backs away.

"Neither. I'm not going to sleep with you. So, it was nice to meet you. Thank you for the cocktail or…eh…water…whatever…bye." She starts to get up from the chair, all flustered, but I catch her hand with mine and there goes that electric shock to my system once again.

Fuck, I am not letting her leave just like that.

Her eyes shoot up to mine and I see the equal parts of fear and desire swimming in those dark pools. She wants me just as much as I want her, but something has her scared and that just won't do.

"What are you afraid of?" I ask without letting go of her hand. I know I was being bold just now, but I simply don't waste time dancing around. Usually.

"Nothing," she says too quickly.

"Come on, you can tell me. It's not like you live here and will see me again. I'm off to college again tomorrow so I am the perfect person to unload to."

"Well, that just solved the problem then because my unloading would take at least two full days. So, it's a no go."

She's sassy, I like that. And not at all the warm sunshine I pegged her to be at the beginning. More like something with claws.

The question is, how sharp?

My lips curve up into a small smile. "Then let's just play the game."

She doesn't seem all too keen on staying but at the same time she is no longer trying to release her hand from mine, and I am not eager to let go. So, we stay just like that. Her watching and calculating something inside her head and me still asking myself: *What was that?*

"Never have I ever slept with a girl," she says all of a sudden, her face all serious but I see the little glint she's got going in her eyes and I like that a whole lot better than the fear that was drowning out all the light from within her.

I shake my head while that small smile turns into a huge grin.

"First of all." I lift up one finger. "We need to get some drinks going if we are playing. And secondly." I lift up another finger. "Really?" I pretend to be offended by her comment while secretly throwing parades inside myself that she is playing along. "Did you have to stoop down to the teenage level?"

"First of all," she imitates after me. Finger and all. "I don't drink alcohol. And secondly, you just crawled out of the teenage crib, so it seemed fitting."

"Oh, you are hilarious, Sunshine." I grin at her. "Please don't hold back," I tell her and pull out the ingredients for non-alcoholic cocktails. But they still have some secret ingredients that I am counting on.

No, nothing illegal. Simply weird herbal concoctions my mother creates to induce them with secret powers. Her words, not mine and I'd question it if I didn't see them actually work.

For example, we have a drink called Downer's Luck. After you drink it, your luck turns up. I swear! Just ask Jimmy Jay who won a fucking lottery after drinking that crap. Or April who got married for the seventh time after drinking those the night before meeting the unlucky dude.

And so, the list goes on. We also have Cupid's Arrow for falling in love, Mellow-Yellows for just relaxing and taking it easy, Fry is very self-explanatory as well and then there is The Eros Spell which we will be drinking.

What? I never said I'll play fair.

6

Zoe

"In case I forget to tell you later, I had a really good time tonight." – Pretty Woman

"**N**ever have I ever seen a dead body."

"I swear I will burst from these cocktails if you keep going like that. Are you psychic or something?" I groan and take another sip of the red, extra sweet drink in front of me that somehow doesn't make me nauseous.

"What?" He gapes at me. "When have you seen a dead body?"

"I'm a pathologist. It's literally in my job description."

"Fuck me. You're beautiful *and* smart?"

"Smooth." I smile back at him, and he winks knowing exactly how smooth he is.

We have been at it for the past hour at least. Maybe more. Time just sort of stopped once I walked inside this place. All of my worries just vanished, and I have been truly enjoying myself. But this whole time he has been trying to weasel out any information about me by the means of this game or using sly follow up questions. I really don't know why he wants to get to know me when I am as sure as a heart attack—as Joy put it the other day—that he is only interested in taking me to bed.

Which is also baffling to me.

I mean...I am just me. The girl who doesn't get chosen, yet here is this sexy bartender who is trying very hard to win a night with me. When there are more than enough other—younger, prettier—girls around. In fact, there is a new one coming up to the bar every few seconds in an attempt to flirt with him.

I mean, I can't really blame them. He's that handsome and wears carefree confidence like his second skin. A perfect cocktail for all of us little moths.

Who I *can* blame, though, is me and my irrational hatred toward each girl who comes up. I almost want to slap their hands away and tell them to back off. Tell them it will be *my* name he will be adding tonight to his long list of conquests.

Yep, I've gone mad.

That must be another symptom of my pregnancy because never before did I entertain even a thought of a one-night stand.

And this fact should be enough for me to turn around and go back to the safety of my cottage, to my romance novels and fucking chamomile tea because wine is no longer an option. It would be enough any other time in my life but for some reason, today, I don't care.

I like his attention. I like it a lot. Our age difference—six years—be damned. And I am here for it. Because this past hour has been the easiest one I've ever had.

Talking to this sexy, shameless flirt is easy. Breathing is easy here. Thinking is easy. And I haven't felt like this in...hell, I haven't felt like this ever. It almost seems like inside LPs I am not a future single mom who doesn't have her life together. I am not a girl who spent her early twenties buried in books and studying her life away.

I am just me. Just Zoe.

So, I stay where I am as we shoot questions at each other.

"Never have I ever gotten drunk."

"Have you been living under a rock?" He takes a sip.

"Nope, in the library."

"Shit, I should do a booze pop-up shop there." He scratches his beard like he's really considering it. And I must admit that does sound like a brilliant idea. When you are five hours into studying soulless subjects, a glass of wine or two doesn't sound half bad.

"Never have I ever been in a relationship."

"Like ever?" I gape at him, but it wasn't anything I didn't already suspect.

"Never."

"Do you want to be in one?"

He takes a second to think about it, puckering his lips as he does so. "You know, I never had a desire for one before." He pauses locking his eyes with mine. "And most likely never will. I like my free-bird style of life."

So, what he is trying to say without saying is: *I am up for one night of fun and that's all, so don't get any ideas.* Strangely, that thought doesn't scare me as much as it usually did because one-night stands were not a part of my vocabulary before.

Now, all of a sudden, I am looking to expand it.

"Never have I ever gone to a club," I say because based on his lifestyle I know exactly the type of questions to ask and smirk at him. "Drink up."

"Evil little Sunshine." He takes a sip of his drink. "Okay, never have I ever sleepwalked."

He notices me thinking and starts laughing. "Okay, I need to hear this! In detail, please."

I roll my eyes playfully. "There is no story. I don't sleepwalk."

"Nuh-uh." He wiggles his finger in my face. "I saw that look on your face. I know you're lying right now."

"Since when do you think you know me that well?"

"Since I've been watching you from the moment you walked up to that front door." He fixes me with a look. "And trust me, I've been watching you nonstop."

I fight an urge to suck in a deep breath.

Yeah, his list of conquests must be a mile long.

"Fine, but I really don't sleepwalk. At least I don't think I do. But I can get a little…" I chew on my lip trying to figure out the best way to say this. "Violent."

"Oh, this just keeps getting better and better." He folds his arms across his chest.

"Next question, and oh look, it's my turn," I deflect, and he shakes his head.

"No, no, no. If you don't want me to dig deeper into your violent tendencies, I get another go."

"I don't remember that being part of the rules."

"That's because it never was."

"Then how come you're switching it up?"

He leans over the bar, bringing his face closer to mine and his sweet breath from the cocktail teaser my skin, raising every hair on my body. "Because I get to make my own rules in life, Sunshine." He winks, leaning back as if he didn't just send that wink all the way to the bottom of my stomach.

Oh, this guy is dangerous. He is nuclear because he represents everything I've never had. He is freedom and danger all in one. Life and death. He is everything I shouldn't want, yet do anyway and I feel my resolve slipping inch by inch.

"Are you holding your breath?" he asks when I don't respond for a few seconds.

"Yes," I quickly say and stop breathing again.

Please don't ask why.

"Why?"

Seriously, universe?

I can lie, tell him I got hiccups or something but for whatever reason the truth just spills out of me.

"So my marbles don't get off their places with a gust of wind." Because I'm *this* close to doing something stupid. Something off the plan.

He tips his head to the side, considering my statement for a bit but he doesn't laugh at me like I thought he would. He puckers his lips in concentration. "What about a tilt of your head? Would that knock them off? Cause you're tilting it now."

"Shit." I blow out the air I was holding. "I didn't think of that. Well, I guess I can blame it on the tilt."

"Blame what?"

I must be losing it. But *what else* do I have to lose?

"This," I say before I can think any better and reaching over the bar I grab a fistful of his shirt, hauling him close as our lips collide.

At first, I stiffen from the shock of my own action but that only lasts a second before wild euphoria takes over my body and both of my hands fist his unbuttoned shirt, drawing him closer to me. I feel pressure, scorching heat and raw desire on my lips as this sexy stranger complies with my insanity and kisses me senseless.

I forget everything. I forget I'm in the middle of a now very busy bar or that I shouldn't be doing this. I forget he is much younger than me. I forget about all the hurts and problems I have waiting for me outside this space.

I forget it all and exist in this kiss as our lips devour each other and before I know it, he slips his tongue past them and tangles it alongside mine, groaning into my mouth and making me shiver with desire.

Dear God, this is the hottest kiss of my life, and I don't want it to stop. But after a few more seconds he slowly pulls away, yet not too far and his eyes are fixed firmly on my now red, puffy lips.

My breathing is labored as if I ran a marathon and so is his.

"Never have I ever wanted someone as much as I want you," he says but I don't drink because the feeling is mutual and he tilts his head to the side, the hunger in his dark eyes now more prominent.

"Never have I ever done something this crazy," I confess, feeling too much at the moment. He watches me for a beat and then instead of drinking like he was supposed to, he pulls me back in for another kiss.

Once he's done, I'm gasping for air. "I don't believe for a second you haven't done something crazy before."

"I have." He grins.

"Then why didn't you drink?"

"I did," he says, and I eye his cocktail in confusion before he adds, "I just preferred drinking you over that."

Can someone help me find my jaw, along with my sanity somewhere here?

Damn it, he's so smooth and he knows it so well. My cheeks are on fire, my thighs are hurting from all the clenching I've done and the more I spend in such close proximity to him, the fuzzier my brain grows.

He keeps watching me with unnerving intensity, like he sees more than I'm okay with. Like he knows more.

And then he brings the pads of his fingers over my lips, gliding over them slowly. "I think I was wrong before."

"About what?" I breathe out.

"About the nickname I gave you. Sunshine is too tame for you."

"Oh?" Never have I ever been referred to as something other than tame.

"Mm-hmm. You are a lot wilder. You are just trying to hide it from the world, aren't you, Beastie?"

Am I?

"Beastie?"

"Yep. That's the one." He smiles at me and then just to spike my heart rate further, he slowly slips back behind the bar, his eyes on mine as he swipes his thumb over his lips, gathering the remnants of our kiss on it and sucking it without breaking eye contact.

"Now, what's your real name, Beastie?" His voice is full of gravel and that sexy rasp.

I'm still panting, and my thighs can no longer keep clenching.

"You decide to ask this now?" We have been together for hours and he only brings it up now.

"I was okay with not knowing before."

"So, what changed?"

"I need to know the name of a woman who's changed my life with one kiss."

I stare at him, my mouth slightly parted. How can he say that? I want to call out his lies, yet something tells me this guy isn't capable of lying. So, I give it to him. "Zoe."

"Zoe." He repeats it slowly as if tasting it on his tongue, and another shiver breaks over my body. "That's okay, you can ask."

"Ask what?"

"My name."

"Why would I need to ask your name?"

"How will you know what to scream later tonight when I will change your life too and make you see the stars and the galaxies above?" I narrow my eyes at him and run my tongue over my teeth.

"Aren't you the cocky one." It wasn't a question. But he leans forward, bringing his face closer to mine once again, as if he can't keep away for that long until he is just a breath away from my swollen lips, and his nose almost touches the tip of mine.

"You have no idea," he whispers into my mouth.

He wants me. I want him. To hell with plans and order.

And maybe, just maybe, Loverly Cave is just what I need.

"Never have I ever seen the stars and the galaxies above," I whisper back.

"Then let me show you."

7

Matteo

"Alcohol is like love. The first kiss is magic, the second is intimate, the third is routine. After that you take the girl's clothes off." – Raymond Chandler

A *thump* sounds as her back hits the wall in my entryway. I should have been a bit more gentle but at this moment that word doesn't seem to register in my head.

Because my need for her is too strong. I ache to taste every part of her as my hands roam over her lush body with curves in all the right places. I don't know where to touch her first. I don't know where to lay my lips first because I want it all.

The second she gave me the green light at the bar, I ran over to her, grabbed her hand and stormed up the stairs to my apartment. I didn't care about all the girls shooting daggers at us. Or who'd be taking care of the bar in my absence as the evening approaches. My brain was in a one-track mode, set on having this gorgeous woman in my bed. Even before we hit the top step my mouth was already on hers. My hands cupping that amazing ass while hers were fisted in my shirt.

Thank God I live so close, otherwise the dirty fucking floor of LPs would have to do because I was not going to wait even five extra minutes to have her.

Every little sound she made throughout the day drove me to madness. Just hearing her talk was enough to make my dick weep for her and it was a strange fucking notion, but I wasn't going to fight it. Needing to feel her wrapped around me was in no way a difficult thought to have.

"Damn, Beastie," I mumble without breaking the kiss. "You taste so fucking sweet. I'm ready to give you the world just so you let me have more of you."

"I'm a virtual stranger, didn't your parents teach you about stranger danger?"

"Nah, they were more into the free-hugs-for-all philosophy."

Zoe chuckles into my mouth, and I bite her lip. "Stop distracting me. I'm on a mission here..." I trail off, finally breaking away from her lips only to drop to my knees and press my nose into her jean-covered pussy. "I need to know if your pussy is even sweeter."

Zoe's already heavy breath hitches as she watches me with propped mouth and hooded eyes.

"I-I guess you'll have to find out and tell me," she whispers unsurely, and one corner of my lips curls up. She has so much fucking fire inside of her, but she is too shy to let it shine. "But..." She stops me just before I'm about to unzip her jeans.

"But?" My hand is frozen in place. I will stop if she wants me to, but I might also die in the process. Because I love eating pussy. It's the best part of sex for me and I could literally spend days and nights with my tongue buried inside a woman. And that was with all of the ordinary ones I've had before. But there is nothing ordinary about Zoe. Something tells me I will simply drown in her. Zoe's will be my complete undoing.

And so worth it.

"But it's been a very long time since I've done this so..."

"Don't continue that sentence," I growl, all of a sudden, a weird, strange and terrifying emotion passes through me. *I could kill every single person who have tasted her. I could.*

Chemistry. This is all just chemistry's fault.

"The only thing I need to hear you say is 'go.'"

Zoe bites her lower lip, nods her head and says, "Go."

The second that word is out, I'm tearing off her shirt, slipping her jeans down her legs and before she gets a chance to step out of them, I slide my hands around her thick thighs and lift her up, carrying her to the bed because she deserves to be eaten out princess style.

Zoe yelps as I do that and her hand grabs a fistful of my hair, holding onto to me and I swear my dick jumps up at that. The fucker loves it rough, and she is just feeding his sick fetishes at this point.

I lightly nib at her soft stomach, enjoying those little yelps she lets out too much right before I lay her down. Without a second to waste, I hook my finger into her soaked, lacy panties, dragging it through her swollen lips before I push them off to the side. "Look at your pretty pussy, Sunshine." As I hold her panties with one hand, I drag the thumb of my other hand through her pulsing clit, relishing the little moans she lets out for my pleasure. "She's so needy for my mouth, isn't she?" I ask, putting a bit of a pressure on her and Zoe's hips buckle, her pussy enchanting me with her scent and the time for playing is over. I need to taste her more than I need my next breath so, I burry my tongue inside her dripping cunt.

"Fuck me," I groan and lick her slit up and down. "You are the epitome of delicious, Beastie."

"I am?" She lifts, propping herself up on her elbows as she watches me.

"Yeah, now, shh, let me enjoy my pussy." With that, I go back and suck in her clit, getting lost in her as I feel her hips lifting off the bed and I grab onto her legs, spreading them wider and pinning her to the bed at the same time.

I need unrestrained access.

Every moan and gasp from her mouth makes my already hard cock weep with need, and I push my tongue inside her as deep as I can as she grinds over my face. Zoe's back arches off the bed as her hand finds my hair again, pulling on it with a death grip, and she comes with a loud moan and a string of, "*OhmyGodohmyGodohmyGod.*"

She's holding onto my head as she rides my mouth through each wave of her climax and I feel more sweetness explode over my tongue.

"Fuck yes, baby. I need it all."

"Shh, don't get distracted," she pants, and I have to fight an urge to laugh at her sassiness. Instead, I smile and insert my finger just as she's climbing down her high, curling it inside her tight walls as my mouth closes in on her clit and she shoots off the bed once again. That new orgasm hitting her just as I wanted it.

"Your name!!!" she yells out. "I need your fucking name."

"It's Matteo, Beastie."

"Matteo!" she screams and moans until she drops back to the bed, sated and panting but we are so far from being done, we haven't even started.

I push up to my knees, taking off each and every piece of clothing I had on. Suddenly, Zoe is no longer lifeless, as she pushes to her elbows once again, watching me undress and her eyes on my body are doing things to me.

I am used to women gushing over my body, my abs, tattoos, and my cock but something about having her gaze on me hits differently.

It feels…right?

"God, do you have to be this gorgeous?" she groans and flops back to the bed with a sigh that makes me chuckle. I climb over her body all the way until my face is hovering over hers, but I support myself on my hands.

"Is that a problem?"

"Of course it is. How am I supposed to go back to average after this?"

I bite my lip and laugh. "Then I guess I need to fuck you good enough for it to last a bit, yeah?"

She swallows hard and gives me a tiny nod.

I rip off the bra holding the most amazing tits I've ever laid eyes on. Once she is fully naked, I sit back and just stare at her dumbfounded. "Talk about ruining things."

Zoe, naked, is what my wet dreams are made of.

"What?" she asks, confused.

"I am the one getting ruined here, Beastie," I say and wrap my mouth around her nipple as my other hand palms her tit, squeezing it in my hand and Zoe moans in answer.

My cock is about to burst from how badly I need to be inside this woman, so reluctantly I pull away, grab a condom from my nightstand and get back on top of her, lining my cock with her entrance.

"Ready?" I ask, and as soon as she nods, I crush my lips to hers and thrust inside her tight pussy in one fast go.

Zoe moans into my mouth as I groan and freeze inside her. "Fuck, fuck, fuck. You are so fucking tight baby." I close my eyes and will the eager bastard not to shoot his load just yet. Dear God, please not yet.

"Matteo," Zoe whispers full with need and lust. "Baby, you need to move. Please."

Yep, that's it. I'm done for it. Hearing this gorgeous woman beg for my cock is my total undoing. I lift up from her to my knees, hook my hands under her thighs to have full control and start thrusting with madness as she holds to the sheets around her for dear life.

"I can't look at you." My head is thrown back.

"Why not?"

"Because the sight of your tits bouncing as my cock gets swallowed up by your pussy is illegal. Completely fucking illegal," I growl, yet I can't resist and look down again, groaning as I do. Seeing her stretch to take me all the way in is so fucking hot. Watching as those lips glide up and down my hard as steel cock make me lose my mind and I know I won't be able to last long.

But then the vixen brings her hands up, cupping her tits in them and says, "Harder, Matteo!"

Fuck. I'm holding on by sheer will at this point, but I give her what she wants. I slam inside her so hard, I'm sure both of us will wear some bruises as reminders tomorrow and the headboard is, without a doubt, leaving holes in my wall.

"Yes, yes, yes," she chants. "Just like that." Zoe pinches her nipples just as I pinch her clit—hard and she detonates. Her hot walls squeeze me in a vice grip and my own orgasm hits me right that second, making my cum shoot out like fireworks.

For a second, a fleeting, crazy second, I wish I could paint her walls with my cum. Mark her. Claim her.

I've gone mad.

I bottom out inside her and stay rooted as she keeps pulsating around me, milking every last drop I have left and with a groan I fall down on top of her but quickly roll us around so Zoe's the one on top of me with my cock still buried deep inside her cunt.

We are both slick with sweat and breathing hard. Her head is resting on my chest and my hands can't seem to be able to stop touching her body as I glide them up and down her back.

"That was…" She trails off and I finish for her. "Fucking best sex of my life."

"Yeah," Zoe agrees and I can hear the satisfied smile in her voice.

I've been with my share of women—more than a share if we are being honest here—but never has it felt like it did with her.

Nothing has come close to her.

To her body.

To her tits.

Her lips.

After another few seconds she starts getting up and I halt her in her escape plan. "Where do you think you're going?"

"Um, home? Isn't that how it works?"

Yeah…I guess it does. I mean, I know it does. That's how I operate every time yet…

"Nuh-uh." I shake my head, pull on her hand until she falls back on top of me and roll her onto her back. Her sun-kissed blonde locks get tangled up over her face and I gently push them off her face.

Damn even her hair is soft as silk. And smells so sweet.

"You are not going anywhere, Beastie. At least not until you come another three maybe four times."

Zoe's eyes grow round and wide. "Are you insane?" she hisses. "That's not even possible."

Nope, I've just gone mad.

My face breaks out in a triumphant smile. "Well, look at that. I accept your challenge, my lady."

And I do just that. We fuck like there was no tomorrow. Because let's face it...there actually isn't. Not with Zoe. And not that I'll ever be able to commit to one woman.

That was never on the horizon for me, yet waking up to the sound of my alarm and finding the other side of the bed empty feels awfully wrong.

8

Zoe

"Never chase anything but drinks and dreams." – Unknown

As soon as I am in the safety of my little beach cottage, I allow myself to breathe and slip to the ground.

What the hell happened to my brain last night and how do I recover from it?

But do I want to?

I run the pads of my fingers across my still-swollen lips where I can still feel him and taste him. I slip my hand lower over my neck that he peppered with kisses and surely left some marks on.

God, I hope he did.

I run it over my somehow still tingling breasts that he worshiped late into the night. And I look down between my legs where it seems my thighs have made custom indents for him to fit in between.

"Dear Lord," I groan to no one at all. The man can fuck. No, not just fuck—ravish, and destroy you in the best way because that's the only explanation for what I am this morning. Or who was I last night when I asked him to fuck me harder, faster and more.

I've never said the things I said to him. I didn't even think I wanted them. Yet one touch from him and I lost myself, shed that old shell I was wearing and dove off the deep end. No, he didn't just ravish my body, he reset my whole brain.

I've never had so many orgasms in one night. Hell, it was a whole process to reach at least one most of the time. Yet it took exactly zero effort on my part with Matteo.

Matteo. I never thought I'd find a guy's name beautiful, edible, and dreamy but here we are. He surprised me from the first moment with his looks, he then won me over with his wit, charm and being unapologetically himself.

And do not even get me started on his cock...even if he would've been a complete fool, that stick between his legs would have won me over.

I didn't even know they could be that big.

And I have seen a lot of penises as a doctor, okay?

He never promised me anything beyond this one night and that's why I high tailed it from his apartment at the crack of dawn because *he* might not be a relationship kind of a guy, but *I* happen to be a commitment whore and staying with him even another second was too dangerous for me.

I was fighting an urge to thread my fingers through his dark, long hair as it was before I left.

But I don't regret last night. Not one bit.

He's set me free. Free from the haunting thoughts I've lived with for the past couple months. Because after just one night with a stranger, I could finally see it.

What Justin and I had wasn't love. It wasn't even lust. It was a disease I willingly contracted.

During the whole year of our relationship, Justin never once took care of me like Matteo did tonight. Never showed me that kind of devotion and adoration. Never made me feel so desired I could smell it off him.

No, I'll never settle for a disease again. I'll never settle for anything less than what I had with Matteo.

Even if deep in my soul I already know there's no one else like him.

"What is she doing?" A somewhat familiar voice sounds from behind me, and I turn around noticing Hope, Grace and Joy standing in my—well Joy's—living room, all wearing varying expressions on their faces from confused (Hope) to happily grinning and moving her head along to the beat (Grace) to scowling and frowning (Joy).

"I like this song," Grace tries to yell over the music, but I can barely hear her.

Nope, I'm not turning it off. My favorite part is about to come up. Plus, Grace likes it too.

"Here I am, looking everywhere for her, and she is dancing her life away in the kitchen?" Joy's booming voice somehow *is* louder than *Panic! At the Disco* playing out of my speaker as I'm living it up to the "House of Memories" by them.

What? It seemed like a very fitting song for this morning, and I needed a dance party. No, I deserved one because today is the first morning in over two months where I didn't have the urge to puke my guts out, got so many orgasms my horny pregnant body is well sated for the remainder of this pregnancy, and I didn't want to cry even once.

Looks like the sexy, younger bartender was exactly what I needed.

"I'm dancing," I yell back to them. "It's good for the baby."

"Dancing? Sure." Joy comes over to my phone and with one finger shuts it off. "Practicing exorcism while you are pregnant? Doubt it."

"Ha ha, so funny." I stick my tongue out, and if someone told me I would be comfortable enough to do so with my boss a few months back, I'd tell them to go check their head. "I was simply caught in the moment."

"So, care to tell me where you were last night as I search the whole damn town for you?"

"I was at the bar," I answer and turn the song back on.

"What bar?" She shuts it off again.

"Are there many bars in Loverly Cave? LPs, of course." The music is back on.

"I checked there. Three times. You weren't there."

I shake my hips with my hands above my head as a wicked grin spreads over my face. "Did you checked upstairs?"

Right away the music is off again and this time she grabs my phone so I'm not able to turn it back on. "What upstairs?" Joy asks, narrowing her gaze on me.

Crap, I forgot how frightening she can be.

"The only upstairs they have there."

"Zoe, I swear to God if you don't start talking right now, I will sick Jacob on you and trust me, that man can get the dead spilling their guts out," she threatens me with her fiancé.

"Is it just me or does she threaten everyone with Jacob?" Grace whispers to Hope.

"She totally does. You'd think he was some kind of a creep instead of the most lovable guy in the world," Hope confirms but Joy snaps her fingers in front of my face, bringing my attention back to herself.

"Start talking girlfriend," she says but turns her head to Hope. "Did you already forget that it was that most lovable fiancé of mine who made your boyfriend tattoo his name on his ass?"

Hope scrunches up her nose. "Yeah, you're right. Jacob is very evil."

"Do I even want to know?" I ask them and all three of them shout, "NO!" in unison.

"Shame. It sounds like a good story." I shrug, knowing I'll get it out of them later.

"You know what else sounds like a good story? Your night." Joy smiles that evil forced smile of hers and I groan.

"Fine, I was having the best sex of my life with the hottest, too-young-for-me guy."

Silence and three stupefied faces.

"Wait, what?" Grace recovers first. "Was it Griffin? He's the only good-looking single guy left," she asks, meaning her boyfriend's friend who I met briefly yesterday. And sure, he is very good looking, with all that tall, dark and handsome thing going on for him, but my guy was hotter.

Or I'm biased because of the million orgasms. Whatever.

"She just said too young for her, and Griff is what? Her age? Plus, that guy clearly has it bad for another girl," Hope whispers back to her.

Also true. I saw how he was looking at Julie—Hope's friend and the local coffee shop owner—yesterday.

"No, it wasn't Griff but I'm not giving up his name. No matter how many Jacobs you set out on me." I point to Joy who only shakes her head.

"You do realize what town you came to, right? There is no such thing as secrets in here and your night with this 'mysterious' guy is probably already broadcasted all over Love Hive."

"What in the world is Love Hive and why would it be up there?" I frown but before she gets to answer me, my front door bursts open as four ladies I met a few days ago at Fifi's store walk in and one of them does it for her.

"Because we are a nosey bunch and Love Hive is an in-town chat we have to share all of the important news and events within Loverly Cave bubble."

"What's going on here?" I ask, confused at this intrusion and how freely everyone seems to be moving around my personal space.

Seriously, what is going on?

Grace comes to my side and pats my back with sympathy written all over her face. "My deepest condolences," she says and then turns to the lady in the neon Adidas track suite. "Fanny, you could knock for a change, no?"

"Tootsie roll, where would the fun be in that?" They start going back and forth between each other, but I am not paying attention because another older but very pretty woman with two braids, a whole bunch of dangling, colorful jewelry who I've also met before comes right up to me, placing her thin hands on my shoulders and kisses both of my cheeks.

My stunned brain somehow remembers the name of the woman in front of me who is still holding me and blinking rapidly. "Willa, right?" I ask with even more confusion than a few moments ago.

"Oh darling." She smiles sincerely with tears in her eyes. "Please call me mama."

That exact moment of dead silence is pierced with a loud spitting sound as Joy chokes on her coffee she just made and looks at me.

She hides her face behind the said coffee mug and mouths to me, "You fucked Matteo?"

My wild, one-night-stand-Matteo ended up being Willa's only son who she loves dearly and desperately wants to see in love and married. And it only took us all an hour to console her when I broke the news that I'm leaving to go back to Chicago in a few days, and Matteo and I are most definitely not together.

"Don't you worry, Willa," Jenny—the other lady from Fantastic Four aka Joy, Hope and Grace's mother—pats Willa's back lovingly. "It will all work out, you'll see."

And it wasn't just me who thought the tone of her voice was oddly suspicious because Joy zeroed in her gaze on her mom and said, "Mother, whatever it is you are planning, stop immediately!"

"I'm not planning a thing," she says sweetly, batting her lashes at her daughter but none of us miss the smirk that passes between her, Nina Colson, and Fanny Lovesil.

God, what have I gotten myself into?

The next few days pass in harmony all the while I avoid Willa and her gang. Their watchful eyes are still giving me the creeps.

But I must admit, leaving LC was a lot harder than it should have been, especially knowing that Joy is not coming back with me no matter what she says. She belongs here.

And maybe so do I because I have been miserable ever since I got back to Chicago, to my apartment and the work routine I used to love so much yet now it felt wrong.

Everything feels wrong.

I also got reacquainted with my old friend, the toilet bowl. Is it something in this air here that makes my nausea so bad? Why didn't I feel like that in Loverly? Or is it simply being in Justin's vicinity that churns my stomach nowadays?

Two weeks later, I finally decide I've had enough and made an impulsive decision I hope I won't come to regret.

"Hey, Dad."

"Hey, Zoe bug, how are you feeling?" I have been calling my dad religiously every day since I came back because for another odd reason, I've been missing him more than ever. Maybe it was seeing the easy relationships the Levine's had with their parents. Maybe it was missing that feeling of belonging with them as well, to have someone care for me. And don't get me wrong, Dad has always been there for me despite the distance. Always. But here in Chicago, I was too busy to be there for him as well.

"It's the same old, unfortunately, but that's not why I called."

"Oh?"

"Yeah…so, I think I'm moving to Loverly Cave."

"Thank God! Finally! I almost ran out of plastic plates and didn't want to buy new ones." My dad exhales with relief and sounds all too happy about this weird comment.

"Um…what? What are you talking about?"

"I've packed my dishes along with all other stuff three weeks ago and I was just waiting for you to finally give me the go-ahead, so I've been living off plastic plates."

"The go-ahead for what?"

"To move to Loverly Cave with you, of course," he says as if that was perfectly clear from the start, but I am standing here shocked and speechless.

"You mean to say you're moving with me? And that you knew I'd be moving there this whole time?"

"Honey, I knew it after the first call you made when you just arrived there. I've never heard you sound so happy. So yes, I knew and was waiting for you to catch up. But I was also going to move to Chicago if you decided to stay there."

Happy tears are gathering over my eyelashes, "I love you, Dad."

"Love you more, Zoe bug, "What about your job? Are you going to be fine doing something else? I know how hard you worked to be at KePah."

"You know, I thought I'd be a lot sadder about leaving it. I thought there would be tears and devastation. Yet the only emotion I feel is elation. I'm free, Dad."

"That's all I've ever wanted for you, honey." My throat grows tight at his words. I don't deserve Kevin Holsted. I don't deserve a father like him. "So, what are you thinking of doing now?"

"Joy and Jacob offered me a position in their new clinic they are starting down there. So, I guess it's time to brush up on my family medicine books."

My dad chuckles. "Knew you wouldn't be able to sit still for long."

"Never."

"Then let's go start our new life."

My Life Plan Two Point One:

1. *Call my landlord.*

2. *Hand in mine and Joy's resignation letters.*

3. *Pack my stuff.*

4. *Dream some more of the sexy bartender.*

5. *Buy a one-way ticket.*

6. *Repeat step number four again. Because why not?*

7. *Never look back at my old life.*

WELCOME TO LOVERLY CAVE TOWN WHERE LOVE IS THE ANSWER TO ANY QUESTION.
POPULATION THREE THOUSAND ONE HUNDRED and Six.

Love Hive:

CookieJ: Attention, attention. I just received news that Zoe is officially moving to Loverly Cave.

Ninasunshine: Which means operation "Tame the Beast" is officially on.

Willoflove: Thank Rainbows! I did not think this day would come.

Toughtolove: Calm your chakras, Willa. We still have a long road ahead of us.

Therunawaybride: And where, pray tell, were you with this advice when you were meddling in my love life?

Toughtolove: You're welcome, Tootsie roll.

Therunawaybride: That was not what I meant.

Willoflove: I've waited this long, I can wait another six months.

Joydontpissmeofflevine: You all need help!

Joydontpissmeofflevine: And also stay away from Zoe!

CookieJ removed Joydontpissmeofflevine from the group chat.

Love Hive: (Fantastic Four group chat)

Toughtolove: Stay away from the newbie!

CookieJ: Who? Zoe? I thought we were going to help her.

Toughtolove: No, not Zoe. Her very handsome father with a cute butt.

Ninasunshine: Dear Lord...have mercy for that poor man.

CookieJ: Isn't he a little too young for you?

Toughtolove: A little age gap never hurt nobody. Don't you read romance? And I'll have you know my lady parts are as good as new. Very well-oiled. In full bloom.

Ninasunshine: Dear Lord...you just ruined flowers for me.

Willoflove: I've heard he's very content with his bachelor status.

Toughtolove: See, I knew he needed me.

CookieJ: How in the world did you get that from Willa's words?

Toughtolove: Who wants to live in contentment??? That's just another word for boring. Or a secret SOS signal, which I'm good at reading.

Ninasunshine: Should we warn him?

CookieJ: Definitely!

Toughtolove: You three stay away from Nerds. Nerds is mine.

Willoflove: He's doomed. She's already given him a nickname.

Toughtolove: I think I hear the Universe crying, Willa from your foul words. Go clean your chakras and stay away from mine.

CookieJ: And now she's territorial.

Ninasunshine: Before you pee on the poor man to stake your claim, make sure you ask him how he feels about golden shower kink.

CookieJ: I see you and Sam started that book we gave you last week. *Wink face*

Willoflove: I will go light a protection candle for Kevin.

Toughtolove: Go light a need-sainthood one for Nina and Jenny with their book choices.

Toughtolove: You have been warned.

9

Matteo

"Sometimes. Life gives you great things. So here I am." – Unknown

Six Months Later

Hello, Loverly Cave, I hope you are ready for what I have in store for you.

After spending five years majoring in Chemistry with a minor in business, I am more than ready to put my new knowledge to the test.

I always knew I wanted to come home no matter what. I always knew that LPs would be mine eventually, just as I knew I wanted to bring it to a new level—hence my chem degree. Over the years, I've created and perfected many drinks, most of which are new, modern twists on good old classics as well as a few completely new creations by me.

Just imagine your beloved dirty martini now in a purple ombre look, with slight undertones of blackberry and mint. Or an old fashioned that doesn't just have the smoke around it for a few seconds for looks, but one you can actually taste, along with bergamot notes throughout every sip, all the way to the bottom.

And don't get me started on the holiday or summer themed drinks I have lined up.

I'm seriously getting hard just thinking about how sexy those will be.

Yeah, you can say I'm passionate and excited about this new chapter of my life and I'm eager to start right away. Only, as soon as I step through the front door of Love and Peace bar, my whole body freezes.

How the fuck is this possible?

The space is the same as always with the same mismatched furniture, karaoke station on one side and the long bar on the other. The same pictures that've been here for ages, cling to the walls like second skin. The board above still has the same cocktail names on them as the day my mom and dad wrote them out years ago. Yet at the same time, nothing is the same.

Not the laughter I still hear echoing through these walls despite the empty seats.

Not the tentative smiles reflecting from the clean glasses.

Not the scent.

How the fuck can I still smell *her* in the air here when it has been over six months. Her scent shouldn't be here. Neither are the echoes of her smiles nor laughs. They *cannot* be here. Yet I swear to God, I can not only smell her sweetness but taste it on my tongue and down in my core.

To say that Zoe messed with my head is not to say anything.

What started as a physical desire for her, became my every waking thought since the morning I woke up to find her gone, leaving just one stray blonde hair on my pillow and that sweet scent in every inch of my space. Or maybe my lungs.

She nestled her pretty, sassy self deep inside my head and refuses to vacate the premises to this day.

In fact, she is responsible for all of the new cocktails I've created recently. It was simply enough for me to think of those deep brown eyes for an idea to pop into my head or remember her sweetness and looking through every ingredient until I found the one that reminded me of it.

Hint: Way too many cocktails include lychee and mint combo.

Because that taste is so uniquely her, I had to recreate it.

I often wonder where is she now? Is she still sad like she was that day at the bar or has she found someone to make her days bright and shiny, allowing him to see that secret beast inside her.

Fuck, why does the thought of some other man around her sweetness makes my insides churn.

I am not that guy. Never was and never will be.

Plus, I have no way of finding her anyway, so there is no point in these inner monologues. *Yeah, I've been trying to persuade myself for the past six months.* Newsbreak, it still hasn't worked.

"My baby boy is finally back home." My mom rushes from the back, breaking the little daydream I shouldn't be having and a huge grin breaks over my face.

Willa Loverson might be quirky, a little crazy, a lot hippy and too obsessed with my love life but she is the best human out there. And the most amazing mom anyone could wish for. She worked her butt off to make sure I was able to go to the college I wanted and pursue my dream while taking on the bar all by herself.

Love and Peace was started by my father's parents and passed on to him when he married mom. They were the happiest couple of Loverly Cave who did everything together and when Dad passed away unexpectedly, Mom never even considered remarrying.

I was ten at that time and saw how many men tried to date her over the years. She's always had that natural beauty and kindness in her heart that drew everyone to her flame. *Much like someone else I know.*

But she always told me, "Soulmates happen once in your life, and it wouldn't be fair to some other man to love him only with half of my heart." And maybe that's why I'm not even trying to find mine.

Why allow that kind of heartbreak into your life when I can give them my all for one night? Isn't that a better trade off?

"Hi, mom." I wrap her into a hug, kissing the top of her head. She is one tiny woman, plus I know how much she loves it when her son allows himself to show love. Her words, not mine. So I do it. Just for her.

"We are all so excited to have you back! The whole town is buzzing!" she squeaks excitedly, her long, graying hair bouncing around along with the million trinkets she wears around her neck.

"I'm happy to be back too. Even though I downgraded on my dating pool significantly," I say it with a pout to tease my mom, because sure, I'm a good son—mostly— but I still like to give her a hard time here and there and there's nothing that makes her more mad than my sleeping around.

I will never forget the day when she found out what I do and called me with panic, yelling frantically, "I raised a manwhore!"

It was quite hilarious.

The thing is, however, that I don't feel as sad about my dating prospects in LC as I should have. In fact, I haven't felt like dating—or my version of it—in quite some time. Well, my dick hasn't really felt like it...moody bastard. He has been giving me a hard—or rather, soft—time anytime I tried to take a girl home.

A little over six months to be exact. And no, I refuse to believe it has anything to do with the blonde perfection I had in my bed all those months ago. I refuse it.

My mom smacks my shoulder and narrows her eyes at me. "Your dating pool here will be just fine."

"Whatever you say, Ma." I kiss the top of her head again and pick up my bag to head back upstairs to my apartment. "I'll go unpack and I'll be back to help you set up for the day."

Yeah, unpacking can wait for another day. After I air out this place because if I thought her scent clung to the busy bar, it has nothing on its concentration in here.

Zoe is not just the trace in the air. She is the fucking air here.

Did my dick just twitch in my pants? Fuck, no! You don't get to do this to me! You don't get to go on boycott for her. She is not here.

I rush to open the windows to make sure her scent washes out of the room and go back downstairs before I need to take a cold shower.

As soon as I come back, I get to work busying myself with unloading the glasses and prepping the ingredients we will need when mom's phone dings with a text and she yelps.

I raise my eyes to her and see her smacking her forehead. "I am getting too old and senile!" I chuckle at her dramatics a little because she's hardly old or senile, but I don't say anything to her and apparently that was the wrong thing to because suddenly I feel her tiny finger poke me in my ribs and now, I'm the one yelping.

"Jesus, mom, are you trying to make me holey?" I grin. "Get it? Like poke a hole in me but make me holy? Cure me of my man-whoreness?" I scrunch up my forehead. "Is that even a word?"

"Matteo!" She pokes me again, this time with a serious face and I lift up my hands in mock surrender.

"Fine, fine, no jokes. What has got you all worked up?"

"I completely forgot to get the mint from my friend's house for tonight. She has been growing it for us for the past half a year. I need you to go pick it up."

"Alrighty, I'll go as soon as I'm done with the lemons here."

"Now!" she yells out, and I jump, sending the perfect slices of lemon to the floor period. What the hell has gotten into her?

"Jesus Christ, woman! Since when are you so passionate about fucking mint?"

"Language, Matty!" She swats me with the towel. "Since it's a special mint and I need it for my cocktails."

"Ah, of course." I roll my eyes. Mom and her cocktails. That's actually the only thing she won't let me change when I take over. The special, magic cocktails must stay. But seeing as I had the best sex of my life after drinking the Eros Spell that night, I might be partial to them too now.

"Fine." I set the lemons I was cutting aside. "I'm going now."

Mom smiles, but it's not exactly her normal smile.

It's very creepy, actually. "Be a good boy when you meet my friend. She's special."

"Okaaay," I draw out and hightail it out of there before she comes up with any more errands for me.

"Oh my gosh, Matty baby!" I hear Lindsey's squeaky, all-too-excited voice beam behind my back when I'm no more than five steps away from the bar and fight the urge to cringe then run away screaming. She was probably about to come inside right before I left.

And we are not open yet.

Great, it seems the whole town already knows I'm back. How the fuck does that girl still not understand we are not going to sleep together again let alone have a freaking relationship.

"Hey," I answer back without an ounce of enthusiasm. I'm not usually an asshole kind of a guy. I'm fun and easy but some chicks just don't get the memo.

Zoe got it. She got too fuckin good, I grumble to myself because I would not say no to another night—or two... fine, ten—with her.

"Oh, I'm so happy you are finally back." She beams at me. "I reallyyy missed you." She bats her eyes at me as her fingers trail over her overly exposed breasts and I fight the urge to throw up.

I'm really fighting that shit right now because even though I like easy fun, I don't enjoy overly eager participants. Or more like desperate hindering on the edge of bat shit crazy.

What the hell was I thinking when I slept with her last year?

Yeah, it was that long ago, and she still hasn't gotten the memo...

I exhale, rubbing my eyes with my fingers because there is no nice way I can go about this – I tried that already. Let's try rude and see if that works. "Look, Linsey, you and I"—I point between us—"are not going to happen. Ever. Okay? So, please drop it."

She looks at me with tears in her eyes and I want to feel bad but then her nostrils flare, she fists her hands and stomps her foot. Yep. Stomps. Her. Fucking. Foot. "Never!" she yells loud enough for the whole Love Street to hear. "We are meant to be, Matty baby!"

"Never," I deadpan and turn around, heading over to the address mom gave me without giving the "Stomping Larry" a second glance.

I swear this happens way more often than it should. I'm always so honest and straight up with them, yet still each one thinks she can be the one to take on a project called Matteo. Won't happen, damn it, not to mention I'm way too young for that shit. I still have a lot of wild oats to sow and all that.

But despite Linsey putting a little damper in my day, I am still enjoying this little walk through my hometown. Loverly Cave is like nothing you'll ever see anywhere else. It's happiness and craziness bottled up into one and capped with a rainbow at the top with its cheery residents, colorful buildings, little out-there-named stores, and nature for days. I never thought my town was special until I left for college and discovered how rude the outside world is.

It takes me twice as long to get to Mom's friend's house because everyone stops me on my way, saying hello, shaking hands and telling me how excited they are for me to be home.

Like I said, LC is one of a kind.

Eventually, I reach the destination for this special mint, and it happens to be one of the old cottages up on the beach that the Levine sisters bought when they moved here in the spring.

I only met them briefly when they came to the bar, but I've known their boyfriends who are now their fiancés/husbands my whole life and those men are the-fucking-best! Alec and Jacob were my role models growing up and Luke always seemed very cool, but he left town when I was still a kid, so I don't know him that well. But it's clear they all remodeled these antiques and turned rotten, paint-peeling shoe boxes into chic, beach retreats.

The cottage I'm headed to is the bright pink one and right in front of it is a huge firepit I imagine they all use daily since the logs seem to be still hot from the night before. I should ask if I could join them one of these days. Sure, I'd be third—or seven—wheeling but whatever, I could use some friends since all of mine are back in college.

I climb up the few steps to the front door and gently knock. It's still pretty early and I don't want to wake anybody up. I turn around taking in the rest of the surroundings but curiously enough there is not one mint stem growing around here. There is not even a stray planter in sight.

Weird.

Maybe she grows them inside the house?

Oh hell, I don't even know who I'm meeting here. Mom never gave me the name. I don't think it's Joy Levine who owns this place since she lives up in the woods with Jacob, plus from what I know about her she does not seem like a green thumb at all.

She's more likely the one to pluck it all out.

A few moments pass and I knock again, this time a little louder because no one is answering the door and I have a feeling mom might make mint out of me if I don't deliver this one. She was that eager to have it.

I blow out a tired breath, turn around and just start rubbing the exhaustion from my face with my hands when the door behind me squeaks and I quickly turn around. "Hey, thank God you answered." My eyes are still a little blurry from all that rubbing. "My mom, Willa from LPs, which I'm sure you know, ignore me. Anyway, she asked to pick up some min—" The rest of the words die on my tongue because finally I see clearly who is standing before me, gaping at me with those big, magnetic, brown eyes, the softest blonde hair, in a messy bun atop her head and her mouth propped open in what I think is a silent "what the fuck"—because that is what I am mentally mouthing to myself.

Zoe.

My Zoe.

My beastie.

At least I think that's who I'm seeing right now because a second later my eyes are registering what I am *really seeing* in front of me, and every ounce of breath is knocked out of my chest. Literally. I have nothing to breathe with, staggering backward in my steps until I feel the porch banister behind me, and I grab onto it with my dear life before my knees give out.

"Matteo?" a very pregnant Zoe whispers. YES! Pregnant! "Are you all right?"

Am I all right? Am I fucking all right??

I'm peachy! Just about to become a dad. But all is well here.

Wait, take a deep breath in, Matteo, you cannot scare a pregnant woman with your internal shrieks. Especially one who is most likely carrying your child.

My face pales further from the realization. I can literally feel the blood from it vanishing as I'm hyperventilating.

"Jesus Christ, Matteo," Zoe yelps and rushes to me.

"H-how? W-we used p-protection, d-didn't we?" I'm stuttering, my voice shaky and I feel that full-blown panic attack about to take over me.

That is until her skin touches mine. Just one little touch of her fingers on my arm and my eyes snap up to hers, locking in on them and just like that I am able to draw a deep, full breath in, steading my erratic breathing as my heart rate slowly slows down that instant.

That. That is what she does to me. No fucking wonder my sperm found a way around the fucking condom all those months ago.

And why doesn't it sound half as bad?

"I'm going to be a dad?"

10

Zoe

"Honestly, if you're not willing to sound stupid, you don't deserve to be in love." - A Lot Like Love

"I'm going to be a dad?" Matteo leans into me, whispering as if it's some kind of a secret. His eyes are huge and wild and up until just now were full of so much terror, it was almost comical. While now they hold some other weird, unexplainable emotion in them.

To say I'm shocked to see him standing in all of his handsome glory at my door step the morning of my first day of my official maternity leave is an understatement. And even being on a brink of delivery didn't stop my pussy from throbbing at the sight of Matteo. That long chocolatey hair in a low, loose bun, his beard as perfect as that night and that silver chain peeking from underneath his half-way buttoned shirt same as last time.

And yes, it was doing things to me, it had no business doing. Especially when I have been feeling crappy since last night. Well, it's more of a permanent type of feeling since I hit the third trimester.

Seems like I have just used up all of those sex memories from that night I used to fuel my horny, pregnant self with for half a year and I'm in sudden need of new ones.

Sure, I've heard rumors that Willa's son is coming back to LC to take over the family bar but with everything going on in my life, I didn't pay attention to those as much as I should have. Plus, I know how rumors work in this town.

Half were fantasies with a dash of delusion, so I stopped listening to them a while back.

Yet here he is, the man who turned my life around flesh and blood, freaking out on my porch over his impending fatherhood that is not going to happen since the child is obviously not his. Not only did we—indeed—use condoms that night but it has only been about six months from that night, and I would not be this big yet unless—

"Wait, but that was only six months, two weeks and three days ago," he says, breaking my own thought process, his forehead scrunching up in confusion as he looks me up and down. I want to tell him he is right, but my brain is stuck on the fact that he has the exact number of time memorized just like that. So, he continues coming up with his own ideas without my input. "How come you are so big already?"

Anddddd the adoration of the man stops right there as I arch one, unimpressed eyebrow at him and he pales again, scrambling back up to his feet and pulling me with him. "No, no, I didn't mean it like that!" he says with a somewhat panicked voice. "You are gorgeous. Not big. Jesus. That's not—"

Suddenly, that already pale face, pales further as he sucks in quick, deep breath and blinks rapidly. "Wait. Is it twins? Are we having twins?"

Oh my God, the look on his face right now...I am trying so hard not to laugh, I have to purse my lips together because this should not be a hilarious moment. The boy is literally about to pass out, yet I haven't had so much fun in a while.

Six months, two weeks, and three days as he so kindly pointed out just minutes ago.

"Breathe, Matteo." He starts talking to himself, closing his eyes, inhaling, and exhaling rapidly. It's quite a sight to see this big, bearded guy trying to meditate or whatever the heck he is doing. "It's okay. It's all going to be okay. You will be a dad. To twins. Soon. It's all totally fine. So what that you are only twenty-three. At least it's with Zoe."

What does "*at least it's with Zoe*" mean?

He clears his throat and looks at my swollen belly that has been hard as a rock this whole morning. "Um, can I...can I touch it?"

I regard him with pure amusement. I should really say something but let the miserable, pregnant cougar have her bit of fun a few seconds longer. So, I pucker my lips to hide the smile and nod.

Tentatively, very slowly and carefully he extends his tattooed hand toward me until just the tips of his fingers graze my stomach. Just a graze yet it feels like he set me on fire.

No, not fire, it's like he sets the world right.

Just like back then. Just like a moment ago when I touched his arm.
I suck in a sharp breath at the contact, and he retracts his hand right away.

"Did I hurt you?" His eyes are wide.

"No," I whisper and clear my throat, no longer in a laughing mood because I should not be feeling anything toward him. Nothing at all when I know where I would end up.

Alone and miserable all over again.

Without asking, Matteo places both of his palms around my belly and our gazes lock just for a second, yet it's enough for me to see the shift within his eyes. There isn't an ounce of fear in them.

My throat goes dry, and I open my mouth to finally put him—and myself—out of his misery but before I can utter a word, a piercing pain shoots through me, followed by a *pop* sound and a whole lot of water gushing from between my legs.

11

Matteo

"You're the best surprise I ever had. And sometimes the biggest shock." – Rachel Green, Friends

P^{op.}

"Oh my God!" I shriek like a high school girl that went to prom with me. Just for the record, I'd like to blame her for teaching me these sounds, not that this fucking matters right now because all of a sudden, Zoe is almost losing her balance, catching onto my forearms with strength she should not possess and lets out a horrible, painful howl.

"Beastie!" I'm full on freaking out now, my heart beating out of control because she's clearly hurting very badly and there is all this water at our feet. So much water. Where the hell is it coming from?

"What's going on? Shit, I did hurt you, didn't I? Fuck!" I curse and then wince, bending down to her stomach without letting her small hands slip from mine, and say, "Dear, kids, please forget you heard daddy say that, okay? I promise I'll put a quarter in the swear jar. Once you are born." I stand back up and see Zoe regard me with what I think should be a smile, but her face is currently unable to make that happen.

"Please tell me what to do, Zoe?" I plead, and she whispers in a barely audible voice.

"Hospital. My water broke."

Damn it, of course that's what it was! I should have known! Look at that, I have been a father—or known that I'm going to be one—for all of five minutes and I'm already fucking up.

No wonder she didn't reach out to find me and tell me about the pregnancy. Who would want a clueless manwhore for a father of their baby. Babies.

Fu...fuuuudge. There, that's better.

"Car! W-we need a car. Mine is parked at LPs, stay here, I'll be right back." I look around for a chair where she can sit, and I can run when she tugs on my arms.

"Matteo, don't be an idiot, a fucking watermelon is trying to come out of my vagina!" She hisses, and I wince from the visual she's pained. Ouch! "You are not running any-fucking-where! Mine is behind the house. Go grab my keys from the house, they are right here by the door." I nod like a bobble head and start to run when she tugs on me again. "Get my purse and my phone too."

Zoe pushes herself off me, leaning against the railing and I dash inside, grabbing the keys and her phone right away but where is the freaking purse? Or rather which one?

I groan. There are at least ten of them hanging by the front door.

"Matteo!" Zoe screams, and I grab whatever one my hand lands on first and run out finding her hunched over, her eyes shut hard. "Breathe, my fucking ass," she mumbles to herself. "It's a gradual process...it will take hours with your first child, my fucking ass...walking around helps with the pain, my fucking ass. A bunch of liars! I had a plan! This is not going according to a plan," she hisses out in pain and then yells, "Matteo, where the fuck are you?"

I jump from my stupor watching her curse whoever told her all those things, wrapping my arms around her waist, and help her down the few steps and around the house so we can get to the car.

The hospital is right smack in the middle of LC and while our town is small, this drive feels like it's taking forever. Especially when Zoe cries out in pain every few minutes and even I know—from the movies—that it means the babies are coming soon!

Zoe texts someone as we drive but it takes her a lot longer than normally because the contractions are hitting her more and more.

See, I know stuff.

Fifteen minutes later I park like a maniac you see in those same movies right at the entrance of labor and delivery, barely putting the car on park before I'm out the door and opening hers, yelling out to anyone who can hear. "Our water broke! We are having the babies!"

"Me," Zoe says through clenched teeth as a nurse runs out with a wheelchair. "I'm having a baby."

I level her with an affronted look. "What kind of a dad would I be if I wasn't involved in the birth of my children!" She gets into the chair.

"Matteo, you—" But whatever she was going to say gets cut off by another contraction and only a string of curses makes it past her lips at the same time as she grabs my hand, squeezing the life out of it and I let out a silent scream.

I'm a man. I can take this. I can be strong for her, but dear God, where is all this strength coming from?

"You're the father?" the nurse asks me calmly, still standing here like we came in for a fucking Band-Aid and not pushing a watermelon out of our vagina. TWO watermelons!

"Of course I am!" I shout. "Do you mind moving, maybe? Can't you see my girl is in pain?"

"First baby?" she asks with that same tone, and I narrow my eyes at her.

"Yes," I hiss.

"Don't worry, next time will be easier." She pats my back and finally starts rolling Zoe in and I follow, seeing as she's still clutching my hand that is already numb.

Next time?

I don't know if I will survive the first one, she's already talking about a next time! I swear if I see her in LPs, I'll make her the worst cocktail of all cocktails. With that cheap, diluted liquor.

We don't carry any at the moment, but I will buy some. Just for her.

"Dad, go park the car and bring in all of the stuff inside." Right, I should do that.

"I'll be right back, Beastie, don't push the watermelons without me, okay?" I lean in, kissing the top of her head and feel her give me a slight nod before I turn around, running back to the car.

Wait, what stuff? I look up to ask Zoe, but she's already in.

Quickly, I park at the nearest spot and search the car for any "stuff," finding two packed bags in the trunk. I grab those and hurry back inside.

Damn it, I don't have any of *my* stuff with me because when I woke up this morning, becoming a dad wasn't on my agenda.

Mom. I should call Mom and ask her to bring me what I need. What the hell do I even need?

This is why normal people have nine months to prepare for the baby, not thirty minutes and a crash course in contractions.

Oh God, are the babies okay if they are born so much earlier?

Come on, pick up, I chant to the ringing phone which she finally picks up a millennial later. Fine, it was just a few beeps, but currently I exist in a different universe, okay? One where my whole world has been upturned.

"Mom," I yell out.

"Rainbows, Matty, don't yell at me! I was doing it for you! Mama knows best." She starts spewing some crap my way, but I have no idea what's she talking about, and I don't have the time for her riddles right now.

"Mom, listen! I need you to pack me a bag and get to the hospital right away."

"Oh my God, Matteo!" she gasps. "Did you guys have a fight?"

"Mom, I swear I don't have time for your rubbish right now! I need to go in! Just bring me my stuff, okay?"

"Wait, Matty, what stuff? What am I supposed to bring you? And what are you doing at the hospital?"

"Becoming a dad."

All I hear is a hiccup before I disconnect and rush inside.

Love Hive (Fantastic Four group chat):

Willoflove: SOS!

Toughtolove: Willa, I already told you, it doesn't mean what you think it means *face slap emoji*

Willoflove: Fanny this is a real SOS!

CookieJ: What happened honey?

Ninasunshine: Tell us what do you need?

Ninasunshine: Fanny @toughtolove can't you see she's really freaking out!

Willoflove: I think I'm going to be a grandma?

CookieJ: Um, is that a question?

Toughtolove: How should I know, but it would be safe to assume that Matteo knocked someone up.

Ninasunshine: Rainbows, Fanny! Would you stop?

Willoflove: He just called me from the hospital, all frantic and worked up. Asking me to bring him his stuff because he's about to become a dad!!!

CookieJ: Dear Lord! I thought you sent him to see Zoe on the pretense that he's picking something up from her!

Willoflove: I DID!!!!

Toughtolove: Well, that plan failed…

CookieJ: Poopie crap.

Ninashine: Okayyyyy, first of all, breathe! We will figure it all out!

Willoflove: I don't want to figure it out! I wanted Zoe to be my daughter-in-law. Not some hoochie he met along the way!

CookieJ: Um, ladies…

Willoflove: What? What else is happening? I don't think I can take much more today. I'm already one Downer's Luck in.

CookieJ: Stop drinking woman!

Ninasunshine: You all see that? See how she withholds something from us! And then you all say I'm overreacting.

Willoflove: You are definitely not overreacting, Nina. Jenny, I know I'm very lovable and generally don't like violence but I'm (this) close to…letting Fanny kick you.

Toughtolove: Wow…that is some next level violence, Willa…

CookieJ: Ladies!

Willoflove: I know, my hand is still shaking after typing that out. I should go meditate and clear my chakras of this bad energy.

Ninasunshine: Are you sure it's not that cocktail you just drank at ten AM?

CookieJ: LADIES!

Willoflove/Ninasunshine/Toughtolove: What???

CookieJ: It's Zoe. Her water broke.

Willoflove: Say that again.

Ninasushine: Does that mean what I think it means?

Willoflove: See you all in ten!

Toughtolove: See, now we are talking. I love me some plot twist.

12

Matteo

"It is a curious thought, but it is only when you see people looking ridiculous that you realize just how much you love them." –Agatha Christie

"Zoe." I slap my hand on the counter. "Where is my Zoe?"

"Last name?" the receptionist asks with a smile. Jesus, why are they all so happy here. This place could give the Fear Factor a run for its money.

Last name. I don't even know her freaking last name! I scrub my face, "Are there many Zoe's giving birth at the moment?"

"Just one."

I snap my fingers and point the index one at her, "Bingo. That one is mine."

"And you are?"

"Father of the baby, babies," I amend. "Matteo Loverson. Where do I go?" The girl slowly lifts up her eyes to mine, regarding me with a shocked expression.

Yes, yes. Me, Matteo is becoming a dad. The playboy days are over. Can we get on with it?

I give my head a slight, impatient shake, bulging my eyes at her as if to say, "*Any day now*," and she clears her throat, quickly looking up the room number.

"Room 105, down the hall," she says, and I'm running that way before she finishes the sentence. I'm almost at the door when Zoe's agonizing scream pierces through me.

Fuck!

I burst in, seeing her changed into a hospital gown with something strapped around her belly as she stands by the side of the bed, her hands fisting the sheet.

"Beastie, I'm back!" I run over to her, dropping the bags in the corner. "What should I do? Tell me what you need, Sunshine? Where is the fucking doctor? Can't you do something to help her?" I glare at that same chilled-out nurse, sitting by the monitors.

Forget cheap, diluted liquor. She's getting the dish water.

I place my hand on her back, rubbing it and it seems to do something because she takes a deep breath and releases a soft sigh.

"It's all going according to Zoe's plan. The midwife will come when it's time. Just breathe, Zoe, this is a natural process."

"Fuck the plan," Zoe seethes through her teeth. "I want the epidural," she says, yet the nurse is not moving.

"She said she wants whatever that is! Why aren't you moving yet?" I yell out.

"Zoe, you don't really want that. You have a plan and it's important we stick to it."

"Dear God, I'm going to die!" Zoe cries out, and I'm about to throat punch someone if they don't give my Zoe what she needs.

"Here, why don't we try the ball while your husband rubs your back, okay?"

Zoe doesn't correct the nurse when she calls me her husband.

And neither do I.

Maybe the world did flip over today after all because just an hour ago I'd run out screaming if someone called me the word that up until now shared a spot with pineapples on my "top hated" list.

In case you didn't know, I'm allergic to it and break out in hives when I eat it. Yet now I'm waiting for her to call me that again.

Yep, the world is about to end.

The next hour is spent just like that. Zoe on the ball, me rubbing her back and it does seem to work a little. The contractions are close, but the first baby seems to be stuck in the wrong place—or something like that. So, we are trying to twist and turn Zoe so the baby moves, each time with a whole lot of pain for my girl.

"Matteo, I need some water," Zoe whispers, and of course the useless hag is not here when we actually need her.

"I'll go get you some." I kiss her sweaty forehead and take off, looking for a vending machine or a cafeteria when I come to a screeching halt at the scene in the waiting room.

"What the fuck is this?" I extend both of my hands toward the seven elderly members of Loverly Cave—my own mother amongst them—who are sitting right there, a blanket in the middle of them with sandwiches, fruit, and fucking cookies laid out neatly as if they are having a picnic! "Are you out of your minds? Wait, what am I asking...of course you are." I pinch the bridge of my nose.

"Well, we are going to be stuck here for hours, might as well eat," Fanny says and takes another bite of her sandwich like it's a completely normal thing to do.

"Oh, Matteo!" My mom jumps up right away, running to me and cupping my face in both of her hands and the second I see that too-sweet smile on her face I know I'm in for it. "Where did I go wrong in this life?"

Here we go...

"Apparently, at every corner if my only son doesn't think to call his own mother and put her out of her misery thinking she raised a manwhore."

"Jesus, mom." I pinch the bridge of my nose. Again. "Tell me how you really feel."

"Oh, I'll tell you."

"Can it wait? I'm kind of in the middle of something here."

"Yep. I'll just be right here, eating this garden sandwich with the knife in my back." Leave it to my mom to make this life-changing day about her...why not?

She pats the wrinkles out of my shirt. "How is it going? Is my favorite grandchild that I will raise much better than you, here yet?"

"Wrong question, Willa," a grumpy, threatening voice sounds from behind me, and I swear a chill runs through my body. I turn around to see a pregnant Joy Levine glaring at me, with her arms crossed at her chest while her fiancé, Jacob is rubbing her back and giving me a *I'm sorry, man* look.

"The real one is what the hell are you doing here? And go tell that nutwit at the reception that you are leaving so I can go in and be with my friend."

"Wildflower, you need to calm down." Jacob tries to coax her, but she only gets more fired up.

"I need to calm down?" She points to her chest and then redirects it at mine. "He has no business being in there! Zoe needs me and they won't let more than one person to go in."

Hope and Grace, her sisters, try to calm Joy as she keeps yelling and threatening the whole hospital if they don't let her in. Come to think of it, there are a lot of people over here.

"The hell I don't!" comes out a lot harsher than I thought it would. "I'm the father! So, you all can go home or sit here quietly and wait."

Dead silence fills just now a very noisy waiting room as all eyes descend upon me.

"What did you just say?" Joy asks slowly.

"I don't have time for this right now," I snap. "Zoe needs water." I start moving but before I can turn around, a hard fist connects with my jaw and a little crunching sound echoes around us as I feel the coopery tang of my blood over my lip.

Who the fuck just punched me? Pressing my hand to my mouth I turn my head and see an older guy standing there, his nostrils flaring, his hand still balled into tight fist as he glares at me before thrusting a water bottle into my hands. "Go give this to my daughter, then come out so I can hit you a few more times."

Whoa...this is...Zoe's dad?

Fuck...that's not how I planned to meet her father. Well, I wasn't planning on it at all before just a second ago, but what else is new today?

"Kevin." My mom places her hand on his, gently tugging him away from me. "Why don't we all take a moment to breathe, yeah? Right now, we need to focus on Zoe and the baby. Let's light up some healing essence, shall we?" Mom proceeds to take deep breaths and I see Jenny and Rick Levine, Nina and Sam Colson along with their son Alec, Jacob and Grace all take a deep breath too.

"Okay, you all keep breathing," I turn my head toward Zoe's father. "Kevin, I'll let you punch me some more after my babies are born, okay?"

As I'm rushing back to the room, I hear Fanny say in sultry voice, "My, my, Nerds, if you wanted to impress me, you did it."

"Fanny! Leave the poor man alone," someone hisses back.

Did she just refer to Zoe's father as Nerds?

"Did you go to the Alps for this water?" Zoe grumbles as soon as I walk in and then her eyes widen slightly. "What happened?" She tries to get up but immediately cries out in pain and slumps back onto the bed.

"Zoe! Don't move like that by yourself." I rush over, lifting the water bottle to her lips so she can take a sip.

"Why is there blood on your lip, Matteo?"

"Um, I just met your dad," I tell her, wrinkling my nose slightly. "It's safe to say, he's not my biggest fan."

"What? Why? And you mean to tell me he...punched you?" she asks through labored breaths.

"He did. And to be fair, I'd punch me too if I was in his shoes."

"Why?" Those magnetic brown eyes bore into mine.

"Because I wasn't there for you. Because you did all of this on your own. Because I didn't hold your hair when you were throwing up in the mornings or got up in the middle of the night to chase down whatever it was you craved to eat."

And up until just now I didn't realize how much I missed out on. Or how much I wanted to be a part of all of that.

What is happening to me?

Her eyes soften with tears gathering there. "Matteo, you..." She starts to say something but once again the contraction cuts her off. "Oh God, oh God! This is a bad one!"

I grab her hand, letting her squeeze the life out of me again because it seems to help her.

"Come on, let's breathe."

"Matteo, why are you breathing like that too?" Zoe asks when I expressively fill my lungs and stomach with air.

"Moral support."

"Aha. It's totally working."

"It is?" I do it again, and she smacks my stomach with her hand.

"Not in the slightest so stop it! It's pissing me off," she hisses and grunts, squeezing my hand.

Why the fuck did my dick twitch just now? It's her violence, damn it. It did me in last time too but now is so not the time. What's also not helping is how beautiful she looks even now with her hair a mess, her face red and peppered with precipitation while wearing this hideous gown.

"Did I tell you how gorgeous you are?" I say, brushing away a sweaty lock of her hair from her forehead.

"MATTEO!" she screams.

"What, Beastie?"

"Stop. Talking. And using that stupid nickname. Oh God, it hurts so so bad." She squeezes her eyes shut hard and all I want is to take away her pain.

"Remember that night? Our night?" I ask her, and she opens her eyes, looking at me in confusion. Honestly, I'm not really sure why I brought it up either, but she needs a distraction and sex is the only distraction I know. Sue me.

"Why?"

"Because I need you to remember it right now, Zo," I whisper into her ear. "I need you to remember the way my tongue slipped over your sweet pussy. Need you to remember the way my teeth grazed over your sensitive, hard nipples. Damn, those fucking nipples of yours," I growl, feeling my cock growing hard just at the memory of her buds in my mouth.

Who am I trying to distract again?

"If you had any idea what a mere thought of you does to me."

"What...what does it do to you?" She looks at me, her hand still squeezing mine.

"It makes me hard. So fucking hard, it's almost unbearable. And needy. I am fucking needy for you, Zoe." Her breath catches and I'd like to think it's in reaction to me, not the pain. "I am needy for a taste of you. Needy to get my cock back inside your sweet pussy. To slide in and out of you. Slowly at first, teasing your little clit and then thrust all the way back until you feel me in every inch of you, until my balls are slapping against your wetness, making a fucking mess on the sheets."

My lips are now hovering over hers, desperate for a taste and I've never been the one to deny myself much—even now—so, I do just that. I press my lips to hers in a slow, sensual kiss. Just one. Just for a second.

But that's a lie.

One second was never enough with her, even the universe knew it and brought us together, so I linger on her lips a little while longer. My free hand now cupping her beautiful face.

"Did it work? Did I distract you?"

"Matteo," she breathes out, closing her eyes. "I fucking hate you."

"What? Why?"

"Because only you could make me horny while I am thinking of the fastest way to die!"

"Want to kiss again?" I wiggle my eyebrows, silently hoping she says yes but Zoe just shakes her head with a small smile and goes back to breathing.

"Oh God, I think she's coming!"

"The watermelon?" I squeak, my heart jumping to the bottom of my stomach.

"The baby! The baby is coming Matteo!"

"Right! Right, the baby, babies. Oh God, I don't feel so good." All of a sudden, the realization of what is about to happen really hits me and I feel my legs shaking, but before I can think of fainting, Zoe grabs my hand and pulls me to her with inhumane strength.

"I swear to God, if you think of fainting, I will kill you!" she hisses and then starts crying. "I can't do this alone, Matteo! I'm scared!" she sobs and just as quickly as I was falling apart, I'm put back together.

I bend, leaning over her and press my lips to hers in a gentle kiss while my fingers caress her cheek. "You are not alone. Never again." I make that promise knowing I will keep it until the day I die.

I might not have been ready for a family. Might not have ever entertained the mere idea of kids, but here and now, with Zoe...I want it all.

13

Zoe

"Swoon. I'll catch you." –The English Patient

"Hello, mama," the midwife says with a smile. "And dad." She nods to Matteo, and I feel my already fragile stomach, churning. Why haven't I told him this whole time? "I hear we are ready to meet this baby."

"Yes, yes we are!" He jumps up, knocking the chair over. His eyes are a little frantic and he holds my hand back just as hard as I'm holding his.

I'm not sure when or how but somewhere along the way, letting go stopped being an option and I'm a horrible human being for using him like this but it seems *I need* Matteo. This amazing guy who is so young, yet so ready to take on the role he decided was his. When he left to get me water, I thought I was going to die. The pain became too much to bear alone, and I was a second from passing out. However, as soon as he stepped back inside, I drew a long breath in and my heart rate slowed, my tense body relaxed a tiny bit and as soon as I could, I grabbed his hand again.

And then he proceeded to take my mind off all this in the filthiest way possible. And it worked. Thinking of that night, of the things he's done to me felt like taking a shot of the best drug. It took it all away.

Until now.

"Let's do this." The midwife claps her hands, pulls out a little speaker from her coat pocket and turns on music. "The Final Countdown" by *Europe*.

"What the fuck is wrong with people in this hospital?" The look on Matteo's face is priceless. "They are either too fucking happy or too crazy?" he muses to me, shaking his head as we watch the doc start shaking off her hands and legs as if preparing for a fucking fight and I can't help it. I burst out laughing despite the pain.

He's right, this is batshit crazy territory and so ridiculous I can't stop giggling.

I'm in so much pain I can barely see straight, yet with him here it feels manageable and watching his *what the fuck* face does me in, reminding me of the best night of my life and it's like he can read my mind, locking our eyes on each other.

"Never have I ever given birth while 'The Final Countdown' is playing, and the midwife was high on something," I whisper, and watch his beautiful face stretch into a huge grin. Matteo lifts up my hand he's holding and kisses the back of it.

"Never have I ever felt like killing so many people at once," he answers with that same grin which now is a bit more frantic, and I laugh again.

"All right, let's do this," the midwife interrupts our conversation and thrusts one of my legs into his arms.

Matteo looks at the leg, then at me with eyes as wide as saucers, leg again and to the midwife.

"What am I supposed to do with this?"

"Hold it, Dad, so you can get a better view of your baby being born into this beautiful world," she says casually, bobbing her head to the music, totally oblivious to this "dad's" fast-paling face. Oh, Jesus, he's so going to pass out now.

"Y-you want me to s-see that?" He motions with his finger to where she just raised my gown and started probing around my vagina. I'm in so much pain, I no longer feel anything.

"Don't you?" the midwife asks with a raised eyebrow as she stretches me down there. "Are you not man enough?" she challenges him, as if she knew exactly what to say. Right away, Matteo's back snaps up, his eyes narrowing on her.

"I'm man enough for anything," he protests and says something else, but my mind is growing fuzzy, and I no longer keep up with the conversation.

I think he's talking to himself, because I swear I hear, "*It's okay. Man the fuck up, Matteo! You are about to become a dad!*" Following with the freaking breathing exercises I was supposed to do as if he's the one pushing this baby out.

The midwife and the nurse are telling me to push, and I get a glimpse of Matteo getting all up and personal with my vagina as he yells for me to do the same, his head hunched over to see what's going on between my legs.

Oh well, if he wants to be traumatized for life it's not my fault.

Somewhere along the way I hear him call out, "I see the head! Beastie! I see the head, but I can't tell the color of the hair. It's too bloody."

"Jesus Christ, Matteo, stop looking at my vagina," I manage to mumble as I push again and again until the pressure is gone. The pain is gone. Everything is gone apart from a piercing cry from both Matteo and my baby girl at the same time.

"IT'S A GIRL!" he yells out as she wails.

"Congratulations, parents, you have a beautiful baby girl." My little bug gets placed on my chest and all the worries I've had about being a single mom vanish. She's my entire world. Just like that.

Tears are streaming down my face as I lift a shaky hand to her back, gently caressing the soft as silk skin.

"Where is the second one?" Matteo asks, bent over me, looking in between my legs.

"What second one?" the midwife asks.

"The second baby! Did you forget to get it out?" he hisses out, and she raises her eyebrow at me.

I smile, placing my hand on his and his eyes snap to mine, immediately thawing as he takes us in. "Matteo, there is no second baby.

I was only pregnant with just one. This one." I kiss the top of her head as she's resting on my bare chest.

"No second baby? So, no twins?" he asks, drawing his eyebrows together and I think he's…sad about it?

"Nope."

"Oh." Yep, definitely sad, which is crazy! The guy didn't want a relationship not even six months ago, and now he's disappointed that I had only one kid?

"One is enough." He nods to himself and bends over to us. "Can I…can I touch her?"

I should open my mouth and tell him he's off the hook, but those eyes…the way he's looking at her…I can't.

"Yes." I smile, and he settles his head right over my shoulder, watching her with adoration as if she's really his. As if she's his whole world just like that too. As if he will love and protect her until his last breath while gently drawing his fingers over her back.

More tears stream down my face because there's nothing, *nothing*, I wouldn't do to have this. For this to be real and not a dream that's about to end as soon as I tell him the truth and he runs for the hills. Thanking his lucky starts it was all a misunderstanding.

"Dad, do you want to cut the cord?"

Matteo gulps, nods and with tears in both of our eyes makes the cut.

Mine are from happiness mixed with longlining like I've never known before.

His?

I'm not sure.

14

Matteo

"I did not give you the gift of life. Life gave me the gift of you." – Unknown

God, she's so tiny. How is it possible for her to be so small? What if something happens to her? How is she supposed to survive in this vile world all alone?

No, she'll never be alone. Time for a career change I guess, because I ain't gonna leave her side. Like ever.

Maybe I can set up the bar at the cottage? To-go bar? Yeah, that's what I'm gonna do.

While I was lost in my planning, Zoe took off her shirt, her gorgeous full breasts spilling free and as my mouth watered my little girl got busy latching onto her nipple.

How normal is it to be jealous of your own child?

Yeah, thought so…get a grip, Matteo! But there is no gripping what I'm feeling right now. There is no containing the explosive, confusing emotions coursing through me.

There is everything in there, but the most prominent one is longing. A sense of rightness. Of being at the right place at the right time. And an attraction to Zoe that goes way past simple, trivial lust. Sharing this experience with her…it was…it was everything I never knew I wanted. And now I'm afraid there is no going back.

But is it really fear I'm feeling?

Because it feels awfully a lot like excitement and…love?

I'm not sure how much time passes as I just lay over Zoe's shoulder, watching our daughter munching on her breast happily as I stroke her soft skin when the nurse comes back and takes her away from Zoe's chest. A feeling that has my heart squeezing painfully sets in. Panic. I'm panicking.

"Matteo?" Zoe's arm lands on mine. "Are you okay?"

"Why are they taking her away?" I ask without moving my eyes from the tiny bundle.

"They need to clean and weigh her."

At that moment she starts wailing loudly and I tense up.

"Are they hurting her?"

"No, no. This is normal."

"But they will give her back, right?"

"Yeah." I can hear the smile in Zoe's voice. "They will."

"I'll just go stand over there." I point to my baby and march up to the table thing they have her at. "Beastie, just look at her!" I exclaim, gazing at the tiny bundle. "Have you ever seen a prettier baby? What am I saying? Of course you haven't. No one is as perfect as my Mellie," I tell the nurse who smiles at me.

"Did you just name my daughter?" Zoe's question sounds from behind me. I look over my shoulder, shooting her what is considered my signature smile and nod. "Sure did."

Zo raises her eyebrow. "And what if I don't like the name Mellie?"

"What's not to like?" I ask with mock offence. "She's our little watermelon that you so bravely pushed out of your beautiful, sweet p—"

Zoe interrupts me before I can finish. "Please for the love of all that's holy, do not"—she shoots me a pointed look—"continue that sentence." She's trying to scold me, but I don't miss the little blush she is now spotting.

"Like I was saying. She's the perfect watermelon, hence Mellie."

"Your logic is unmatched, Matteo," Zoe says in dry tone.

I shoot her a crooked smile, a wink and watch that little blush deepen. "See, I knew you'd love it too."

A nurse confirms we are going with that name and runs to get the paperwork done, handing me a swaddled Mellie to hold. For a second when she was carrying her my way, I thought how bizarre it all is.

Me, about to hold my daughter. Talk about life curves.

But then a warmth so bright spilled over my heart, I felt it bursting through me as soon as she was settled in my arms.

That feeling of rightness is back.

"You are so, so tiny Mellie. But don't worry, Daddy will be here to protect you. Always," I whisper to her and gently kiss her cute, button nose.

I'm still rocking and gazing at her when I hear Zoe clear her throat and call my name.

"Matteo," Zoe says a little unsure, making my eyes snap to hers. Those beautiful eyes that are filled to the brink with tears and I rush over to her.

"Hey, what's wrong, Sunshine? Why are you crying?" I ask, whipping the tear sliding down her cheek.

"Because I'm an idiot."

"What?" I ask, confused what's she talking about.

"I really should have told you right away, as soon as I saw you this morning but..." She trails of cryptically.

"But?"

Zoe exhales. "You were so funny and sweet and caring that *I* got carried away with this. Pretending this was something it was never meant to be." She exhales some more. "You are not the father."

What did she just say?

"What?" I hear myself asking, but my brain is stuck somewhere else.

"Matteo, I really *really* appreciate all your help and support here today." Zoe leans into me, placing her hand on mine. "I'm not sure I could do this without you. I'm sorry I didn't tell you right away."

"Hold up here one second." I swallow the thick lump, stuck in my throat while feeling my world tilt upside down for the hundredth time today. Yet this one feels the fucking worst. "You are trying to say that that sweetest little bundle I just watched being born, the one I'm holding, is not mine?"

Zoe sighs, lowering her eyes. "Yes. Unfortunately, she's is not."

My heart squeezes painfully, doubling over inside my chest, and I start breathing heavily. "Matteo?"

"One second," I whisper, my voice growing coarse and drawing Mellie a little closer to my chest as if afraid that someone will come and steal her away from my arms. "I just need one fudging moment over here."

Not Mine.

"Shouldn't this be a dream come true? You, not being stuck to one woman who you barely know because you knocked her up?" Zoe asks without looking at me, hiding away her face.

Yeah, it should be.

But it sounds more like a nightmare at this moment.

I'm a fucking idiot.

I look down. Of course she's not my baby! Our night was six months ago, yet I somehow convinced myself that it was enough time. Zoe did nothing wrong, come to think of it, she did try to tell me something a few times but every time she was interrupted.

Happy. I should be happy. I should hand over the baby and run the hell away from here.

I should forget all that nonsense that I've conjured up in my head over the past few hours. I should go celebrate that my fun and easy days are not over. I should go out, drink, and get laid.

I should not be fighting this tightness in my chest. Or look at the most perfect woman who was—after all—just a one-night stand and has a whole beautiful life without me. I shake off the ease with which I came into this role that was never mine, just because it was Zoe who was pregnant.

I lower my eyes to Mellie, memorizing every little detail about her.

Fuck, Matteo, what the hell? This is not you. You were never meant for this kind of life.

Then why does it feel like I've just ripped away a part of my soul when I passed a peacefully sleeping Mellie into Zoe's arms?

I clear my throat, force a smile that has no business being forced and get up from the bed.

"Yeah. Of course. I really shouldn't have jumped to weird conclusions like that." I wet my lips, fighting the urge to scream or throw something at the wall or better yet, curse myself for putting me in this situation.

Snap the fuck out of it, Matteo.

I take one last look at Mellie, force another smile for Zoe without really seeing her and turn for the door. "You take care, okay? And I guess...I'll see you around."

I don't look back. I don't wait for Zoe to say anything back. She probably thinks I'm batshit crazy, thinking I'm the father of her baby. Hell, there is a real dad somewhere out there who would probably kill me for sharing this special moment with *his* girls.

Fuck...why does that thought hurts so bad?

As soon as the door behind me closes, I fall against the wall, sliding down until my butt hits the floor, close my eyes, and take a deep breath. "This is the best-case scenario, Matteo."

But then my little girl sends a piercing cry that shoots straight through my chest and I'm wondering who the hell am I trying to fool...

***

"Matteo? Son?" I hear my mom's voice and turn her way where she is standing with the same group in the waiting room.

"Oh, hey, you guys are still here?" I know I shouldn't sound like my world has just ended but for the love of cocktails, I cannot muster a single smile. Even the forced ones I just gave Zoe.

It seems like I'm all out.

"Of course we are. How is it going in there?" They are all looking at me expectedly and I realize no one has told them that the baby—Mellie—was born. All seven pounds zero ounces and nineteen inches of her. With fuzzy blonde hair and the softest skin.

I blink back the stupid emotion trying to break free. "Oh, sorry, I thought someone told you. The baby was born," I tell them, and hear the collective sigh of relief. "She's healthy and beautiful."

"Now, can I go in to see my friend?" Joy narrows her eyes at me, and I simply step aside, gesturing for her to go ahead. She looks at me for a second and then starts walking but just as she's passing by me, some insanity takes over my limbs and I grab onto her wrist, halting her.

"Take care of them, okay?" I whisper, holding her gaze until she nods and starts walking again.

I turn to see everyone watching us curiously, but I just don't have the mental capacity for anyone else today.

I need to go sleep and wake up back to my old, usual self.

Love Hive:

Kevini'mnotNerds: Where is that little bastard? How could he leave her all alone again?

Thoughtolove: God, I love it when you get all angry.

CookieJ: Who do you mean, Kevin?

Kevini'mnotNerds: The little shit that got my daughter pregnant and left her.

Willoflove: The father of the baby is here?

Kevini'mnotNerds: Sure is! In case you missed him, he's the one you call your son.

Ninasunshine: Great. Now you made her cry again after I just spent an hour on meditating with her.

Toughtolove: Don't take that tone with him.

Kevini'mnotNerds: So? Where is he?

Ninasunshine: Kevin, Matteo is not the father of Zoe's baby.

Willoflove: He's not the father *crying emoji, wailing emoji*

Kevini'mnotNerds: But he said...and he looked...

CookieJ: Like they were his?

Kevini'mnotNerds: Yeah.

CookieJ: They will be.

15
Never Have I Ever

*Matteo: Never have I ever wanted to be someone I'm not.
Until today...*

16

Zoe

"You are the only person who can make me feel like I'm dreaming and awake at the same time." –Unknown

As soon as the door to my hospital room closed with Matteo on the other side of it, seemingly calm and peaceful Mellie started crying and still hasn't stopped three weeks later.

And not just her.

I have been an emotional mess from that same moment too. But I blame the hormones and Mellie's fussiness and not the fact that I miss a guy I have no business missing.

"Shh, Mel baby, what's wrong? I don't know what else to do!" I break out in another fit of sobs because I've tried it all and she won't stop. I rock her, walk around with her, breastfeed her—I tried the bottle too—and bought all possible pacifiers for her to take but she refuses them all.

Joy thought it could be her tummy and we tried all the possible remedies for that too and nothing...nothing works. Her pediatrician says it's normal even though I did notice the crease in her forehead when she was examining Mellie.

The only time she stops is when she falls asleep on my breast and then I don't dare to breathe too much to not wake her. I'm exhausted and sleep-deprived and even though I've expected it all, I did not imagine it would be like this.

"My God, Mel, you are scaring the ducks out of me," Joy says as she walks into our home. She is pregnant herself, with twins, and seeing how difficult I have it with one is not helping her own anxiety.

She is the best friend I could ask for, though. Joy came in as soon as Matteo left, saw us both bawling our eyes of, cursed the local bar and men in this town and stayed with us till now. I keep sending her home, to her husband, but she refuses to leave me alone.

"Joy, I don't know what to do anymore," I confess, and Joy must see the last shred of desperation in my eyes because my stoic friend softens and sighs with compassion.

"If anyone can do it, it's you Zoe Holsted. This is just a phase. It will pass, you'll see."

"Do you even believe the crap you are trying to sell me yourself?"

"Don't curse in from of my goddaughter." She narrows her eyes at me. Yeah, Joy declared herself a godmother that first day too.

Alec, Hope's husband, and Jacob rock-paper-scissored who will be the godfather. No lie. They stood there for a solid hour, playing to the tune of Mellie's wailing until Alec won and Jacob is still pouting over it because he already bought a shirt that said: *Best Ducking Godfather.*

So, a day later he showed up in another shirt that said: *Uncle – 1 Godfather – 0.*

When Alec asked what is that supposed to mean he pulled out a onesie he had made for Mel that said: *Uncle is my hero. Not that ducking godfather.*

And so, the war began.

I'm guessing that's part of the reason why Joy is still living with me.

"Crap is not a curse."

"If I say it is, it means it is and now it's banned from this house," she says with a straight face, pulls out her phone and start typing away.

"Great," I groan. "Let's add on to my misery. Who are you texting?"

"Help."

"What help?" My back straightens. Joy knows perfectly well how I feel about anyone helping me. I made my bed when I decided to raise my child all on my own and I will lay in it until the end.

"The one you desperately need."

"Joy," I growl.

"Oh, shut up." She throws her arms up. "This whole 'I can do it all' crap stops now. You have a whole town waiting to come over and help, so you will take it."

"So much for banning the word crap in this house," I mumble. "And I do take their help or at least the meals they cook for me." Joy ignores me and keeps texting. "Please, don't tell me you literally texted the whole town?"

"It's like you don't know me at all. Do I look like I'm insane or have a death wish to you?"

"Well, you did marry Jacob, so I guess that's up in the air at the moment."

"Oh, look at you being funny." She mock-smiles at me, and I fight the real smile trying to appear. "Your mommy is real jokester when she's sleep-deprived, Mel." Joy kisses the top of Mellie's head. "I only texted the Fantastic Four."

"Only?" I gape at her. "You might as well have posted it on Love Hive.

"Stop being dramatic, it doesn't suit you."

Not five minutes later, my front door flies open, and Fanny, Jenny, Nina, and Willa come inside.

"Nerds tagged along with us, hope you don't mind." Fanny throws her thumb over her shoulder toward my dad who just walked in as well. And yes, apparently Fanny likes to give everyone a candy nickname and somehow my dad received that one.

"That woman will be the death of me." He sighs and embraces me in a hug, cooing to crying Mel in my arms.

"Baby, you really shouldn't flirt with me like that in public." Fanny waggles her eyebrows at him. "I have nothing against exhibitionism."

My eyes grow wide. "Dad? Is there something I should know?"

"Nothing at all," he answers too fast, raising my suspicions to a whole new level. It's not that I don't want him to be happy with someone, I'd love it, actually. He deserves it.

"Don't worry." She winks at me. "I'll fill you in as soon as I wear him down."

"Dear Lord," I groan. "Please don't. You guys are big kids, you can do whatever you'd like just without me knowing, okay?"

"There is nothing going on," Dad snaps. "Now give me my granddaughter and go rest."

"Go, honey." Jenny pats my arm. "We got this for a few hours. And by this, I do mean Fanny."

"Har har, Snickers, you are just jealous of my game."

"Fanny, the only thing I'm jealous of is your big head and karate skills."

"What about my impeccable style?" She points to her neon orange track suit and Jenny wrinkles her nose.

"I am saying this with all the love and care." Her smile turns saccharine sweet then drops. "No."

I watch in fascination as they all start bickering with each other and even Mel seems to be interested in their ridiculous conversations because she's slowed her crying and now only whimpers quietly. How are they all best friends?

"Go." Joy pushes me out and I head to the bedroom at the end of the hall.

Having these amazing people come to my rescue fills me with both gratitude and guilt. I shouldn't have to rely on others to help me with my daughter.

I can do it all.

Except, as that thought goes through my head, a whole other one overshadows it. It's not really a thought, it's a memory of Matteo and his excitement to be a dad. I bet he wouldn't let anyone near Mellie. I bet he would want to do it all by himself too.

And I wouldn't say no to Matteo's help. Not that he would be interested. What twenty-three-year-old wants to get involved with an older woman who has a baby on top of that.

Yet as I fall asleep, I imagine his strong arms wrapped around me, telling me to rest while he takes care of our daughter.

I'm aware it's a dangerous dream to have, but that's all I have left, so let me cherish it a while longer.

Love Hive:

Willoflove: Did you all see how tired my poor Zoe is?

Ninasunshine: That girl was about to pass out when we showed up.

CookieJ: She is also stubborn as a mule, refusing to accept the help.

Toughtolove: When did that ever stand before us, ladies?

Willoflove: You are right, Fanny. We took a step back after that day at the hospital, but I think it was a mistake.

Toughtolove: That's what I've been telling you all for the past three weeks! But noooo, no one listens to little, poor old Fanny.

CookieJ: Please don't be modest on our account. You forgot to add terrifying, delusional, crazy, and a few more adjectives.

Toughtolove: Snickers, are you still salty that your youngest daughter loves me more?

CookieJ: SHE DOES NOT!

Toughtolove: Whatever you need to tell yourself.

Willoflove: Okay...let's all inhale and exhale a few times.

Willoflove: Jenny, please go make yourself that Calming Spirit tea I got you. Fanny, you should finally try that Humble Garden I made specially for you.

Willoflove: Should I make some tea for Zoe?

Toughtolove: Only if it will include a few drops of your son in there.

Ninasunshine: Fanny is right.

CookieJ: What?

Ninasunshine: Zoe needs someone to be there for her. Someone she can rely on and not feel guilty about asking for help like she does with us.

Joydon'tpissmeofflevine: Zoe is fine. Whatever you are thinking, stop it right this second.

CookieJ: Oooo, you guys I have the perfect idea!

Joydon'tpissmeofflevine: Mom what did I just say a second ago? None of your ideas are perfect.

CookieJ: Shush, yeh ungrateful daughter of mine and remember who you have to thank for that sexy husband of yours.

Tinyhousebigheart: Mama J, trust me, I am grateful for the both of us.

Joydon'tpissmeofflevine: Traitor @tinyhousebigheart, next time there is a spider in the house I am not killing it for you.

Toughtolove: How many times do I have to remind you all that the sexting chat happens on Wednesdays.

Joydon'tpissmeofflevine: We are NOT sexting. I was threatening him.

Toughtolove: Your form of foreplay is none of my business.

Toughtolove: Snickers, tell us that plan of yours.

17

Matteo

"Any man can help make a child, but it takes a special man to help raise a child." –Tony Gaskins

I watch as my mom walks into LPs, wearing a happy, dopey smile after she went to see my girls.

Jesus Christ! It's been three damn weeks of trying to kick those words out of my head. Every day I've been convincing myself there are no *"my girls."* I even took to repeating it in front of a mirror every morning and night, followed by a pep talk that I'm too young and free to want that.

That I love my one-night stands and that any day now I will jump back into the game.

If only I actually believed a word out of my mouth, it would be great.

But not only do I not believe it, I also started being jealous of my own mother who got to spend time with Zoe and Mellie. Became a scowling prick that patrons started to avoid and to top it all off, completely and utterly uninterested in anyone who's name is not

Zoe, is not a curvy blonde with dark eyes and who doesn't have the most perfect daughter in the world.

Yeah...I'm fucked. And I don't have a damn clue what to do with that.

It's not like I can just walk up to her front door, knock, and say what? Can I have a play date with you and your kid? How about a sleepover, I can take the floor? Take me back, I promise, I'm potty trained?

Jesus, Matteo, you are totally losing it, aren't you?

"Hey, son."

"Hey," I greet her without looking up from the glass I've been cleaning for the past two hours since I found out where my mom was headed and was not able to concentrate on anything at all.

"That must be the cleanest glass we have." Mom smirks at me.

"Just taking care of our bar." Her smirk vanishes, replaced by a scowl she's been wearing ever since I walked out from the hospital.

"When you should be taking care of something completely different," she says under her breath, but I still catch it. "I went to see Zoe," she says louder, making sure I hear. As if I'd ever miss that name being called out.

My ears seem to be trained to it.

See what a good dog I'd make?

"Great."

"Mellie is so adorable."

I huff. "Of course, she is," I tell her with a weird sense of pride I should not be feeling. Have no right to feel. But that little girl is the most perfect creation. Just as her mom is.

God, they were so beautiful when little Mellie was nestled on her chest right after she was born. My eyes still sting every time I remember that moment. Which is why I try to avoid any mention of those two.

"But she's been fussy," mom continues, and my spine snaps up. That's the first I hear of Mellie not doing great and it's partially because anytime someone around me started talking about them, I immediately left, not wanting to torture myself.

Despite tiny alarm bells going off in my head that I should leave like I always do, this time I stay. Silently listening for any nugget of information about my little watermelon.

"I guess it's a good thing Jenny decided to call that guy to come and help Zoe."

"What guy?" The question flies out of my mouth like a bullet after passing through my insides, grazing that hole that's already been there since that day at the hospital.

"Oh, the one she was seeing before she left."

Is it just me or is there an annoying ringing sound over here? It's so loud I can't hear what else my mother is saying. Did someone turn off the lights too? Why has everything suddenly gone dark?

Most importantly…did someone just punch me in the gut?

Some random guy thinks he can just show up and be what? Zoe's boyfriend again? Mellie's father? And what the hell is wrong with my mom and her friends for encouraging this?

The roaring in my ears intensifies and I have to grab onto the table, my knuckles turning white.

"Did she?" I grit through my teeth without looking up because I love my mom dearly but right now that fact seems small and unnecessary with all the anger coursing through my veins.

"Did she what?" Her voice is so calm like we are talking about next week's menu and not about my life crumpling to the ground.

"Did she already call him?"

"Oh, yeah, I think she said he's coming later today." That's it, that roaring in my head is a full-blown explosion now.

"What the fuck, mom?" I roar, snapping my eyes wide to her so she can see the bloody murder written in each speckle of my irises.

"Language, Matteo!" she snaps back. "And what does it matter to you, anyway? It's not like you wanted a family ever in this lifetime, no?"

She's baiting me. I know it. My brain understands it.

The only problem?

My heart doesn't give a single fuck. Too bad it doesn't get to call in the shots here. It doesn't know what's best for me. Or more importantly, what's best for Zoe and Mellie.

So, I just hum in response, ignoring the tiny cracking noises coming from that glass in my hands.

It's for the best.

That guy is probably older, has a respectable, stable job and doesn't think monogamy is a curse word. Someone who can take care of Zoe and Mellie. He must have his shit figured out and knows what he wants in life.

Maybe he's even the one who is the real father to Mellie.

Fuck, I pause for a second, breathing hard through the burn in my chest. Why do I feel so irrationally pissed right now? Of course there is a real father somewhere out there. The one who actually has the right to be there for Zoe and their daughter.

"I don't," I finally respond to mom, but don't lift my eyes up. "Hope he can help her."

I hear a long sigh from mom, but I don't have the time to decipher it. I have to clean this glass.

Then I'll clean one more. And another. I will keep cleaning these fucking glasses until the roaring in my head and the tremble in my hands stops. Until that simmering range settles down.

An hour and fifty-six glasses later a female voice calls out my name, pulling me from my destructive thoughts that haven't settled one bit. I look up and see Linsey waving me over.

She's wearing a too-tight-for-her top once again, the one that barely contains her tits inside. Her lips are painted a bright pink, the same color as her nails and she is looking at me like I'm to be her dinner tonight. Or she is to be my desert.

My very first thought is how fast can I run to make it to the bathroom to throw up, but then I stop. Maybe this is what I need.

Zoe is clearly moving on, so should I, right? Granted, Linsey is not the best choice for that but at this point I will do whatever it takes to stop that roaring in my head and burn in my chest. So, I stroll over to where this Barbie-wannabe is sitting, trying to concentrate on her tits. Because tits are tits, they always do the job for me.

Except the longer I look at hers, the stronger the urge is there to throw up. Unfortunately, Linsey interprets my twisted face as one for wanting her and leans even more over the bar.

Jesus Christ, I can see her nipples.

Breathe, Matteo. Don't you dare leave. You need to get out of that stupid funk and get laid again. You need to get back to your normal lifestyle.

"Hey, Matty baby," she says in her overly sweet voice.

"Hey, Linsey." *Concentrate on her lips. Maybe those will be better.* Nope. They are not. "What can I get ya, darlin?

Oh hell, why did that taste so sour on my tongue? That is the most innocent line I've ever used on the ladies.

Linsey's eyes light up and I watch as her chest expands, breathing heavier. "You, Matty."

"Um, what?" *What do you think she means, idiot?*

"Come on, Matty, you know what I mean." She draws her pink nails over her pink lips, and I feel my dick not only *not* getting hard, but I'm pretty sure he's shrinking in size. "I knew you still want me the way I want you. I saw you checking me out the whole evening." She giggles while I'm trying to figure out when did I look at her before a minute ago. "Let's go up to your room, Matty."

Well, talk about being straight forward.

Say yes, Matteo. Say fucking yes and get over whatever hang up you have in your stupid head.

Only the mere thought of touching her makes my skin crawl with disgust. I look up to the heavens, silently asking "why me" then sigh, and pinching the bridge of my nose, turn back to Linsey. "Sorry, that won't be happening."

"What?" she shrieks, loud enough for the whole bar to hear. "But you want me!"

"Um..."

"Um? What is um supposed to mean, Matty baby?" That stupid nickname.

"Jesus, stop calling me that. And I'm sorry, but you got the wrong impression, Linsey. You are a pretty girl and all, but I'm..."

I'm what? Hung up on someone who is never going to be mine? Thinking of being a husband and a father? I'm fucking what? None of that is what I actually want so why was is the first thing I've thought about?

"You need more time?" Linsey asks, her brows pulled together. "Because I'll wait for you, Matty baby. I'll wait forever."

I wince. "Please don't." I'm a dick but no matter what, Linsey is not the girl I am going to sleep with ever again.

She opens her mouth to say something but anther voice from the other side calls me over. "Hey, son." I know that voice and when I look his way, I see Zoe's dad sitting on one of the bar stools, waving me over and I gladly take the escape he unknowingly provides.

I feel Linsey fuming in the back of me. What the hell was I thinking coming up to her and even considering sleeping with her again. *Ugh*, I fight that shudder again.

"Hello, Mr. Holsted. What can I get ya?" He's been to the bar a couple of times since Mellie was born but he was always in the company of his friends, Rick Levine and Sam Colson, or with Mrs. Lovesil and we haven't spoke again since the day he punched me.

"A beer would be nice, your choice."

"Coming right up," I tell him and go to pick one of those sparkling clean glasses, filling it up. "There you go." I slide it over to him. "Anything else?"

"Yeah," he says but instead of continuing he just looks at me long and hard.

Why is he looking at me like that? Is it hot in here all of a sudden?

Kevin Holsted is not a huge guy, more like a teddy bear kind and not someone you would find threatening, yet here I am, basically shivering from the assessing look he's giving me.

The pause stretches, making me squirm under his gaze, and mind you, I'm not easily intimidated but I haven't been myself in a long while so maybe I need to get used to this new version of Matteo. I'm about to turn around and flee when he says, "You can tell me if you are done being a chickenshit yet?"

"Um, what?" I gulp. That's not what I thought he was going to say. I expected an order of wings with a side of fries, instead I got served a hot one myself.

"It's not a hard question, Matteo." He takes a sip of his beer. "You can even use only one word for the answer. A yes or a no."

I look at him, sputtering over my thoughts inside my head. What the fuck does he mean am I done being a chickenshit? When was I ever one?

I feel the heat inside me rising up, bristling out of me.

"I'm not a fucking chickenshit!" I don't mean to snap at him, so I take a deep breath and add, "Respectfully, sir."

Kevin raises one eyebrow at me, taking another sip. "Good job reining yourself in there. You'll need it in the future."

What is he talking about? What the heck is going on here? But before I can ask anything, he continues. "Did you know Zoe is not my biological daughter?"

"What?" I frown. "No...no, I didn't." And I would have never thought that. From what I've seen—which granted, wasn't much, he loves her like his own flesh and blood.

"Didn't stop me from loving and taking care of her like she is," he says while casually drinking his beer. "It also didn't make me run away as fast as I could from her mom with my tail tucked between my legs. Even though that woman didn't possess half the good qualities my Zoe girl does."

I narrowed my eyes at him, was that a dig at me?

"I didn't run away as fast as I could with my tail tucked between my legs, if that's what you implied," I say through clenched teeth.

"Oh? Sure could have fooled me." The man is on a roll here.

"I'm not boyfriend material, let alone a father. It was never what I wanted."

Kevin regards me with an assessing gaze, then turns back to his beer and keeps drinking like nothing is wrong.

"What? That's it? No more comments my way?"

"No point. You are not the man for my Zoe, so maybe it's for the best they called that other one."

Again, with this fucking phone call bullshit. *I don't care. I don't care. I. Don't. Care.*

"I knew it the second I saw her that she was my daughter. Zoe was peeking from around the corner, assessing me, when her mother invited me over, and just one look into those curious brown pools and I knew," he says with a smile, clearly reliving that day right now.

"Smart as a whip and cutest kid I've ever seen. Then she smiled at me, and my heart was hers from that moment on. I knew it."

Fuck, why does it feel like there is not enough air in this bar? And my gut feels like I've been sucker-punched right through it again because everything Kevin just said? That's what I felt. Those were the feelings that ran through me like a hoard of wild horses as soon as Mellie let out her first cry.

Those are the thoughts that I try to shoo away every morning and every night for the past three whole weeks. The thoughts I've been fighting since I first met Zoe because this is not just about Mel. This is about my family.

Mellie is mine. Zoe is mine.

Mine.

Kevin leans back, and I swear I see a small smile pull up in the corners of his mouth while I'm on the verge of a panic attack over here. "There. That wasn't so hard now, was it, son?"

No. It's all way too simple, actually. It was right there in front of me seven months ago, yet I was too blind or too lost in my ways to notice the gift that I was given. The gift that walked through my door.

Because yeah, I never wanted to dip a toe into monogamy. Until that ray of sunshine with an identity of a feral beast, parted my clouds with her mere presence and I won't allow some uptight bastard steal my thunder. Or my family.

I have no idea what I'm doing or how to do it, what I do know is that no one will love my Mellie more than I do. No one will touch my Zoe the way I do. And I won't give them the chance.

I don't bother answering Kevin, I simply step out from the bar and run upstairs. Moments later, I'm headed out the door with a packed bag in my hands and determination written all over my face.

"Matteo? Where are you going?" I hear my mother call out from somewhere in the back.

"You better have bail money saved up, mom, because if I'm already late, I won't go down without a fight."

18

Zoe

"When you realize you want to spend the rest of your life with somebody, you want the rest of your life to start as soon as possible." -When Harry Met Sally

Impatient knocking sounds at my door, making me frown. Did Joy forget something?

I finally managed to get her out of here and go home to her husband. She put up a fight, but I already feel guilty enough for stealing her from Jacob for this long and besides, I really need to figure out how to be a single mom sooner rather than later.

I look around for something she could have left behind, but nothing catches my eye so after another fit of knocking mixed with Mellie's wailing, I open the door and freeze. Apart from the chilly, fresh autumn air, I am greeted by the furious eyes of Matteo Loverson.

What is he doing here...looking like he's about to kill someone and feel no remorse for it? But then in a blink his eyes shift to the fussy, crying baby in my arms and his demeanor changes just like that.

The tension seeps out of his shoulders, dropping to a relaxed position. That sexy body of his stops vibrating and those brown eyes filling up with love and mushy emotions instead of ones that could land him in jail. His balled-up fists uncurl, making the bag he was holding in one of them drop to the ground—why does he have a bag with him?

Is he leaving town again? Oh God, he is, isn't he? He probably came over to say goodbye. And why does that make me feel like curling up into a ball and crying myself to sleep? I have no claims on this man or his young, free spirit. I could never be the one to tame this beast and won't try it.

But why was he so mad when he got here? None of this makes sense to me and before I can even open my mouth to say hello, he reaches for Mellie, taking her from my arms and instantly, my crying daughter stops.

She just stops. As if she wasn't screaming her lungs out since she woke up and nestled her little nose into his half-covered, tattooed chest. I can't even blame her or call her a little traitor because given the chance I'd gladly nuzzle into his warmth as well.

Damn this man and his unbuttoned shirts.

I must be too stupefied about this whole ordeal because I just stand there and blink, watching him slowly rock her, cooing some gibberish that she listens to intently.

I didn't even put up a fight when he pulled her out of my hands. What kind of mother am I?

The wake-up call finally rang, snapping me from Matteo-trance and I go to take her back, narrowing my eyes at him but just as my fingers graze her, she gives out a tiny cry sound, protesting my action and I retreat with a sigh.

Great, he got us both eating out of his hands now.

Way to go, Mellie...

"Matteo, what are you doing here?" Do I sound detached? Like having him stand in front of me, holding my daughter with a look of pure love and adoration does nothing to my heart?

"Moving in," he says casually without taking his eyes off Mel. I blink and open my mouth to say something, but nothing comes out and I look like a lost fish. Matteo uses that moment to scoop up his bag and push past me into the house without an invitation.

"Sure. Come on in. Make yourself at home."

"Thank you." He flashes his dazzling smile and starts looking around the house like he belongs here, strolling toward my bedroom in the back.

Well, that makes me move, blocking his way. "What do you mean you're moving in? Did you get kicked out of your apartment?"

There must be a logical explanation for all of this.

"Nope." Again, with that casual tone as he sets up his stuff by the couch and wanders off into the kitchen, which is now a beautiful, warm part of the cottage instead of the seventies gone wrong situation it was before. I completely remodeled the whole place after I moved to LC, including building an additional bedroom downstairs for Mel since originally the house only had one, which Matteo is off to next.

"Then I don't understand. And stop snooping.

"I'm not snooping. I'm looking." He keeps going, peeking into the brand-new bathroom. It's pink. To match the house. And to make me smile every time I walk in there but seeing this hunk of a man in the cotton-candy world, nearly breaks out the giggles out of me.

"For what?"

"For whom," he counters, and I draw my brows together.

"And who is that 'whom?'"

"Someone who shouldn't be here."

"Wow, Matteo. You impress me with your solid logic once again," I tell him, crossing my arms across my chest and Matteo turns his gaze to me, one that starts roaming over my body and that's when I realize I look like crap in front of possibly the hottest guy I've ever met.

No, there is no *possibly* in this equation. He is the hottest, and I'm the biggest mess wearing a milk-soaked shirt—with what smells like throw up too on my shoulder—my hair in a wet bun atop my head and sweatpants that barely cover my postpartum body. Nothing in those baby blogs I've read bothered to mention how atrocious this part of having a baby is.

Yet the way he looks at me...is not with judgement or disgust. It's with pure heat...Dear Lord.

Without a single warning, he starts advancing my way, with Mellie happily sleeping in his arms and his dark eyes eating me up.

Fuuuuticle on a cracker—yes, I'm trying not to curse over here—why does he have to look so hot holding my baby? Why is he even here? He cannot. Cannot be here.

My throat goes dry, arms uncross and flop down. *Don't whimper, damn it! Don't you dare whimper.*

Matteo comes right up to me, lifting his free hand up to my cheek and gently brushes his thumb across it, eliciting a damn whimper out of me that unfortunately does not go unnoticed by him and one side of his mouth curls up into that sexy, dangerous smile of his.

But only for a second, before it drops, and he grows serious again.

"I'm moving in because this is where I'm meant to be. With you and Mellie. And if some prick thinks he can take that spot, he is sorely mistaken, Zoe." The storm is back in his eyes.

What is he talking about? What prick? But Matteo locks his eyes with mine, stealing my breath and says, "I don't share, Zoe."

"Since when?" My voice is barely above a whisper.

"Since seven months ago." Then he looks down at my daughter. "And since three weeks ago."

He can't mean what I think he means, right?

I can't have him here. Absolutely not! I can't fall for another guy only to have him leave when he gets tired of playing house with us. Because he will.

Everyone does.

I've never been good enough for anyone to stay let alone for a guy like Matteo who could have any woman. Younger. More beautiful. Without a kid.

"Matteo, you don't know what you are talking about." My tone is defeated. It's better to end this charade before it starts. "You can't really want this." I motion between myself and the baby in his arms. "That's not the lifestyle for you."

"And why the heck not?" He sounds offended, and I didn't mean it like that. I simply want to protect myself and Mel from future heartbreak.

I sigh, taking a step back from him because I can't think clearly in his vicinity. "We are not even dating, for Pete's sake." I throw my arms up. "And here you are talking about moving in."

"Be my girlfriend," he throws out right away with ease and not as a question. "Okay, so what's next on your list?"

"Matteo, you can't be fucking serious right now."

"Ouch." He glares at me, covering Mel's ears. "That will be twenty-five cents in the swear jar." He points to me in all seriousness then looks down on her. "Look at that, by the time you turn eighteen we just might have enough to cover college expenses seeing as your mommy loves them curses and"—he stops, looks up to me and mouths—"fucks."

I narrow my eyes at him, drawing my tongue over my teeth. My hands firmly planted on my hips because the audacity of this man. "Look who's talking, Mr. Prim and Proper. If I remember correctly, you owe at least a dollar from three weeks ago."

"It's already in."

"What?"

"The dollar." He nods toward the bag at my feet. I bend down, unzip it, and find a little mason jar, covered in watermelon stickers, right at the top. It's filled with four quarters and labeled, *Dear curses, thank you for your contribution to Mel's college fund*, and my heart freaking melts, damn it.

"Now that that's settled, what else, Beastie? I gotta warn you, though, I'm here to stay. So, throw it all at me."

I collapse on the floor next to his bag, holding the swear jar in my hands. I have no clue why he's doing this. What he wants from me, but I am too exhausted to fight him right now. And let's be honest, that needy bitch inside of me is not really trying all that much. No, she is screaming for me to shut up and keep him with us a little longer. Possibly forever, if she has any say in the matter. Which she doesn't. It's sensible Zoe time.

"Fine, you want to stay and play with Mellie, that's fine. Hope you like that couch right here," I tell him.

"It's a nice couch." Matteo shrugs.

"Glad you think so. It's all yours." I get up, walk over to the kitchen counter and set the jar there.

I'm waiting for him to start throwing protests about it, reminding me that we already shared a bed before but when I turn around, I find him simply staring at me, his head cocked to the side. "If you thought that will make me back out, sorry to disappoint. I'll gladly sleep here."

Honestly, I did think that because my couch is a small three-seater and not the most comfortable one.

After the complete remodel of Joy's cottage, I had to also furnish my little house from top to bottom apart from the bed and mattress Joy got for me when I visited that first time, and it was not very budget friendly. So, I got whatever was on sale. Hence the couch in the color of Mellie's poop that no one else wanted.

And I guess that makes it two people. Me and Matteo.

I quickly turn away to hide the small smile I'm wearing now.

"But," he adds, yet I don't look back, "just for now. Until you realize how much better I'll fit in that bed with you."

Sigh, meet Zoe.

Because there's no realization needed. It's a damn fact.

"Matteo, put her down," I ask for the millionth time.

"No."

"Jesus Christ, give me patience." I pinch the bridge of my nose. "She has to sleep in her bed, not your arms!"

"Yeah, that's easy for you to say. You had her all to yourself for three whole weeks, now let me get my fill." He pouts. He freaking pouts and then has the audacity to glare at me.

And what the heck am I supposed to make of this? Since when does a guy like him care about time with a newborn baby?

"Matteo." I try to calm my voice down and reason with him. "You will get Mellie used to sleeping in your arms and when you leave, she won't go back to the crib." Only instead of seeing reason, that glare of his intensifies and he draws her even closer to his now bare chest.

Oh, did I forget to mention that little and very distracting detail?

One I am pretty sure he's figured out I am weak for because no matter how hard I've tried, I can't stop ogling and salivating over him ever since he came out of the shower, smelling illegally male with that woodsy, spicy scent, wet hair in a low bun and bare-chested with only that silver chain glinting on his golden, tattooed skin.

"Look at that. It's settled then. She is sleeping right where she is because I'm not leaving."

"I can't wait to tell you 'I told you so' later on."

"Not gonna happen, Beastie," he fires back without looking my way. "Also you still haven't answered my question?"

"What question?"

"About being my girlfriend."

"Um, maybe because it didn't really sound like a question?" I widen my eyes slightly at him. "More like delusional, fairytale statements." Matteo looks down at Mellie, says something to her in a hushed tone and turns back to me.

"Nothing delusional about it but let me rephrase then. Will you be my girlfriend?" he asks with that sinful smile of his. The one that lit up my path to his bed seven months ago.

"No."

"No?" He furrows his brows at me. The expression on his face says that he's not used to hearing that word all that much. "And why not?"

"Because I'm a twenty-nine-year-old single mom and I don't have the time or mental capacity for games. That girl you met at the bar back then, she's gone."

"Thank you, Jesus, for that." He rolls his eyes but not with annoyance. "She was sad and terrified of life ahead of her. Only allowing me the tiniest of glimpses of the real, strong beast on the inside. I prefer this spit-fire version of you much better, but just so we are clear before you jump for my throat"—he sends a pointed look my way—"I would take any and all versions of you."

"Matteo, snap out of this!" And I really do snap my fingers at him like that will help. "I'm being serious!"

"And I'm not?" he calls out louder with a slight hurt undertone, making Mel twitch in his arms to which he immediately reacts. "Shh, sorry my little watermelon. I didn't mean to scare you." He rocks her. "Your mom here is just being exceptionally difficult over here."

I huff. "No, I'm not. I'm being realistic. Look, you are an amazing guy and you stepped up at the hospital for us which I'm still very grateful for, but you are not cut out for relationships." Matteo narrows his eyes at me, but I keep going. "I saw how many girls came up to the bar that night trying to get your attention. How many made comments about a repeat of the night you had with them."

He cuts me off before I can continue. "And what did I do?"

"What?"

"What did I do, Zoe? When those girls approached me?" Matteo asks with hidden furry that I can see simmering underneath his skin.

I swallow. "Um, nothing at that moment." I want to say more but he cuts me off again.

"Exactly. Nothing at that moment or any moments following that night."

What is that supposed to mean?

"Ask me why?" He moves closer to me.

"Why?" I follow his command, my voice no longer as confident sounding as I was a minute ago, my heart beating out of my chest in anticipation of his answer.

"Because since the moment you opened the doors to my bar, they all disappeared." A moment of tense silence stretches between us. "I don't know what kind of magic you wielded over me, but since that day, I've only had eyes for one girl. So, all those others? They could parade naked and do splits right on top of my bar for all I cared because all I saw was that damn sunshine sitting in front of me."

"You can't mean that, Matteo," I whisper.

"I do. I know you probably think I'm young and naïve and that may be true, but what I'm not is an idiot who lets the only girl who made him feel walk out of his life twice. Or let someone else come swooping in and being the dad to this little watermelon when that role is mine. So, if I must spend days, weeks, and months proving that I am boyfriend material, I will." He is so close his breath fans my face, making me grow drunk on him. "Or scratch that. I will make sure I'm daddy material."

He's nuts.

He's lost it.

And maybe so have I, because all of a sudden, I'm rooting for him to pass this test yet that fear of mine is still overriding my senses.

But I like order. I like my plans for the now and for the next five years and Matteo wouldn't fit into those. Right?

"Everyone always leaves. And so will you." Somehow that comment makes him put Mel down in the little cot on the coffee table and I'm waiting for her to start wailing again just like she always does when she's in it, only it doesn't happen.

Did he put some kind of voo-doo spell on my daughter? Ever since he came into our cottage and took her in his arms she hasn't cried. She was a little fussy when he went to take that shower but nowhere near her usual shenanigans.

Matteo covers her with a blanket, kissing the top of her head and I'm too mesmerized by it all to see him prowling toward me. Yes, prowling, with that sexy swagger of his and by instinct I start to backtrack which only makes him smile and keep going until my back is plastered at the wall.

"You say everyone always leaves?" he asks me, his head tilted to a side but my throat is too dry from having him this close so I can only manage a slight nod. "You know why?"

"Because I'm not good enough. And that's not self-pity. It's a fact."

"Oh no, my ray of sunshine." He smiles again as his fingers come up to my face, gently grazing my cheek and it's almost embarrassing how quickly I am falling apart at the feet of this twenty-three-year-old cocky player. "They all left because they knew you were never meant to be theirs."

His dark eyes connect with mine. "You were always mine." And before I can suck in that breath I desperately need, his lips crush against mine as his body pushes me deeper into the wall, squashing me with his power and heat.

I know I need to push him off me. I know this should not be happening and I'm headed into that land of tears and devastation after he crushes my heart but...but one kiss won't hurt, right?

His hand on my neck tilts my head up, giving him full access to my mouth and as soon as his tongue slides against mine, I get lost in him.

Kissing Matteo is like breathing and drowning all at once. It's a pleasure and pain. The carefree summer and the blistering winter.

His other hand digs deeper into my ass, drawing me closer until his hard cock digs into my soft stomach, sending waves of heat across my whole body.

I've never wanted another man like I want him, and that alone should be enough for me to pull away and run as far from him as I can. Yet I'm still here because I've never been kissed the way he kisses me, and I know without a shred of a doubt that I never will be.

I'll take one for the road, is the last thought I have before rising on my tiptoes, digging my fingers into his still-damp hair, and returning the kiss with the same ferocity. This was never about cute or sweet. This is raw and unhinged and a little bit mad.

I've never thought I'd enjoy kisses and sex on a rough side, but it seems that everything with Matteo is quickly becoming my new favorite thing.

Dreams. That's all this is. That's all I have. That's all I *can* have and that thought pulls me away from his sinful lips. His eyes are hooded and filled with lust, and I desperately want to get back to what we started. But I can't.

I've fallen for too many men with pretty words and nice bodies who had no intentions of growing gray and old with me.

And Matteo is just another one of those. Only so much worse. So, I place my hands on his chest and will myself to push him away.

"Matteo." His name is barely a whisper—or a plea—on my lips. "Please, don't."

"Don't what?"

"Don't say that anymore. D-don't kiss me like that anymore. Don't...just don't." I need him to do this for me. I need him to obey these rules because...because otherwise I'll fall right into his pretty promises and sweet touches.

He pulls away slightly to look at me, the lust in his eyes replaced with something hard. "Fine. I won't kiss you ever again."

"R-really?" Damn it, why does it hurt to hear him say that when I was the one demanding it just now.

"Really. I won't kiss you until you beg me to do it." He pinches my chin with his fingers. "And trust me, you will beg."

I swallow hard, somehow not even doubting the truth in his words. However, he won't ever hear it.

"I have all the time in the world too because I'm here to stay and claim you as mine."

"You don't know what you're saying. You want to spend some time with Mellie, that's fine, but that's all there is."

Matteo stares into my eyes without letting me go. "Never have I ever met someone who likes to lie to themselves as much as you do. But that's okay, I'll wear you down."

"Matteo, this is not a game. We stopped playing it back at that bar."

"Never have I ever said it was just a game, Beastie."

19

Never Have I Ever

Matteo: Never have I ever spent a night with a girl and didn't touch her once.
Zoe: I don't even know how you survived it.
Matteo: Right! I should be given a damn medal for that. Especially when you decided to parade in front of me half naked.
Zoe: Matteo, I was in a tank top and pajama pants.
Matteo: Like I said, I'm basically a saint.

20

Matteo

"You're the only person who can make me feel like a teenager again. And sometimes, like a toddler too." – Unknown

I've been having the best dream where Zoe finally admits she wants me just as madly as I do her and was about to wrap her pretty lips around my cock when sharp poking into my ribs wakes me up. I try to slap it away with my hand, but it doesn't disappear.

"Wildflower, maybe you should stop poking him?" I hear a familiar male voice through my sleepy haze.

"You know what? You are right." Is that Joy?

"I am?" Comes out surprised from Jacob.

"Mm-hmm. Now, where is that cast iron pan we got her last month?"

"Joy, why do you need a cast iron pan?"

"To hit the intruder on Zoe's couch. Thank you for giving me the idea, baby."

"I did no such thing!" Jacob protests. "You know I don't condone violence, and this is not an intruder. It's Matteo!" I open my eyes slightly, and see Joy raising an eyebrow at her husband.

"Fine, not an intruder. More like a random stray that got lost at my friend's house."

"I'm not a stray," I mumble from my not-to-comfortable spot on the couch. Where did Zoe even get this thing? It should be illegal to sell bricks disguised as couches.

"See, Wildflower?" Jacob grins. "He's not a stray."

"I'm her forever," I mumble some more, still partially in my lovely dream and turn around to try and go back to sleep, but that poking comes right back. Only now it's ten times stronger and is coming from a frowning Jacob.

"Ahh," I shriek because that's a totally normal reaction to having the Viking of LC looming over me like an imposing mountain with his nose practically touching mine.

"Who's forever? Because if you think for a second you can hit on my wife, I will twist you into a pretzel faster than you can say quack."

I swear, I hear Joy whimper somewhere in the background.

"Jesus Christ." I jump up, but Jacob's face doesn't leave mine. Literally. His nose is still right over mine. "Dude, I might have a reputation but I'm not into married women." I chance a glance at Joy.

Sure, she's hot but everyone pales in comparison to my Zoe. I meant what I told her last night. Ever since meeting her, I simply don't see other women and for the first few months after my spring break in LC, I was freaking the fuck out.

All my outings to bars and clubs were fruitless. All the girls rubbing themselves over me on a dance floor made me want to go scrub my skin clean, and what's worse my dick was enjoying life in a permanent state of flaccid.

I even saw a doctor, but he said my equipment should work just fine.

I didn't understand what was happening until thoughts of her would cross my mind and all of a sudden, I was as hard as a rock and ready to go, painting my shower walls with a fresh coat of my cum.

It finally all clicked in for me when I saw her again. My dick fell in love with Zoe's pussy. But what's worse...I think *I* fell in love with her that night too.

Which is madness and what's even crazier, not once since the realization kicked in—or since her father smacked it into me—did I get scared of such commitment.

I tried. I tried to talk myself out of it for these past weeks, but it was utterly useless, because for the first time in my adult life, I understood what my dad meant all those years ago before he passed away.

Fate. Bloody fate.

Now, I just need Zoe to snap too. To realize that as much of a player as I was and was allergic to relationships, none ever felt like this before. And I'm all in.

Jacob immediately straightens up, the intimidating mask replaced with a huge grin on his bearded face. We could pass for brothers if he wouldn't be a giant and have blonde hair. "So, you mean Zoe."

"Duh." I rub the sleep out of my eyes which I didn't get that much of because as soon as Zoe took Mellie away for the night she started crying and I'd like to think she was protesting being torn away from me.

Mellie.

I shoot up from the bed, not caring if these two *intruders* get an eyeful of my morning wood—especially after that dream—and look around for my baby.

I ended up taking her away after about two hours of wailing so Zoe could get some rest and she was sleeping peacefully on the coffee table next to me. Now she's not.

Did she roll out of there?

I drop onto my hands and knees, searching the floor but there is nothing. Wait, she's too little to do that, no?

"What is the stray doing?" Joy whispers to Jacob.

"I have no idea."

"I'm not a stray," I repeat again. "And I'm looking for my baby."

"Wait, you have a baby?" Jacob asks, but I don't get to answer because the door to the master bedroom opens and Zoe walks out looking like an angel from heavens with her blonde hair in disarray, her tank top twisted around her waist and the cutest pillow mark is on her right cheek.

What's not cute is the murderous look she's giving us, and my dick—of course—twitches. Sick fucker. "What's on the agenda today?" she asks with zero humor. "Alien invasion? End of the world? Or the usual LC nonsense like the last time you all barged in telling me about my dad and Fanny."

"Well, now that you mention, I am concerned about crocodiles—"

"Jacob," she interrupts at the same time as Joy slaps his stomach. "That was a rhetorical question. What are you doing here at six-thirty-three in the morning?"

"Apparently, saving you from a stray who probably has flees and needs a tetanus shot based on his roster," Joy says, and I glare at her.

"For the last time, I am not a stray. I'm a good puppy." For a good measure, I let out a few barks, and Jacob gives me two thumbs up and a huge grin that his wife slaps away.

Zoe looks heavenward, rubbing her face. "He's not a stray, Joy."

"See?" I smile with glee at her. "Now that that's settled, where is my baby?"

As if my Mellie can hear me, she lets out a loud piercing cry and I take off after her, finding her fighting against the swaddle in her cot as she lays on top of Zoe's bed. "Shh, my little watermelon, I got you." Gently, I slide my arms underneath her, lifting her up and onto my shoulder and she immediately nuzzles into my neck, making me smile.

"You really like to do that, don't you, Mel?" I breathe her in and wince. "Watermelon, you have no business smelling like that. Let's go change your diaper," I tell her and lay her on the changing table Zoe has in her bedroom, since Mellie is not using her own yet.

I've never changed a diaper before, but I was watching Zoe do it last night and later I totally watched some YouTube videos on how to do it. So now is the time to test my knowledge.

I open it all up and lean away slightly. "Jesus, Mellie, you are lucky you are so cute," I tell her and get busy wiping all the yellow poop. I freaked out seeing the color yesterday, but Zoe assured me that was normal.

It's not that I didn't believe her…but I definitely looked that up as well. Hey, I needed to make sure my baby was all right, all right? I made quick work of the diaper change, smiling as I was zipping her back up.

"See, baby girl? I've got you. Always," I kiss her forehead and come out of the room to hear Joy saying, "*My baby?*" she hisses.

"I leave you alone for one night. One, Zo, and you manage to find trouble."

"I didn't find him, he came all on his own and declared he's moving in."

"He's what?" Joy shrieks.

"Moving in, yes," I confirm for everyone who still didn't get it, and stroll up to Zoe with Mel in my arms. "When did you take her? I didn't hear you at night?"

"A few hours ago. I needed to feed her."

"See, this is why I need to relocate to your bedroom. That way you wouldn't have to get up at all. Just roll over and pop the boob out. I assure you, both Mellie and I will appreciate it." I wink at her as she blushes but tries to hide it with a cute scowl.

"There will be no relocating anywhere unless it's back to your apartment."

"Nah, Beastie, it's too small for all three of us there."

"Shut up," she murmurs under her breath but none of us miss how much deeper her blush has gotten or the way she averts her eyes. My girl is too stubborn for her own good. "Give her to me, I need to change her diaper." Zoe leans in, intending to take Mellie away from me, but I turn from her hands.

"No need. I already did."

"You changed her diaper?" Zoe looks at me like I just told her I flew to the moon and back. "A poopie one?" She accentuates that point.

"Yep," I tell her, kissing Mel's head, and Zoe visibly relaxes right that moment, watching us with longing.

Hell yes, I'm wearing you down, woman, and I haven't even started trying yet.

"Oh hell," Joy groans. "This is so much worse than I thought. I warned you." She points her finger at Zoe. "Damn it, I warned you! I told you to stay away from that cursed bar, didn't I? And you didn't listen. Congratulations"—she throws her hands up—"you are screwed big time."

I'm still trying to figure out what she means by all that when Jacob's strong hand lands on my shoulder and he grins at me. "Love the nickname! Call me for tips." Then adds more quietly, "And don't give up, brother. It's all worth it."

"Stop fraternizing with the enemy, Jacob," Joy snaps. "Where are Hope and Grace? I need reinforcements."

Love Hive:

Joydon'tpissmeofflevine: I don't know how you did it, but this was a terrible idea! Undo it right this second.

CookieJ: Did what honey? Are you talking about our tandem swimming classes we are starting on Thursdays?

Joydon'tpissmeofflevine: Mom, aren't you all tired of meddling yet? Wasn't last year with Hope me and Grace enough for you?

Ninasunshine: There is never enough love Joy. And we, as the righteous guardians of it, need to make sure it flourishes and prospers in our town. Can't leave no stone unturned.

Joydon'tpissmeofflevine: Turn Zoe's back around, Matteo is not for her.

Willoflove: And why not? What's wrong with my boy?

Joydon'tpissmeofflevine: Willa, I say this with as much love as I can muster...

Joydon'tpissmeofflevine: Your son is a manwhore and I won't have him mess up my friend's head. He's been filling it with nonsense already, and she started getting that dreamy look on her face that means trouble to her heart later on.

CookieJ: So, what you mean to tell us is that operation "tame the beast" is already a success?

Ninasunshine: I must admit, I thought it would be harder to crack that tough cookie.

Willoflove: I need a moment here. These happy tears won't stop.

Toughtolove: Hold your hippy horses. I have solid intel that Zoe has walls up higher than even Joy did.

CookieJ: Fanny there are no hippy horses.

Toughtolove: Are you suffering from selective reading?

Joydon'tpissmeofflevine: Are you all suffering from selective hearing?

21

Never Have I Ever

Matteo: Never have I ever made breakfast for my girl.
Zoe: Matteo, we are not playing that game.
Matteo: Never have I ever enjoyed someone scowling at me.
Zoe rolls her eyes
Matteo: Never have I ever gotten hard from an eyeroll before.
Zoe: You need help.

22

Zoe

"Love is shown more in deeds than in words." —Saint Ignatius

Two days of this man living in my house and I am already losing it.

He's everywhere I look. His scent is in every corner of every room. His voice fills the once empty space with life and laughter as he plays with Mellie. Those winks and crooked smiles he throws my way every time he catches my eyes on him have a toxifying effect on me.

As in, they light my insides up, setting a kaleidoscope of butterflies over the wild, long-forgotten hills.

I'm limping, for Pete's sake. From how hard I've been clenching my thighs every time I hear that husky timbre of his voice.

This was not the plan. This wasn't even in the "possible complications" column of the plan.

Because falling for Matteo Loverson could not be classified as a complication. It's a full-on disaster waiting to happen.

Yes, my physical body has a reaction to this young and extremely handsome guy–stupid hormones and muscle memory. Yes, I will blame it for still keeping the memory of his glorious cock inside me.

Seven months and a whole child delivery later, I can still feel him deep inside my pussy. I still relive that night—the way we fit together, his groans and the pulsing of his cock as he comes inside me—on daily basis.

However, that doesn't mean I need to let him get into my head, or God forbid, my heart.

I walked away from him that morning fully aware that there was no future there. I was committed to my first—and only—one-night stand.

Too bad the other guy apparently didn't get the memo because at this moment my one-night stand is strapping my daughter to his chest with a wrap I was sure I'd thrown away last week because it pissed me off.

"What are you doing?" I ask him, eyeing the perfectly wrapped carrier. "Where did you get that and how do you even know how to use it?"

Jesus, it took me a solid week to use these mummy tapes and not look like one after I was done wrapping it, yet here is Mr. I-am-allergic-to-commitment-and-monogamy, using that Tetris equivalent of a baby carrier like a seasoned pro.

Hold on a second, this is not the same wrap I threw away.

"Did you know carrying your baby like this enhances your bond between the two of you?" he asks me, but doesn't wait for my response before continuing. "So, I got one this morning while you guys were still asleep. I need to rebond—is that a word?—three weeks' worth of lost time. Oh, and I learned it from YouTube. It's so easy." He grins eagerly.

Can you tell my eye is twitching? Because it is. Easy, my ass. He is just an insufferable, hot show off.

Apparently in every area.

"So, you are going to carry Mel like that around the house?" I ask him with one eyebrow raised.

"Nope, we are about to head out for a walk down the beach. My little watermelon needs fresh air and I need quality daddy-daughter time," he says proudly.

"You know what? I think you should allow me to do a check up on your head. I'm convinced you are suffering from contusion or memory loss."

"Why?" He narrows his eyes at me with genuine curiosity.

"Because this has got to be the millionth time I am reminding you that she is not your actual daughter. And you are free to leave any time, you know."

"So, I see we are both going for that checkup," he responds.

"And why would I need a checkup?" I cross my arms.

"Because this has got to be the millionth time I am telling you that she *is* mine. No matter what that DNA test says." He starts to leave but turns back around. "And I'm not leaving. So, how about you finally accept the fact, and we can get to the good part?"

I'm not sure I am ready to hear what else he has to say. My heart is beating out of my chest as it is, but since I like to torture myself, I ask, "Which is?"

"You. Me. Mellie, and a few years of practicing making a brother or a sister for our girl."

Nope. I was not ready for that. Mentally.

Physically? My pussy is screaming, *"Let's get this party started,"* and she hasn't even recovered from the labor yet.

"There will be no practice happening, Matteo."

"If you like the taste of denial, please, by all means, continue. I, for one, cannot wait to paint you with my cum," The bastard smirks and ducks out the door, leaving me standing there, gaping at the closed door, my jaw on the floor and heart in a race.

That arrogant, cocky, confusing, young, stupidly hot, ridiculously sexy man.

I need him gone.

Really, really need him gone before I do something stupid.

Only just twenty minutes later, I am running out of excuses as to why I can't, eyeing that bathroom door and the nice new shower head I had put in as soon as I moved here.

Fuck it. I dart from my bed, slamming the bathroom door closed and stripping with a whole new sense of urgency because this guy turned me into a needy idiot.

Good thing knowing Matteo, he will be out there "rebonding" for a while, so I'll have time to go through the whole circle of hell from feeling good to guilty and then to pissed and finally back to needy all before they are back.

23

Matteo

"When you're a kid, you assume your parents are soulmates. My kids are gonna be right about that." –The Office

Thieves. Bloody thieves.

Leave it to my own mother and her gang of peace-loving girlfriends to steal my own baby right from my hands.

Mellie and I were enjoying our conversation—well, more like she was enjoying sleeping soundly to the sound of my blabbering—when out of nowhere the four little devils disguised as silly grandmas attacked me and told me to go rest while they spend some time with Mel.

What makes them think I need rest?

In fact, I don't remember the last time I felt as refreshed and happy as I have been since moving in with Zoe and Mellie. Even sleeping on that awful couch because my woman is too stubborn to let me into her bed. Yet.

I am still pouting and mumbling about bloody thieves when I enter the house and stop.

"Matteo!" Zoe calls out loudly, and the blood in my veins freezes. Oh my God, did something happen? That sounded like a cry for help!

Quickly, I drop the wrap to the floor and dash for the bathroom from where the sound seemed to come from. What if she fell and broke something? My heart drops to the ground as my mind thinks of every possible worst-case scenario. And my mind can be a dark place when it wants to be dramatic like that.

"Zo?" I call out, but she doesn't respond. I test the handle, but it's locked, of course, and I'm about to bang on the door, or better yet, break it down, when she calls out my name again.

"Matteo. Oh God, ohmyGodohmyGodohmyGod."

Oh…

Oh…it's *that* kind of cry for help… My hand on the handle freezes. My jaw dropping and that blood that froze in my veins earlier?

Yeah, it's no longer cold or still because it has all traveled to my cock.

That was not a damsel-in-distress kind of shout. Nope.

That was my little ray of sunshine pleasuring her little pussy with my name on her lips.

I swallow the groan that rises out of me. God, what I wouldn't give to be in that shower with her right now. To be the one who makes her see the stars instead of the thoughts of me she is using. I guess it's the next best thing, though, since Miss You-and-I-are-just-friends won't admit she wants me. Won't admit how badly her pussy aches for me.

I drop my forehead to the closed door, palming my aching erection through my shorts while my ears are eagerly picking up any tiny sound she makes. And she makes a lot.

Fuck, I should give her some privacy. I shouldn't be standing at her bathroom door, touching myself like a stage five creeper.

Only, when have I ever done what I *should*. There is absolutely no fun in that. Or pleasure. Plus, she's mine anyway. Only because Zoe doesn't want to admit it, doesn't make it less true. So, by that extension, I am entitled to her moans and orgasms. Especially, the ones she uses me for inspiration.

Fuck, talk about an ego boost.

With my conscious cleared by my own very sound logic, I pull the string on my linen pants and slide them off just enough to take my cock out, squeezing it tightly with my hand while imagining it to be hers.

There is a whole new set of pleasure sounds coming through the door and I revel in each one.

"Yes, yes, just like that," Zoe moans, and I repeat the exact same words as I work my cock, imagining that lush, curvy body naked and wet on the other side. It only takes me seconds before the beads of precum spit out over my head.

That is what this woman does to me. I can't even see her, yet I am harder than I've ever been for anyone else, ready to unload my seed and paint her bathroom door with it any second. And then when she reaches her peak, so do I.

Moaning in unison with her as my fist pumps every drop of cum I have for this woman.

Now, that's a morning I could get used to.

24

Matteo

"Relationships are like puzzles. Sometimes they're fun and sometimes they're frustrating, but when you find the right piece, everything fits perfectly." –Unknown

"Aren't you supposed to go to work?" Zoe asks me, looking up from the rim of her teacup.

"Eager for me to leave, Beastie?"

"Matteo, I don't care whether you leave or not. Your presence makes no difference for me personally."

My mouth curls up into a small smile and I lean into her, whispering, "Little liar."

"Am not," Her eyes flare up in an attempt to seem threatening but all it does is just make my pants feel tighter.

Damn that woman and her silly no-kissing rule.

"Then why are you trying to get me out the door so badly?"

"Um, because you need to work, maybe?" She rolls her eyes at me.

"Orrr, it's because having me here affects you. Makes you want to break down those silly walls you have put around yourself and get down and dirty?"

Zoe has been on a "Move Matteo Out" mission for the past four days since her little bathroom show.

"Definitely not," she says but her voice is a touch breathy.

"Definitely yes."

"You think too highly of yourself."

"Apparently you do too." I wink at her and watch those rosy cheeks grow pinker. She doesn't know I was there when she played with herself, coming with my name on her lips. Three times.

Little naughty girl.

And I wasn't going to bring it up, but my Zoe needs to start admitting these feelings she has, and I am all too eager to help her.

"Trust me, I don't."

"That's not what you said four days ago." Her eyes snap to mine in a flash, her mouth slightly agape. And biting my lip I go for the kill. "I distinctly remember hearing your praises—three loud, expressive times."

The cup she's holding slips out, rattling off the table.

"Y-you…h-how…Matteo! OhmyGod, kill me now."

She's so cute when she's flustered and embarrassed, slapping her palms to her face to cover it from me. And then she gets even cuter and starts talking to herself out loud as if she forgot that I am still here.

"No, you know what? You are not going to be embarrassed by it. So what, you pleasured yourself. It's normal. Hot."

"Oh, I happen to agree." Her hands fall off her face, shooting daggers at me with her big, brown eyes. "It was very hot. I came twice within minutes while listening to you."

Zoe's mouth drops open. "No, you didn't."

I arch one eyebrow with a smirk on my face. "Want me to prove that I can?"

"That's not what I meant." She sucks a deep breath, closing her eyes. "You didn't think to—I don't know—maybe give me some privacy?"

"I had that thought for a fleeting second."

"And what happened to it?"

"I remembered that you are mine and there is no such thing as privacy between us," I tell her and take a bite of the breakfast croissant.

Zoe shakes her head, pinching the bridge of her nose. "For the love of... Matteo, go to work before I kill you."

"I can't."

"And why the hell not?" She narrows her eyes at me but once again there is nothing threatening there since that blush is still firmly intact on her cheeks.

"That will be a quarter from you." I point to her. "And I'm on paternity leave." Those narrowed eyes disappear as she rolls them and sighs.

"Matteo, you are not on a paternity leave, and you've already been here for a week. It's bad enough I'm intimately familiar with your horrible eating habits, I don't need to know anything else. Go to work." She points to the front door.

We were having such a great morning with me making her breakfast she moaned over, then having such a lovely conversation about her extracurricular activities in the bathroom while Mellie is sleeping soundly in my arms, but she just had to go and burst my happy bubble.

Tough shit, I have plenty of tape to seal the holes.

"And what is wrong with my eating habits?"

"Nothing apart from being as ridiculous as you."

"Hmm, I don't think so."

"Matteo, just last night you were eating an apple and chasing it with a Coke. When you don't like apples."

"What? I really wanted that Coke but it's bad for you, so I had to add something healthy in there." Zoe looks at me from underneath her eyebrows. "What? It's all about the balance."

"Like I said, ridiculous. But since you are such an advocate of the 'balance'"—she puts quotation mark around the word—"go to work so you don't lose it."

I don't know why she says it like it has been any kind of hardship for me to be here. I've been enjoying every second of these past six days.

"See this baby in my arms?" I reference to Mel. "Paternity leave."

"Lord give me patience. Matteo, Mellie will be here when you come back. I promise. So, put that baby—my baby—back in her cot and stop being ridiculous. Aren't you tired of us yet?"

"Tired?" I gasp, press her closer to my chest, looking at Zoe like she's grown a few heads this morning. "How could I ever tire of my perfect little watermelon or my future wife who puts on a show for me."

"Jesus Christ. Now he escalated it to a wife," Zoe sighs. "And that show was *not* for you." She shakes her head and takes a sip of her tea but that little blush she's spotting doesn't escape my attention. "You are impossible. When are you going to drop that girlfriend—excuse me—wife crap?"

"Crap?" I shriek. "That is a very serious business, Zoe Holsted. I will not have you belittling it."

"Okay, okay." She holds her hands up in mock apology. "We can postpone that conversation to when you come back from work."

And she's back at it. The truth is my heart aches at the thought of leaving them. "What if she forgets me? Or does something cool while I'm away?"

"Matteo, she's a month old. The coolest thing she could do is sleep for solid four hours at a time."

"See? I could totally miss that." I bulge my eyes out at her because solid four hours of sleep is badass, and I need to be here for it. I need to be here for all of it.

Zoe sighs. "I promise I'll FaceTime you if that happens, deal?"

"What about the part where she forgets me?" I ask, chewing on the inside of my cheek. Part of me understands how ridiculous I sound but there is this other part that refuses to listen to any logic where Mellie and Zoe are concerned. I want to be with them twenty-four-seven. I want to be the man they rely on. The one they turn to if there is a spider in the house or another silly reason.

I may not have been ready for any of this, but that doesn't mean I don't know how. My dad showed me every day how to be a great husband and a dad. In fact, he still is, thirteen years after he passed away.

And maybe I want to stay around and make sure no other fucker comes around to steal my girls.

"She won't."

"She might," I press on.

"Jesus Christ. What do you want me to do? Print out your picture and tape it to my face?"

"That's an excellent idea." I snap my fingers, snatching her phone off the table and hold it up to snap a selfie.

"Matteo," Zoe shrieks and lunges for the phone but it's too late. "That was just a joke."

"Where is your printer?"

"You are utterly ridiculous… you know that?"

"Yep. Aren't you happy you won't ever be bored in life with me?"

"I'll settle for sane."

My mood grows from playful to serious in a flash. I stride over to her, tilting her chin up with my finger. "No, you won't. You, my beautiful sunshine won't *settle* for anything in this life."

Zoe swallows hard. "Maybe you just don't understand how life works yet, Matteo."

"I don't need to know how it works. I make my own rules." I send a little smirk her way. "Don't worry, baby, I'll share those with you."

And I would. I'd share anything with this woman. Chocolate, home-brewed beer, my t-shirts, life, bodily fluids—I'm especially interested in that one—and everything in between. *Does she want my social security now or later?*

But despite me being ready to jump all in, Zoe is hesitant to do the same.

No idea why, really. I'm a catch!

Fine, I'm a shit liar but I will do anything to be the one she gets hooked on and not just for a quick pleasure session in the bathroom.

And that's why after another two hours of pushing me out the door, I decide to relent and go to work. For a little bit.

Literally, in and out under one hour.

Me: How are my girls?

Me: I miss you both already.

> **Beastie:** Matteo, the door just clicked shut behind you. I can still hear and see you typing on your phone.

Me: You know what? I don't think I feel all that good, maybe I should skip today.

> **Beastie:** I feel like I am dealing with a child.

> **Beastie:** Oh wait, what am I saying? Of course, I am.

Me: Solid burn, beastie.

Me: Yet I don't remember you thinking that when I had my tongue deep in your sweet pussy. Or when you fucked it with your fingers thinking of mine.

Me: Do you need a reminder?

There was no reply but when I turned my head around, looking through the window, there was no mistaking the desire in her eyes and my pants felt even tighter walking to work.

"Matty, my boy," Mom calls out as soon as I step through the door. "How is Mellie and Zoe?"

"They're great mom." I give her a hug and a kiss on top of her head. I'm not even that mad she stole my baby that day on the beach. It turned out quite all right, actually.

"But I want to get back to them as soon as possible. So, where do you need me while you have me?"

"Oh, there are a million boxes in the back that came in this morning. I assumed those were the supplies you ordered for your new menu and was going to call you to come sort through them, but here you are."

Damn it, I totally forgot about that. I squeeze my eyes shut, groaning. This will take way longer than the one hour I was planning to spend here, and I'm already feeling those withdrawal symptoms being away from my girls for so long. But this must be done.

I may only be twenty-three, but I understand responsibly all too well when it comes to our family business. Especially with a free-spirit of a mother who, if given a chance, would serve the whole town for the cost of one smile.

I take out my phone and shoot Zoe a message.

> **Me:** Hey sunshine, unfortunately I'll be stuck here for a hot minute. So, I'm forwarding you three more pictures to print out and a voice memo you need to play to Mellie every ten minutes at least.

> **Beastie:** So, I just tried to show her one of the pictures, but I don't think she liked it. See the middle finger she's showing you right here?

Attaches a picture of Mellie's hand in a fist except the middle finger that sticks out.

> **Me:** Damn it, I knew she's going to do something cool when I'm not there. *crying emoji* Proud papa. *happy tears emoji*

> **Beastie:** Did you just say you are proud of her showing the middle finger? *unimpressed emoji* Only you, Matteo. Only you.

> **Me:** I knew I was growing on you, beastie.

> **Beastie:** In your dreams.

> **Me:** Nah, in my dreams you are bouncing up and down on me, not growing.

After that there are no more messages, but I just happened to know that it's not because she's pissed at me like she pretends to be. She's turned on and trying to hide it.

That's okay, though; I'm patient. I've waited all these months. I'll wait a few more weeks.

25

Zoe

"You're the closest thing to a miracle in my life. And sometimes the worst thing that ever happened to me." – *Meredith Grey, Grey's Anatomy*

This is all his fault. I knew it would be like this.

And *this* is only after a week with the man. What will happen if he sticks around for a whole month? Mellie will lose her voice from crying as she's been crying ever since he was no longer in the vicinity of the cottage.

I thought the crying fits were over since we haven't had one in a few days. That maybe whatever was hurting her had passed, but now I know better.

It was Matteo magic, and the apple doesn't fall that far from this tree that has been under his spell ever since I've met him.

Bathroom show being the prime example. God, I can't believe he was there, listening and…enjoying it? From the sounds of it.

No. I will not let my mind wander there. I am done. This is done. No more playing for Zoe.

No more Matteo living with us. He must move out—if not for me, then for Mellie who is getting too attached.

How in the world did she know he left, I'm not sure, but just like before I have tried it all and nothing is working.

"Shh, baby girl." I am on the verge of tears myself because I'm her mom and once again, I'm failing. "We are almost there." *And when we get there, I'm going to kill that favorite human of yours. First, for getting me hooked on him, and second, for getting you there too.*

As soon as I fly through the front doors—which unfortunately doesn't have the desired dramatic effect I'm going for because of the soft opening doors, damn it—Matteo's head whips up that second, his eyes zeroing in on the car seat in my hands.

Perfect, there is no one in here yet.

Oh, I am going to hand it to him so bad right now. I will give him an earful for creating this issue for me! You just wait, Matteo Loverson, the baby whisperer.

Next thing I know, that man jumps over the bar top like his ass is on fire. Literally. Jumps over it, Rambo, or was it Jackie Chan-style, and runs to us with wild eyes.

"What happened?" he asks in panic, and before I can open my mouth to start cussing him out—swear jar be damned—Mellie stops crying.

Breathe, Zoe. Fucking breathe.

His voice. That's all that little stinker needed to stop her wailing.

Matteo snatches the car seat out of my hands, lowers it to the ground and takes a now very peaceful Mellie out of it while cooing sweet nothings to her. "What's wrong, my little watermelon?" he asks her in that ridiculous baby voice, kissing her cheek, nose, forehead, and her little fingers as my daughter sniffs and shakes dramatically.

She actually manages to pull her bottom lip over in a pout as he cradles her.

I should consider a career in acting for her when she grows up. Look at that talent at barely four weeks old.

I should be angry at him. I should tell him to move out right this second before my daughter gets even more attached to him but with every second that she gets more settled in Matteo's arms, her little hand resting on his peck and closes her eyes without so much as a drop of milk, my body sags. My brain sighs in relief and my heart is filling with more and more mushy feelings that absolutely cannot be there.

Who's the one getting attached here, Zoe?

"What happened, Beastie?"

"This happened." I point to him holding Mel. "You've gone and done it."

"Done what?"

"Got her used to your arms and now she refuses to sleep anywhere else." I don't mention that it might not be just about sleeping in his arms. The truth is, it's just him. She wants him nearby.

Matteo's body relaxes and he gazes at my daughter with so much love, my heart is about to explode. This is the same way he looked at her at the hospital when she was just born. The same exact way.

"You love me, Mel?" he asks her, gently brushing her little cheek with the back of his finger. "I love you too, little watermelon." Mellie relaxes and nuzzles into him, falling asleep that instant.

"I hate you," I throw out his way, but both of us are well aware there is zero heat behind those words. "You are making my life harder right now."

"Shh, Beastie, relax."

"Don't you dare shush me! This is all your fault! How am I supposed to be a single mom when she doesn't want me?"

"That's because you're not." His hand reaches over to my face cupping it as his forehead tilts against mine and all I can see, breathe and feel is Matteo.

"What?" My voice is breathy just like it always is when he is this close. My body relaxing more and more with each second, turning into a limp noodle in his arms.

So much for handing it to him so bad, giving him an earful and cussing him out. Who were you trying to fool, Zo?

"You are not and were never supposed to be a single mom, Zo. I am here to take on that other half of the equation, remember? And she wants you more than anyone, she simply wants me too. And I mean, can you blame her?" The bastard has the audacity to wiggle his eyebrows at me while wearing the worst smirk of all smirks.

"Wipe that smirk off your face before I do."

"There is my beastie." He smiles. "Threatening me with a good time."

"How is me punching your face a good time?"

Matteo leans over, bringing his mouth to my ear, his lips touching it with just the briefest of touches. "Because I like it rough," he says in a low husky tone, and I fail at my attempt to not be affected. He straightens, sending a wink my way while I'm hyperventilating from one little line.

Matteo places Mellie back in her car seat and moves her to the back where he was doing some sort of inventory. The next couple hours pass with him working, Mel sleeping, and me shamelessly ogling the man I was going to kick out of my house while sipping on a non-alcoholic cocktail he made me. It's sweet but fresh at the same time, just perfect. Everything about my current set up is perfect.

So, why am I fighting this thing between us so much, again?

"Why don't you go upstairs and take a nap while my little girl helps me with these orders over here?" Matteo asks me.

"No, that's okay," I give him the practiced answer I've been giving everyone else when they offer to help me. I should go home anyway. The bar is starting to fill up.

"Zoe." He pins with his brown eyes. "Go upstairs and take a nap. Please," he commands me, and I find myself sliding off the stool despite my earlier answer.

"Okay, are you sure, though?"

"Yes." His eyes are still on me, now growing darker. "Fuck," he utters under his breath at the same time as his hand moves to his crotch, adjusting his suddenly tented pants. "Your obedience turns me on just as much as your violence," he groans but my mouth drops open.

Why does he keep saying things like that?

"Zoe." My name tumbles out of his mouth low and sexy with a slight note of a threat. "Are you trying to kill me, Sunshine? Or are you looking to get your mouth stuffed with my cock?"

My eyes snap to his.

No, no I wasn't looking for that, but suddenly I really want that. I want to feel him slip past my lips as I wrap them firmly around his swollen head. I want to drag my tongue over the full length of him, down to his heavy balls. I want him down my throat, so deep I wouldn't be able to breathe. I want him to spill his cum down it too.

I'm still lost in my thoughts, visualizing him fucking my mouth rough—like he likes—when I hear a long groan and a huge, warm chest crushes against me, with strong arms wrapping tightly around my neck and ass holding on to me like a savage with his prey. Matteo's breathing is just as rugged as mine, his lips a breath from mine but not touching when I want them to—no, need them to—kiss me. Ravage me. Take me.

"You don't understand what you do to me." His eyes are wild, mad and a bit pained. "I exist for you."

"Matteo."

"What, Beastie?"

"Why aren't you kissing me?" I don't know why I just asked that.

I don't want him to kiss me. I made the rule that he can't. So, why does it feel like I will die without his lips right now?

His lips curve up into a small—yet disgustingly smug—smile, and he whispers into my ear, "Beg, Zoe."

"W-what?"

"Don't you remember? I'm not allowed to kiss you but I'm all for breaking rules. I only need a bit of...let's call it motivation." The hand on my ass, squeezes harder as he pushes us closer together. Fusing our bodies.

"And me begging will motivate you?"

"Oh, baby, it just might make me come in my pants like a fucking rookie." Matteo drags the tip of his nose through my neck, from the curve up to my ear and a shudder passes through me and I feel his cock thickening even more against my lower belly.

I did that? I did that to this man who could have anyone, yet for some reason wants me. But it will pass. His infatuation with me will run its course and I'll be left a broken mess again, right?

Then why does it get harder and harder to keep persuading myself in that? Why do I run out of my bedroom each morning as fast as I can just to see him? To make sure he hasn't left yet and when my eyes land on now a very normal routine of Matteo talking to Mellie as they cook breakfast together, it feels right. So, so right, it scares me further more.

Yeah, I'm fucking coward.

"I can't." I make myself say and just as fast as he slammed into me, Matteo steps away, taking all the warmth away with him, getting back to work like nothing happened.

I am still trying to rein myself in—and figure out if I'm making the right decision here—when Matteo simply says, "Let's continue the game."

"What game?" If he means the one about kissing, I'm not playing. Because if he pushes just a bit more, I'll break and fail at level one.

"Never have I ever."

Great, now I'm disappointed it's not the kissing one. Way to go, Zo.

"Fine." I slide back onto the stool, still trying to rein myself in but now it's not the unleashed lust, but rather my irrational irrationality.

"Never have I ever had sex in the shower."

I choke on my drink. That was not what I expected. Why in the world did I think he wouldn't play it dirty?

I guess it's a kissing game after all. And I should not be smiling right now, damn it.

"Hmm, I'm pretty sure jerking off on the other side of it counts." Matteo snaps his eyes to mine as they darken again.

That's right, two can play. Well, I'll only last so long, but it's worth it.

"I guess you are right. What shall I drink then?"

Me. I want to say me. It's right there at the tip of my tongue before I swallow it, pushing the cocktail over to him. Matteo leaves his inventory for a second and takes a sip with his eyes still in mine.

"Your turn."

What a dangerous little game I'm playing. Yet I can't stop my next words. "Never have I ever been in love."

What I said is the truth. One I've come to realize after my night with Matteo and when I said it, I was one hundred percent sure Matteo wouldn't drink. I was confident in that. Yet...

Yet I'm stunned speechless when he takes my drink and drains it full.

He's been in love...

My eyes search his as my heart is racing but whether it's from hurt or surprise is yet to be determined. I have a million questions to ask but don't because the front door opens and loud, joyous laughter fills the whole space and Jenny, Nina, Willa and Fanny stroll in and just as always with Rick, Sam and my dad trailing in behind them.

Who I don't expect are Hope and Alec to walk in as well but the looks on their faces tell me they have been ambushed just as much as I have been and their date night was ruined by their parents.

"Zoe," Willa exclaims happily and embraces me in a warm, motherly hug. "How is my favorite daughter-in-law?" she asks with excitement in her eyes.

"Oh, um, if you mean me, I am good. But I'm n—" I don't get to finish the sentence because Matteo swoops in behind me, drawing his arm around my waist and plastering my back to his front, rendering me speechless while claiming me in front of everyone.

Why would he do that? Isn't he afraid his playboy status will take a beating if others see him embracing the single mom of LC?

"Hey, you all, are you in for an early happy hour?" he asks them.

I try to move his arm off my hip discreetly, but the behemoth won't budge.

He's been in love...

"We sure are," Sam supplies. That man is in abnormally good shape for his age. "Give us those fall specials you've been brewing."

"And here we thought none of you would show up this early," Alec grumbles. "Don't you all have your new rally to plan?" He twists his lips.

"What's that supposed to mean?" Nina asks.

"Means we wanted some privacy for once."

"We always give you privacy," she argues back.

"The events of last night prove you very wrong, Mom." Alec and Nina start going back and forth, and Hope slides next to us.

"They showed up to our place last night. Well, in the middle of it. And while *we* were in the *middle of it*," she says with a small blush and rolls her lips. "Needless to say, they killed the mood and Alec is still very sour about it."

"What did they want?" Matteo asks, confused. Poor guy lived for too long away from these schemers and they have definitely escalated from what he remembers.

Hope sighs. "Well, you see, we were supposed to be out of town last night, and they knew about it. So, they decided it was a perfect time to hang up some weird pregnancy charms all over our house in discreet places so we wouldn't find out about them, yet magically would get pregnant." Matteo looks at her with a stupefied expression. "Oh, and when they walked in and saw that their plan has failed, Nina proceeded to tell us about a position we should try." Hope cringes. "I don't think I've ever heard my husband yell that loud."

"No, they didn't," he gasps. "Please tell me my mother wasn't part of this," he pleads but when Hope scrunches her nose, he gets his answer and groans.

"Um, she was the one who found the charms. So, I recommend going through your house as soon as you can. And look under the floorboards."

"The floorboards?"

"Yep."

After another five minutes, Nina and the rest of the gang are put on curfew. And banned from Alec and Hope's house.

You see, these four ladies want as many grandchildren as they can get and are willing to go to any length to get them. Case in point.

They are not malicious, they're just a little crazy and a lot overboard, but no matter how much Hope, Joy, or even Grace want to complain about their schemes, they did help all three of them to find their husbands and live out their happily ever afters.

Maybe I should consult the Fantastic Four?

26

Matteo

"I love you. I've loved you since the first moment I saw you. I guess maybe I've even loved you before I saw you."
- A Place in the Sun

The day took an interesting turn, and I must say, having my girls with me here was as best as it could go. Now, if my beastie would retract those claws and finally let me in, that would be the cherry on a cocktail, but she's not there quite yet.

For a second there, I thought the walls were crumbling, but then when we played the game and I drank in answer to the question, the tiny crack was sealed so fast, I thought I had a whiplash.

What scared her? Did she figure out I was talking about her, and it spooked her?

Just what the hell happened to her in that past to make her run from love as fast as her feet could carry her?

I'm head over heels for this woman, yet her life prior to living in Loverly Cave is one big mystery. I've been with her, felt her body, seen her naked but not in the sense that matters.

I should say I won't push her and I'll let her tell me on her own, but nah, I'm not that big of a gentleman and Zoe needs that push. Otherwise, she'll live in her shell forever and we can't have that happening.

After all, I've already decided I'm going to marry this girl. So, she needs to get on board.

"I'm telling you, Jenny, this is the one. I've finally mastered that cabbage casserole." The conversation is still alive around us with Nina sharing her new recipe.

"Oh, so that's what that smell was? I was certain it was a dead skunk somewhere in our yard. Good for you, honey." Jenny pats her friend's hand with a sweet, sincere smile.

"Oh, I should bring you some," Nina says to Zoe as Alec dips behind his mom and shakes his head in a violent *no* his eyes big and full of horror.

I look back at him, silently saying, "It can't be that bad, can it?"

He understands what I'm asking and mimics an explosion and us, dead.

Okay, it's very bad.

"Oh, um, that's very kind of you, Nina, but there's no need. Matteo is an excellent cook. So, I'm well taken care of in that department."

Did she just compliment me? And here I thought we weren't making progress.

"What about the other departments?" Fanny asks nonchalantly.

"Which ones?" My eyebrows pull together.

"The sex ones."

"Okayyyy," Zoe's dad says, picking up his beer. "Rick, Sam, we will go over there into the farthest corner of this room right about now."

"Nerds, your daughter is a grown woman. Surely you don't think she got impregnated by the Holy Spirit."

"Nope. But I would like to pretend that she did."

Kevin and the guys take off toward karaoke that is being set up with Sam registering his name first. This is our cue to leave and do it soon—after Zoe answers Fanny's question—because if Mr. Colson gets going, there will be no stopping him, and let's just say he's a man of many talents. But singing is not one of them.

The singing is not the only problem here because from the few times I saw this gang for karaoke nights during spring break, it got very ugly, very fast with Rick being competitive and jumping in to outdo Sam.

Newsflash: He can't sing either.

Yet it doesn't stop their wives from going crazy, rooting for them, trash talking the others' husband and going as far as dancing on the bar to hype up the room. Yep. I've seen it and now I can't unsee it.

Especially when my own mother would join in and Fanny attempting to twerk her behind…never again.

"Sunshine, can you please give that answer real fast because we need to go."

"What answer?" she asks looking all innocent, but those eyes won't fool me, she's avoiding answering. Good thing she has me to push her out of her comfort zone.

"The one about how good my cock makes you feel." In a flash, Zoe jumps up to reach my mouth and I catch her, holding her sweet, curvy body pressed to mine just as her hand slaps over my mouth, her big eyes, growing even larger.

"Are you out of your mind? Your mom is right there," she hisses to me, pointing in the general direction of our spectators and then turns to Jenny, Nina, Fanny and my mom who are watching us with huge grins, looking like four cats who just caught the Canary.

"Well, Fanny, I think that just answered your question," Jenny says with a giggle. "You kids have a good night." She winks and takes off together with Nina to find their husbands who already started arguing which one of them will be singing "Dancing Queen."

"That it did," Fanny agrees and leaves us watching my teary-eyed mom.

"I'm available any day of the week to watch my granddaughter," she says.

"She means Mellie, doesn't she?" Zoe leans in to ask me.

"Yep."

I hear her exhale a long breath and very quietly mumbling to herself as she moves away from me. "Should I even fight it at this point?"

"Definitely not," I answer loudly, and she whips around to send me a cute glare that never fails to make my dick twitch.

"This is all your fault."

"What? You wanting me around?"

I don't expect an answer but Zoe surprises me with a soft, "Yes."

It's sometime after midnight when I hear the sounds of someone shuffling toward the kitchen where I am in the process of cutting up and smashing the watermelon by hand since using a mixer at this time is not an option.

The idea for this cocktail has been brewing in my head for weeks now, but after today, after feeling how much my little girl loves me, needs me, it clicked. All the pieces of the missing puzzle in my head snapped into place when a distraught Mellie nuzzled into my chest, calming down that instant.

Before meeting Zoe, each cocktail I created was based on what people generally like, what's popular and how I can twist it. It was about the chemistry, the composition and surprise. Now? Now, everything I make holds a piece of Zoe or Mellie.

The taste of lychee and mint in my drinks belongs to Zoe. If there is an ice element in there it's because of her ice queen attitude, only the ice has the tendency to melt around fire. And if, while someone drinks the cocktail, it stings them a little, it's because pain and pleasure go hand in hand when it comes to that woman.

And now my sweet little watermelon has left a mark on my creative process as well. Ever since they went to sleep, I've been playing around with ingredients that remind me of Mel and so far, I have a menu of no less than five perfect drinks. All light and fluffy with a touch of fire.

"Matteo," Zoe whisper-yells. "What are you doing still up?"

I take her in, standing there with her hair slightly ruffled from sleep, her tank top twisted as usual and her fucking tits spilling out of the nursing bra she wears, and if that isn't bad enough for my poor, needy cock, the woman is not wearing any pants or shorts. Nope, only a thin layer of lace is covering her sweet pussy.

Apparently, she's done wearing those postpartum things.

Fucking great.

It was hard enough to resist her these past days fully clothed and now she's standing here, practically dangling a delicious treat in front of a very hungry puppy with no self-control.

"Creating, Beastie." My voice comes out sounding strained, but she doesn't seem to notice because she comes even closer until she is standing right by me, leaning over to sniff the drink I just made.

"Mmm, it smells fruity, and familiar." She frowns slightly. It should smell familiar because it smells just like Mellie's shower gel. "But shouldn't you get some sleep? You worked the whole day and when we got home you went straight to playing with Mel. Aren't you tired?"

A small smile pulls up on my lips. "Are you worried about me?"

"Pshh, you wish." She pushes away from the counter, giving me an unguarded view of her perfect, round ass and lowers herself onto the chair across from me. "So? Why the sudden need to pull an all-nighter?"

I gulp and swallow a groan. Does she realize what she's doing to me? How badly my fingers are itching to dig into her soft flesh with my cock buried in her?

Fuck. Down, Matteo, your owner didn't give you the command yet. I shift my cock to the side and clear my throat. "When an idea pops into my head, I can't sleep. I need to keep working it until I get it right."

"Oh, and what is this one about?"

"Mellie," I simply say, and Zoe's eyes snap to mine, her mouth in that perfect O.

"Y-your drink is about my daughter?"

"Yeah, she inspired it. Well, all five of these." I gesture to the line of glasses standing off to the side and she trails her eyes over it, her posture growing softer.

"How come you never asked about her father?"

I shrug. "And here I thought you were sick of my big head. Now you want me to ask you about me? Why would I need to ask about myself?"

"Matteo. Can you be serious for one minute?" I set the knife down and give her my full attention.

"I am. I'm Mellie's father." And I mean that with every ounce of blood in my body. "As for the sperm donor..." I trail off, because yeah, I have thought about him. Especially when I thought another man was coming here but it came to one simple truth.

"He doesn't matter. He's not here. He wasn't here when you walked into my bar or when your water broke or when Mellie took her first breath. And if he was stupid enough not to follow you to the ends of the earth then he doesn't matter. Any more questions?"

Zoe looks at me with her mouth agape. Those plush lips falling apart, filling my mind with dirty fucking thoughts, I can't have.

Yet.

At least she's finally done protesting the fact that Mellie is mine.

"What are you doing up?" I shift the conversation, needing a distraction from wanting this stubborn woman more than my next breath.

"Oh, um..." She tucks a lose strand of her blonde hair behind her ear as she visibly tries to pull those wall back up. "Mellie hasn't woken up yet to eat and my boobs are killing me, they're so full."

I freeze. *So much for that distraction*. "Zoe," I groan, tipping my head up and pinch the bridge of my nose. "One, two, fucking three, four, double fucking five."

"Are you counting?" Zoe looks at me with one eyebrow cocked up and I nod, continuing my count. "Why are you counting?"

"Because." I snap my head down, locking eyes with hers. "You are sitting over here, practically naked, talking about your full tits and I am many things, Beastie, but one who has self-restrain when it comes to you in not really one of them." I clench my teeth. "So, seven, eight, fudging ten."

"You skipped nine," she utters breathlessly.

"What?"

"Your count, you skipped nine." She gets up from her chair and starts moving.

"Zoe." I say her name as a warning. "Why are you moving toward me?"

"You skipped nine," she repeats again.

"So I did."

"You have been there for me every single day." I'm not sure if it's a question but I nod anyway. "You love my daughter." Another nod. "You make cocktails inspired by her. You learned how to change a diaper and cook for me and for some reason you want me. You want my daughter when her own father didn't."

She is standing so close, too close. Our rapidly raising chests practically touching with every labored breath we take. "So, why have I been refusing it this whole time?" Zoe asks but her eyes are locked in on my lips.

"I don't know, Beastie."

She looks up, "Kiss me, Matteo."

"What?" *Did she just really say that?*

"You wanted me to beg, here I am, Matteo. I'm begging you to kiss me."

Maybe someday in the future I will take my sweet time making her beg for my lips, then my fingers and finally, my cock. But today is not that day.

The second the words are out of her mouth, my mouth is on hers, swallowing the gasp she releases. One of my hands goes to her small, slender neck, wrapping it so I can feel the wild pulse beating against my fingers. My second arm goes to that sweet, lace covered ass and I dig my fingers deep into her flesh like I have craved to do.

Zoe jumps at my rough touch but doesn't pull away. No, my girl fists my shirt, dragging me into her body as close as she can while shamelessly moaning and rubbing herself against me. But I have a feeling even if she were painted over my skin, that would not have been enough.

At least for me.

At this point, I'm not sure we are capable of sweet and cute kisses, because every time our lips crush against each other, they engage in a war. Raw, bloody and power-hungry. Each stroke of her tongue against mine sends a zap through my blood and I find myself biting her lower lip, dragging it into my mouth and sucking on it like my personal lollipop.

More. I want—no, need—more. So, I grab her by the waist and prop her on the counter behind her. Zoe's head falls back, and I follow her into it, looming over her as I breath in each of her breaths, wrapping her silky blonde hair tightly around my hand until she hisses at the pressure.

More. I need more. I'm so fucking hungry for this woman; I can no longer think rationally.

I then slide my lips lower, kissing and biting her chin, soothing the stings with my tongue and I keep going down her neck, leaving my marks over her soft, pale skin. I drag my tongue over her collarbone and feel Zoe's body shuddering at my touch, digging her fingers into my shoulders.

Just then, something wet presses against my shirt and I pull away to see what it is.

"S-sorry," Zoe pants, looking down to her soaked shirt. "I told you I was very full."

"Does it hurt?" I ask her and she nods.

I don't think. I don't consider whether it's right or not, all I know is I need to soothe her pain, so I grip her shirt and pull it down with such force, the flimsy thing rips straight through the middle with Zoe letting out a small yelp. Her thin, cotton bra shares the same fate, and I am stuck looking at the most gorgeous set of tits.

They are so much more fuller now than they were the last time I saw her, beads of her milk oozing out of her dark pink, hard nipples. My mouth waters at the thought of having them inside my mouth. Of *tasting her* on my tongue.

"Matteo, what are y—" I don't let her finish her question when I lower my head, grabbing a handful of both of her tits in my hands and wrap my lips around her nipple and she falls back with a moan, propping herself on her arms.

Immediately, the sweetest taste fills my mouth, her milk flooding my mouth as I greedily suck on her nipple while my other hand squeezes her other breast and that precious liquid covers my hand, flowing down my wrist.

Fuck, I don't think I have ever been this fucking hard and there is no stopping the moans that come from me as I devour her tits. I'm throbbing and sure as fuck leaking in my pants.

"M-Matteo," Zoe pants, her voice barely audible. "Please, please..." I'm not sure what is she pleading for but a second later I get my answer when I switch to her other nipple, licking over the pointed tip with the flat of my tongue and she drags her fingers into my hair, slipping the hair tie off my loose bun and wraps her little fists around it. Dragging me closer to her breasts until my face is firmly buried in her, and it's only by sheer will and a fuck ton of luck that I don't explode and paint my pants with my cum right there and then.

Zoe's hips are moving frantically, seeking any kind of pressure and I slide my hand lower, cupping her pussy over the soaked panties and she lets out a guttural moan, rubbing herself over my hand.

I go to pull her panties off when her hand shoots out, stopping me and I break away from her milky tits to see what happened. Does she not want to go further?

"You can't," she whispers, her eyes hooded. "Not yet. We can't go there for another two weeks."

"Two weeks?"

How the fuck am I supposed to survive another two weeks?

"Baby, you are killing me," I groan, tipping my head forward and burying it in between her tits, my hand still over her pussy. "But I can touch you?"

"Please do," she almost cries out, and I don't need anything else to press my thumb to her clit over the thin lace and rub her little nub. "Matteo?"

"Yeah?"

"I need your mouth on my tits, baby. Right this fucking second."

"Fuck," I whisper in adoration, feeling my dick twitch dangerously. "I love it when you're bossy."

I wrap my mouth around her nipple again, sucking it in and this time the scent of her arousal in the air around us, the feel of her wet pussy between my fingers, the sweetness of her milk and the harsh grip she has on my hair does me in.

My whole body vibrates as an explosive orgasm takes over me, shaking me from my toes to the tips of my hair and my cum spills all over my pants. I've never come without a single touch to my cock before and the thought alone makes me feral for this woman.

I start working her clit even faster, my mouth dripping with her milk, and Zoe pants, "Fuck, fuck, fuck, damn that swear jar. I'm fucking coming!" She tightens her hold on me and does just that. Her body shakes, quivering on the counter. I pull away from her tits and slam my mouth against hers, swallowing her sounds of pleasure that are mine and mine alone.

A few seconds later, her hold on my hair relaxes, her body growing lax and she pulls away. Those beautiful eyes now wide, watching me with caution and something else. Something that looks a lot like shame that has no place here.

"Um." She swallows hard. "I...uh, I got carried away over there for a second. I'm sorry," she says, dropping her gaze to the ground but I slip my fingers underneath her chin, bringing it right back.

"Talk to me, Beastie. What is going on in that beautiful head of yours?" Zoe tries to jump off the counter to run away without answering but that won't be happening. So, I cage her with my arms and wait.

Eventually, her body sags as she lets out a sigh and says quietly, "I made you taste me. My milk, I mean," she chews on her lip.

"For the record, you didn't *make me* taste you. You demanded it." Zoe starts saying something back, but I halt her, pressing my index finger to her lips. "And I fucking loved it. In fact"—I grab her hand dragging it over to my linen pants that do nothing to hide the wet spot right smack in the middle of them and place it there—"I loved it so much, I came just like that."

Her eyes snap to mine, that delicious mouth propping open in another fucking O. "Y-you, you came?"

"I did." I give her a crooked smile, my teeth sink into my lower lip. "I came so fucking hard to the taste of your milk in my mouth. And I think we may have a problem now." I lean into her, greedily breathing her in.

"What problem?"

"I want more. I want to feed on you every time. I want your sweetness in my mouth." My cock grows hard again just at the thought of it.

"Feel that?" I ask, because her hand is still touching me, and she can definitely tell something is going on behind that linen. "Just like that, Zo. Just-like-fucking-that, I'm hard for you again."

Zoe's chest starts moving rapidly once again, her eyes growing wild as she licks her lips while her small fingers glide over my spilled cum.

I'm fucking trembling from her touch, watching those beautiful eyes when she brings the pads of her fingers to her mouth and sucks them in, stealing the last fucking breath I had left in my body.

My nostrils are flaring like a wild bull, chest heaving, and Zoe leans in whispering, "Then have some more." And I don't waste another second, pushing her back and feeding on her while she rubs my cock until both of us come once more.

27

Never Have I Ever

Matteo: Never have I ever faked an orgasm.
Zoe: Wow, shocker.
Matteo: Why did you just drink that?
Zoe: Because that's how the game goes, no?
Matteo: With me? Did you fake those that night?
Zoe: Unfortunately, not.
Matteo: Damn right.
Zoe: That will be twenty-five cents.
Matteo: It was worth it.

28

Zoe

"Age is not a number, it's an attitude." –Unknown

Something changed last night.

Noooo? You don't say!

Who am I kidding right now? No shit, something changed last night. My whole world as I know it flipped over and still can't find its way back to the normal position.

I have no idea what came over me, but when he told me the cocktails were inspired by Mellie, I felt my heart crack. Or rather, the control I had over it. But I was going to hold onto it cracks and all. Until he said he was Mellie's father.

And meant it.

The fight was so over it wasn't even funny. I was done and I've allowed my sanity to slip through my fingers.

And now I'm lying here in my bed alone since he stole my daughter sometime early this morning and I'm hiding in my room like an idiot, refusing to get up and face him in the broad daylight, because apparently, late at night it's easy to pretend I can shake off my fears and just *be*. It was easy to get lost in everything Matteo.

His voice. His presence. His scent and taste.

His touch and his lips.

Dear God, what his touch did to me. If you'd ask me before last night what I thought about lactation kinks, I'd call you an idiot and to never mention it to me again. Now? I'm trying to fight the urge to run out and beg him to wrap his soft lips around my nipples again.

It was the most soothing feeling I've ever experienced, coupled with pleasure so deep, I feel wetness pooling between my legs just thinking about it now.

But it wasn't just that. Simply being held by Matteo sends a wave of shivers down my spine. His dark, hungry gaze sets me ablaze and when his lips come in contact with mine, I forget my own name.

Fucking perfect. A twenty-three-year-old has messed with my head so thoroughly, I am hiding under the covers.

I cover my face with both of my hands and let out a silent groan. "Get up, make a plan and stop overthinking it. Last night happened and it won't anymore. It was a fluke. A weird magnetic field misfire crap—if such thing exists but I don't really care if it doesn't. I'm still using that excuse." I keep talking to myself, listing all of the ridiculous things I could blame for what happened when Matteo's voice filters through the closed door.

"Hmm, how about radioactive spiders?" he asks, and I freeze.

Shit, of course he's standing on the other side of the door like a sexy creep and heard my crazy rambling. Let's add yet another item to the list of my embarrassing moments in front of the man.

"Or there is always food poisoning, you know." He stops, and I presume take a bite of something because his next words come out muffled. "You can blame that too. I personally find that one a bit bland," he adds nonchalantly. "I mean, if you really want to go all out you have to *at least mention* alien invasion."

"I'm asleep, go away." I throw the cover over my face, knowing I'm being ridiculous, but what else is new these days?

The next instant, the door creaks open. "Perfect, then I can still wake you up properly," he says, and I tug the cover off my face to see what he's planning to do, but I'm too late.

Matteo has already lunged at me, throwing his massive, shirtless body over mine, and I squeak, trying to get away from him, but once again, am unsuccessful. He pins me to the bed, trapping my wrists in his hands above my head and lowers his face to mine, while his hair falls over my face, covering us from the world.

I see his intent to kiss me, and roll my lips together, hiding them from him. But do you think that deters him? Not in the slightest. "Silly little Beastie." He grins. "As if you could stop me." Matteo kisses me anyway, or more like plants a whole bunch of smooches all over my face.

His lips are everywhere, on my cheeks and chin, on my nose, eyelids and eyebrows. He kisses my forehead and leaning down, just below my ear. He starts moving lower and that's when I buck, realizing his intent and yell out, "Matteo, stop! What happened to no kissing me until I beg?"

The bastard uses that moment to quickly slide his lips over mine, kissing me, instead of answering and I mumble into his mouth, "Morning breath!"

Finally, he pulls away slightly, but still not too much where I could sneak away from him and grins wide at me. "Mm-hmm, love your morning breath." And lowers his mouth back to mine, this time moaning as he slips his tongue past my lips.

I swat at his shoulder. "You are disgusting." But there is zero heat behind my words.

He loves my freaking morning breath...and the thing is, I'm fairly certain he's not joking.

I'm starting to realize Matteo doesn't say anything he doesn't mean. He's...honest.

The thought sends my mind spiraling because that would mean everything else he said was true as well and he really intends on staying with us. He really does love my daughter. He wants me, us, this.

Pull the brakes woman, before your heart trips over your tongue, running to him.

"And that whole beg for a kiss situation was a one-time password deal. You have unlocked unlimited access to Matteo Land. A lifetime pass." He smirks. "Feel free to take a ride anytime you'd like." He presses into me and even through a thick duvet—yes, the one with the cats Joy got me—there is no mistaking how hard he is.

"Oh, really? And how many other women have this special pass?" I quirk and eyebrow at him, and I expect him to make another joke. Maybe even tell me something along the lines of too many to count but instead his teasing features are replaced by a serious, almost grim look.

"One," he says and crushes his lips to mine right away, showing me instead of telling me how true that is. "Fuck...what you do to me. Maybe *I* should be the one blaming aliens for your existence."

His body starts rocking into mine and suddenly I need this blanket off me, I need to feel his body on mine. Need to feel what I do to him, but before it goes there, Matteo pulls away from me, bracing himself on his elbows and to my horror, I let out a whiny noise.

"My needy girl." He smiles, biting my chin. "Do you need me to play with you? Maybe have my fingers on that little pussy? Or"—he licks his lips and my heart starts racing—"do you need my mouth on your tits, hmm?"

Matteo slides down a little bit until his face is leveled with my breasts and just the feel of his breath on my skin is enough to drive me crazy, but he leans in and takes a lungful of my scent, closing his eyes in pleasure, and letting out a husky, "Fuck, that's exactly what you need, isn't it?"

"Yes, yes, God yes," I chant, my fingers already digging into his hair, and Matteo lowers his mouth to my clothed nipple, biting it lightly through the cotton bra I'm wearing, and I feel the milk leaking right through the thin material.

So much for that fucking plan to never do this again...

Only...Matteo pulls away and one word leaves his smirking mouth. "Later."

My eyes snap down to his so fast they hurt.

"What do you mean, *later*?" I sound like a petulant child and I don't care.

Matteo jumps off me, bends and twists a bit to fix the hard-on situation in his jeans and strolls to the door. "Later means after you get your pretty ass out of bed, have breakfast and admit how much you like me."

Oh no, he didn't! I sit up in my bed, crossing my arms across my chest and glare at the smiling, sexy bastard.

"Get back in here, Matteo," I almost growl out, and that stupid smile of his turns into a horrible self-satisfied grin.

"God, I love it when you are bossy, Beastie." He bites his lip teasingly but keeps retreating.

I narrow my eyes at him. "What's your middle name?"

"Orion. Why?"

I will stop to think about his middle name later, for now I'm too angry and sexually frustrated so all I can do is grab a pillow and throw it into his face while yelling, "Matteo Orion Loverson, you are a dead man walking."

Matteo catches the damn pillow, sniffs my scent off it as he rolls his eyes and biting that stupid lip. "Ugh, you are so feisty in the mornings. Just imagine how much fun we will have once you give in."

"Currently, my mind is set on how much fun I will have killing you."

"Promises, promises." He winks and sends me an air kiss, and by the time I send another pillow flying his way he already ducks out of the way, laughing as he does.

Reluctantly, I do get up, running through my morning routine that I now have the time for because Matteo has been the one taking care of Mellie in the mornings. That stupidly hot, sexy, considerate, frustrating, sadistic man.

Just thinking about how amazing he is makes me angrier. In another life, if he would be older, I'd call him the ultimate dream.

"Zoe, stop glaring, my dick can't handle any more blood rushing to it," he says, sliding a plate with a smoked salmon bagel and other veggies on it and a homemade smoothie he just created especially for me—as he put it.

I would protest eating if he wasn't such an amazing cook—because of course the man made the bagels himself—and his drinks taste too good to pass up.

"Is this your thing? Put a ban on something I want until I give in to your rules?"

Matteo wiggles his eyebrows. "It gets the job done, doesn't it?"

Way to go, Zoe, just a few minutes ago you were preaching to yourself about "never again" and "that was a fluke" and "how could I like that," and now you're pouting and irrationally angry he didn't suck on your tits.

Fucking phenomenal.

"No, what it does is make me mad."

"So, what you are trying to say is you want me?"

More than I ever thought was possible. Not that I will ever say that out loud. Mellie gives him enough encouragement for the both of us with her constant need for him. Even now, she is chilling in her baby cot that had to be situated on top of the kitchen counter so she could see him.

"Come on, Beastie." He leans over the counter. "Just admit you like me. It's the truth anyway, you are just a stubborn little cub, refusing to come to terms with it."

No shit, it's the truth, but what do I do? I pick up the bagel and stuff my mouth with it, while still glaring, refusing to answer him and Matteo bursts out laughing.

"God, you are the most perfect woman out there." He puts his hands around Mellie's ears and whispers, "And I will fuck you so good as soon as I can."

Sigh, meet Zoe.

"Please remind me who thought it was a good idea to invite Matteo tonight?" I ask the girls around me while still glaring at that frustrating man who is now happily chatting with Alec, Jacob, and Luke.

"Well, seeing as he now grows on your ass, it would be quite difficult to have you here without him, but also no one invited him. The stray just can't get lost again," my cheery best friend supplies and takes a long sip of her water.

We are all gathered at the beach, around the bonfire that is in front of our houses and the guys are grilling in our plain view.

With no shirts.

And while usually I would appreciate the fine male specimens in front of me…tonight, I only see one. With no shirt. Did I mention that?

Lord help me.

I stayed strong the whole day despite his teasing touches anytime he was around me. A brush of his fingers against mine as we passed in the hallway, his cheek against mine as he leaned in to take Mel from my arms and even the feeling of his front pressed against my back as he pretended to grab something from the kitchen cupboard where I was standing didn't do me in.

But it seems my luck is running out with all of that tan, golden skin, peppered with salty water droplets from his earlier dip in the ocean and his damp long hair in disarray on display for my hungry eyes.

What are the chances no one will notice me licking his chest right about now?

"Don't even think about it," comes from Joy.

"What? What are you talking about?"

"Who me?" Joy mimics my forced-innocent tone, pointing to herself. "I am talking about that look on your face that says 'From which side should I start licking him up first? The top to bottom or bottom to top?'"

"Definitely top to bottom," Grace whispers with a giggle beside her.

"Why are you whispering?" Hope asks her in that same whisper while rocking my daughter in her arms.

"Because my husband is keeping track of all the times I talk about other men and that list is already too long."

"Why is he keeping track?"

"To punish me," she says with a smile that says she doesn't mind those punishments too much.

"Okay, we are not here to talk about you and your husband's perversions," Joy interrupts. "I've heard enough about your broken vagina to last a lifetime already."

"Keep your jealousy on the downlow, sister," Grace shoots back. "But I agree. I'd much rather talk about Zoe and her cougar tendencies."

That gets a groan out of me.

"I hate you. There are no cougar tendencies here. None," I proclaim vehemently, but Matteo choses that exact moment to come running my way, crouching right in from of me.

"Are you all right, Beastie?" he asks, his forehead creased with concern, taking a lose strand of my hair and tucking it behind my ear and all I can do is nod because just the simplest of his touches, set me on fire. "I heard you groan."

Dear Lord, for all that is holy do not whimper. Don't you dare, Zoe.

"I'm fine," comes out a lot squeakier than I want it to.

"All right then." Matteo gets up but not before kissing my forehead and there goes my attempt at no whimpering.

Pathetic, I swear.

"Anything you'd like to say to me?" he whispers into my ear. His manly scent mixed with ocean breeze stirring my insides and with yet another whimper I shake my head. Matteo leans back, that sexy half smile of his firmly intact on his lips. "Take your time, Zo, I'll be standing right there if something. Deciding whether I'll taste your milky tits or your sweet pussy first. What do you think?" The bastard knows exactly what he's doing to me right now.

"You are such a little shit."

"Spank me, Mommy." He winks, flashing me his wide grin and stands up leaving me up in flames over here. And mind you they are not the embarrassment ones. No, sir.

"Let me take my girl." He extends his arms toward Mellie and Hope hands him my daughter who immediately nuzzles into his chest, placing her little hand on her favorite human and they walk off with him cooing sweet nothings to her, as if he didn't just unlock yet another kink I wasn't aware of having!

"No cougar tendencies, she says." Grace cracks up. "So, like I was saying, go from top to bottom," she adds.

"Stop that! I need you to talk me out of it, not encourage me."

"And why would I do that?" she frowns at me.

"Because I can't go there. Not with Matteo."

"And why can't you?"

"Gracie, he's not going to stay for the long run. He's not that type of a guy," I tell her but even I have a hard time believing the words coming out of my mouth.

"Oh, right." She nods, heavy on the sarcasm. "He's just the type of a guy to stay with you through the whole fun that is child labor, jumping right into the role of a dad without running for the hills. The one to show up at your door to help you with the baby who is not his. The kind to keep living there, sleeping on that awful couch, cook for you, create cocktails inspired by you and come running as soon as he hears you groaning. Nooo, he's *definitely* not that type of a guy."

Damn it, why is she making such a good point right now and I have nothing to say back? I look to my best friend whom I can always count on to find the negatives in any situation. "Joy?" But she's quietly wrinkling her nose. "JOY!"

"I hate it when you say smart things that make total sense, Gracie," she finally says to her little sister, and I sag into the chair.

"Then how about the fact that he's younger than me? What are people going to say?" I ask, lifting my hands up in question and all three sisters stare at me with one eyebrow raised.

"Do you want me to call Alec and Jacob over here so they can educate you on how many fucks should be given when it comes to societal norms?" Hope asks.

"God, no," I groan. Those two have a personal issue with how normal people live in this world. So, they took it upon themselves to spread word that we shouldn't give a damn about what is acceptable and not in society.

"Then, I really don't see a problem. I say go for it," Hope adds, and Gracie raises her hand. "I second that." They both turn to Joy who's been quiet, and they have some weird sisterly silent conversation at the end of which Joy rolls her eyes and looks to me.

"Look, I know I have been the one to talk you into kicking that puppy to the curb, but even I must admit that he's good for you, Zoe." She sighs as if it's physically painful for her to admit she was wrong before. "Ever since he strolled into your life, you've been different. More alive. Happier. And that's all I want for you. Life is that simple and not a series of horror films we were used to before."

I look at her, my mouth agape and not believing that it's my grumpy cactus of a friend who is saying this right now.

"Damn it, Joy." I slump into my chair. "I needed you to be my voice of wisdom."

"I am."

"Then I'm doomed."

"Nope, it looks like you are about to be thoroughly satisfied as soon as the doctor gives you a go ahead." Hope giggles.

"How did it get to this? This should not be happening," I cover my face with my hands. I still don't seem to grasp that he really wants me. Us.

I want him. We want him.

"No, that should definitely be happening, because you deserve that kind of a man. Shed your fears off, Zo, they are just shackling you to a world of gray routine."

She's right isn't she? Maybe *I am* enough for Matteo?

"Now"—she narrows her eyes to the scene in front of us—"what shouldn't be happening is our husbands getting all cozy with Matteo. There is enough crazy between Jacob and Alec as it is," Hope adds, pointing to the trio who are all staring at Luke's crotch.

"Did it hurt?" We hear Matteo ask Luke because his voice is higher pitched than the others at the moment.

"Jesus, please tell me they are not discussing your husband's piercing again." Joy sighs, looking over to Grace.

"They totally are." She shakes her head.

"What piercing?" I ask them at the same time as Matteo calls out to me, "Hey, Zoe, how do you feel about dick piercings?"

"That kind." Grace points to Matteo and his question while all I can do is sit here and blink.

"Um..." I clear my throat. "Why are you asking me?"

"Because if I'm going to traumatize him, it better be for a good cause."

"And the good cause being..." I trail off, not really understanding where he is going with this.

"To give you the best orgasms possible, of course," he says nonchalantly while both me and Joy choke on our waters.

"Matteo!" I cry out while coughing and he runs up to help me, slapping my back lightly. "You can't just blurt out that kind of stuff."

"Why not?" He seems genuinely confused about it.

"Because we're not even dating!"

"Of course we are, Beastie."

"Did you hit your head when you were jumping off that cliff earlier today?"

"Nope."

"Then you were probably bitten by a radioactive spider."

"The same one that got you last night?" He smirks, the smug bastard.

"Why? What happened last night?" Joy pipes out from beside me.

"Yeah, what happened last night, Zo?" Matteo parrots her but with a knowing grin on his face.

I chuck my tongue. "So, about that piercing..."

Matteo tips his head up and starts laughing, "God, you are the cutest."

"Jacob, are you sure Matteo is not your long-lost brother?" Joy calls out to her husband.

"Um, I'm pretty sure he's not, Wildflower. Why?"

"Because both of you have no self-preservation skills, thinking you can call us *cute*. We are not cute, we are menacing."

"Sure you are, Wildflower." Jacob winks, and Joy bristles even more.

"Mm-hmm, I do like it when you get violent. You are even cuter then." I feel everyone watching and listening to our conversation intently.

"Matteo, for the love of...stop talking," I shake my head at him.

"So, is that a yes on that piercing."

"Matteo, it's your dick. So, you can do whatever you'd like to it. I don't care," I tell him, but he frowns at me like I've kicked his puppy.

He then looks down to his crotch and says, "Mommy is just joking, she does care about you." He pats his shorts-covered dick, and I wish I could say it was horror I was looking at him with, but nope.

All of a sudden, I have this irrational wish to slap his hand away and comfort his dick myself. With my mouth.

Joy looks from me to Matteo's retreating form. "You were right, he's definitely not a stray. The pup has found his mama. And he is definitely Jacob's long-lost brother. Lord help us all."

"I am so defriending you." I glare at her but my whole body is buzzing with desire for that man.

Maybe it's his nonchalance about the topic or the ease with which he just called his dick mine, but it ticks something off in my head, unleashes a part of me I didn't know about. Because I might like the idea of him belonging to me and only me a little too much.

"Zoe, take it from someone who was stubborn and stupid to keep the most amazing man at arm's length for too long." Hope levels me with a look. "When you find a man like that, don't let your own fears and insecurities to lead your heart. This—he—is worth the risk."

He is, isn't he?

29

Never Have I Ever

Zoe: Never have I ever won a lottery.
Zoe: Why did you just take that drink?
Matteo: Because I have.
Zoe: What? You seriously mean to tell me that you won a freaking lottery???
Matteo: Sure did. The day you walked into my bar.

30

Zoe

"If I know what love is, it is because of you." —Herman Hesse, *Narcissus and Goldmund*

Alone. I've always been alone on these bonfire nights—well, before Mel was born—but even with her, I was alone in the sense of missing that strong, warm hand over my shoulders when the air got too chilly. I've been the one to fetch myself drinks, food or a thick blanket while my friends had their boyfriends, now husbands, do it for them, and I always told myself that I didn't mind.

I was happy for them and resigned to my fate as a single mom.

It was fine when I took walks on the beach by myself or was the only one to talk to the little nugget that was growing in my belly.

That was until tonight. Until *this* bonfire night. Because Matteo just changed it all and I'm not sure how I will ever be able to go back.

I simply don't want to.

Because tonight is the first time it wasn't me fetching my food. First time taking a stroll on the beach hand in hand with a cute guy—who wrestled my hand into holding, because I'm still being a stubborn idiot—while he carries my daughter in his other hand.

First time someone took my hand and told me to sit my cute ass in between his thick thighs, leaning my back into him and using his warmth instead of those thick blankets I have plenty of now. At the same time rocking the little cot with a sleeping Mellie by our side. Matteo never leaves one of us without his attention.

Every day, hour, minute, and second I spend in his presence, I feel my resistance crumbling to the ground more and more. I feel those fears slipping away page by page, and instead this deep-rooted belief that Matteo would never crush my heart blooms inside my chest.

"I can't wait for our babies to be born," Jacob says wistfully, watching us with Mel as he rubs Joy's growing belly.

"It's not all going to be sunshine and rainbows, Jacob. They are *your* babies after all."

"That just means they will be as brilliant as their daddy." He waggles his eyebrows at her rolling eyes but there is also a smile on her face as well.

It still brings me so much happiness to see Joy this happy after the crap we went through with Justin back in Chicago.

"I disagree," Matteo says. "*It is* all sunshine and rainbows; I mean, look at Mellie. She is brilliant!" he proclaims the fact like a proud papa. "You should see how fast she burps after eating! And it's an impressive one too."

I turn my head around to look at him. "Matteo, is this seriously Mel's best quality you could come up with to share?"

"What? It is impressive!"

"Don't bother, Zoe, you and I will never be able to speak Loverly Cave men. It's a special dialect for stupidly hot idiots, who us smart women tend to fall for."

Matteo and Jacob both look at her, squinting.

"I'm one hundred percent confident she just insulted us, but after she called us stupidly hot, I stopped listening." Jacob purses his lips. "But just in case, justice needs to be served nonetheless," he adds and starts tickling my grumpy friend who breaks out in giggles, trying to fight him off.

"Jacob! Stop it! If you make my water break at the beach, I'm going to kill you," she says but it's all muffled by her laughs.

I am so entertained by my friends, I don't notice Matteo leaning into me, his lips right at the shell of my ear, teasing me with his hot breath as his arms tighten around my waist. Instantly, the scene in front of me is long forgotten and my skin breaks out in wild goosebumps. "You know, unlike Jacob, I heard the whole comment," he whispers. "The very last part of it too."

I try to search my brain for what was it that Joy had said. Something about the men in LC being stupidly hot. Well, he knew that part already, that's hardly surprising.

Wait...my whole body freezes.

Didn't she also say something about falling for those men?

"Don't worry, Beastie, this stupidly hot idiot is falling for this very smart and beautiful woman too," Matteo says, making my heart race like a wild horse while his lips are trailing over the column of my neck.

He's falling for me? That's what he said, right? That wasn't me hallucinating things because I'm clearly lacking a lot of oxygen at the moment with his body so close to mine.

"Mm-hmm," he murmurs into my neck. "You heard me right."

Oh my God, did he just read my mind or did I say that out loud? But Matteo doesn't let me ponder it anymore because he starts nibbling on that soft skin of my neck, and I can't fight the small moan coming out of me.

"Hey, lovebirds. Mind rejoining the party over here," Joy calls out to us, and I jolt awake from my lust-dream, Matteo's lips disappearing from my body, and I let out an involuntary groan.

"Um, are you okay, Zo?" Hope asks me.

No, not really. But it's not like I will grace you all with how high my sexual frustration is so, I blurt out, "Yep, just my boobs killing me. Mellie hasn't woken up for a while now and I really need to feed her."

Which is not really a lie, my boobs do hurt, but I'm not sure if it's from them having too much milk or not enough Matteo.

"Zo, that's not good." Jacob says, very seriously. "If you don't get that milk out of there, you can get clogged ducts."

And just like that, all eyes are on Jacob and Joy slowly turns her half frowning, half *what-the-fuck* type of face toward him.

"What?" Jacob asks with innocence. "Why are you all looking at me like that? You know what a clogged duct can do? It will hurt." He nods toward Joy with big, bulging eyes who is still frowning at him. "Yeah, Wildflower. I read about it." Jacob turns his gaze back to us. "You gotta help Zoe out, my man. Gotta suck that milk before it's too late. I bet it tastes good," he muses to himself.

Many things happen at once.

Luke spits out the beer he was drinking, breaking out in a coughing fit.

Alec looks at his friend like he is taking notes for the future.

Grace and Hope are gaping at him with their jaws hanging low.

Joy squints at her husband, running her tongue over her teeth.

And then there is us. Matteo, chuckling quietly into my hair and me, who is thanking the evening hour for the low visibility of my very heated cheeks.

"What do you say, Zo?" Matteo's low, husky voice trails over my body once again. "Want to give that a try? Want me to suck on those pretty little nipples? Just to make sure there are no clogged ducts, you know."

Oh, I can just imagine that smug face of his right now. The way he bites his lower lip when he's up to no good.

"Matteo?" I whisper back.

"Yeah?"

"Shut up."

The bastard only responds with a snicker.

"What? Why are you all looking at me like that?" Jacob seems genuinely confused why no one is taking him seriously—apart from Alec. And to be honest, the guy is right. Not that I will volunteer to say that to the class.

"I'm still trying to figure out who appointed you the main love advisor slash creepy lactology specialist of Loverly Cave." Joy tells him, pinching the bridge of her nose and shaking her head.

"I'm only speaking the truth, Wildflower. Well, apart from the taste thing. I have no idea if it's actually good."

They all start discussing the taste of breast milk but I'm hardly listening because Matteo's hand slowly snakes underneath my shirt, his fingers trailing up toward my breasts as he murmurs, "Oh, it's good. They have no idea how fucking good."

My head tilts back, resting on his chest, my breaths growing more and more shallow with each second as his fingers crawl up and up. My nipples are two hard pebbled stones, leaking milk profusely, soaking my bra and shirt.

"Fuck." Matteo's voice is hoarse as the drops of milk land on his fingers and then pulls them out.

They are shiny with my milk, and I watch as he sticks them into his mouth right away, sucking each drop off them while his eyes are locked in on mine in a silent promise of more. That huge cock in his pants is digging almost painfully into my backside and I can't draw another breath.

Dear God, what is this man doing to me? I am so turned on right now... I don't even care about our friends watching us or noticing what's going on in this semi-darkness.

"Zoe." He whispers my name like a prayer, dragging the three-letter name into a long string, coated in lust and desire.

And I snap.

My body jolts up in one fluid move, standing up and dragging Matteo with me.

"You okay, Zo?" Joy asks, watching me grab my sleeping daughter in haste and I nod.

"Yep. Totally fine. Better than ever. Just need to go deal with these clogged ducts, you know?" I'm talking too fast, blubbering too much, and I'm not sure why everyone always talks about only men having their blood down south when they are turned on because I sure do feel those same effects on me right now.

I don't wait to hear what anyone else have to say. I don't even care that they are very much aware of what is going on between us. All I know is that I need to get Matteo's lips on my body. I need to feel him. All of him. Physically. Since mentally, he invaded my head a long time ago and spread around, growing deep roots ever since that first time we met at the bar.

"Follow me, Matteo," I tell him.

"Until the ends of the Earth, Beastie."

I think someone coos, "Awww," behind us as Matteo swoops in, taking Mel's cot from my hands and we make our way to our house.

Our.

Yes, I really said that and it didn't freak me out. Maybe because it never felt like just mine. Even before Matteo moved in, something was missing and now I know what. Or rather, who.

In the few steps it takes us to get inside, we somehow grow even more impatient for each other, about ready to tear the clothes we are wearing to tiny pieces. But Mellie has a different idea and chooses that exact moment to wake up, screaming for her dinner.

"I gotta go feed her," I tell him.

Matteo can't even utter a single word, simply motioning for me to go do what I have to do while he struts over to the kitchen, pouring himself a tall glass of cold water. He sees me still standing in the hallway, watching him and he groans.

"Baby, go. For the love of my manhood, please go and come back as fast as you can." He sounds like he's in pain and that gets me moving, running through our bedtime routine with Mel as fast as I can.

Thankfully, Mellie decides to play nice tonight and goes to bed without needing to be rocked for half the night. Once I lay her down, I quickly drag my fingers through my hair, trying to make it look as good as it can be after a day spent at the beach.

Well, good luck with that…

I don't look even remotely sexy when I step out of my room, yet Matteo's eyes are glued to my body, watching me as if I just walked off the runway.

Like my own personal predator, he's perched against the back of the couch, his head tilted to the side as he watches me. "Come here," he rasps out, extending his arm toward me, and I walk right up to him.

He is pure sin, confidence, and cocky arrogance personified. Something I'm sure he wielded plenty of times with all the girls before—including me. And I'm falling right into that trap once again.

Only, this time I know I won't be able to climb out. Won't be able to just say, "Thank you for the good time, I will carry this night in my memories forever." Because I want that forever with him.

I come to stand in front of him and Matteo pulls me in between his thighs. The back of his fingers trailing from my shoulder all the way down to my wrist where he wraps them around it and brings it to his mouth kissing the underside while his eyes never leave mine.

"Tell me, Zo." His breath tickles the wet skin of my wrist and I shudder.

"Tell you what?" My breathing is ragged as my legs turn into pure jelly.

"The truth."

I know what he wants to hear. I know he wants me to admit what I feel.

"I thought your manhood was threatened and you wanted me to rush?"

"What's a few more seconds when I've already waited the whole day? This is a lot more important, anyway."

Is he even real? What twenty-three-year-old considers emotional stuff more important than getting to the bedroom part? Apparently, *my* twenty-three-year-old. I search his eyes for a flicker of some hidden agenda, a lie that I somehow missed but I don't find it.

No, there is nothing but longing for me and my answer.

"Tell me you're only here because of Mellie. Tell me I'm delusional to think otherwise." I swallow hard as my nerves betray me.

"Oh, baby." Matteo's posture softens, and he gently cradles my face, bringing the tips of our noses together. "I love that little girl with all of my heart. But *you* make up my soul. You run though my blood. You consume my every thought day or night. You are a part of me. The one who gave me that beautiful baby."

My teeth sink into my lower lip as I watch this man. As I bring my fingers to his face, tracing over his perfect features.

How are you so perfect inside and out?
How did you crawl into my heart so fast?

Matteo stays silent the whole time I'm touching him. Patiently waiting for my very last walls to break off, clearing the path to my heart all the way while handing me the broom to sweep the ruble.

He's just there. Always.

And I want to be there for him. Always.

Without taking my fingers off his face, I whisper quietly, "I like you, Matteo Orion Loverson. I like you very much. Too much. In fact, I'm probably falling in love with you, and I'm too far gone for you to be afraid any longer."

Matteo doesn't let me say anything else. Not a single word as he stands up fully and pushes me against the nearest wall, crushing his soft lips to mine.

He pulls back slightly, only to look at me with reverence and whispering "Zoe" into my mouth before he seals it with a soul-crushing kiss. His touch always had a toxifying effect on me but right now, tonight, it feels downright deadly.

My lower belly clenches as his hand drifts to my neck, wrapping around it and the other one tangling in my hair. My own body shifts closer, flush against his, needing more contact, more of his body, more of anything to do with him, and Matteo doesn't hesitate to do the same.

He is crushing me into himself, almost as if he is trying to fuse us into one.

"My Zoe," he whispers again into my mouth. "The one who stole my heart, my sanity and the rights for my cock who only wants you." He pushes his very hard dick against my shorts covered, weeping pussy.

"You are all I am capable of thinking about, Beastie." He kisses me hungrily. "I'm in so deep. My heart is yours."

This time it's me who pulls back and Matteo frowns a bit. "What's wrong?"

"I wasn't the first one to have it like you have mine."

"What?" He looks confused.

"Your heart. You gave it away to someone before me." Matteo visibly relaxes and smiles.

"No, I didn't." He plants a kiss on my lips, and I press my palms to his chest to halt him.

"But the game, you said you've been in love."

"I was." He pushes past my hold and lays another kiss on me. "I am. I've been hopelessly and utterly in love with only one woman. And that's you."

Me...

I stare at him without blinking. He's been in love with me?

Mine. He is mine. And I am his. That's all I can think about before losing it completely because I am in desperate need of this man. For his heart and soul. For every inch of him.

Matteo's confession set the last of my fears on fire. And my sanity. I pull away slightly, just enough to reach into the waistband of his shorts, slipping my hand deeper until my fingers are wrapped around him.

"And this cock is mine, Matteo?"

He whimpers, sucking my lower lip into his mouth as his hips start grinding into my hand.

I pull on his hair until his head snaps up. "Yours. He is only yours."

"Then no piercings, Matteo. And no other women. I won't allow anyone else to see it but me, got it?"

"Fuck, Beastie," he breathes out. "He is your slave for life."

"And don't you forget it." I sink my teeth into his lip.

"Damn it, Zo, I was gonna go do this thing all sweet and romantic. But my girl doesn't want sweet and romantic, does she?"

"No." I shamelessly grind into his body, clutching his hair with all might in one hand as my other one stroked his cock. "No, she wants you. Real and raw."

"Oh, baby, then hold the fuck on."

In one swift move, Matteo picks me up, grabbing two handfuls of my ass as I wrap my legs around his waist and walks up toward the stairs that lead to my unfinished loft.

"Where are you taking me?" I breathe out. "There is nothing up there." But Matteo doesn't stop.

He climbs up the old, rackety steps with me in his arms—God, this man is strong—and I'm about to start protesting again but all the words get stuck somewhere in my throat.

My no-good-for-use loft looks like a scene out of a romance novel. There are string lights hung up across the ceiling, some with plain bulbs, some heart-shaped. The whole area has been cleaned of old paint buckets, ladders and moving boxes, instead featuring a made-shift bed of what looks like hundreds of blankets and pillows. And off to the side of it is a small tray with two glasses that have some cocktail in them.

I slide off his body, staring—no, gaping—at what he has done. "Matteo," I whisper in awe.

His arms wrap around me from the back, his chin resting on my shoulder. "You like it?" he asks, kissing the curve of my neck and I suck in a sharp breath. "I was going for sweet and romantic before you ruined my plans." His kiss turns into a bite, sending a jolt through me.

"Like it?" I ask breathlessly, turning my head toward him and he captures my lips in a kiss before I can say anything else. Placing my palm on his cheek, I brush it lightly and pull away. "Baby, no one has ever done anything remotely close to this for me." I can hear all of those sacred emotions slipping through my voice. "When did you do this?"

"When you were putting Mellie to sleep. Well, I started planning it the day I moved in and saw this space. I was going to do a little date night for us in here since we have a baby and leaving her alone is not an option."

"There are always babysitters."

"Like I said"—he looks at me with a pointed glare—"leaving her is not an option. But I still wanted to do something to thaw that ice around your heart."

This man...always thinking about my daughter.

"I'd say it worked." I pull his face to mine and kiss him as his hands travel down to the hem of my shirt, lifting it up.

"I'm glad to hear that. Now, let me cash in my winnings," he says before slipping my shirt off my body and pushing me back until I fall into the heap of blankets with a small yelp.

Matteo unzips my shorts, pulling them off me and all I'm left in is my bra and panties. He climbs over me, his hot breath on my skin, his magnetic eyes set firmly on mine as his hand reaches underneath me, professionally unclasping my bra one-handed.

"Show off," I mutter, and he flashes me that sexy grin of his.

"I've been practicing my whole life for you," he says, and I roll my eyes.

"Sure, you were."

Matteo shuts me up with another kiss, dragging his hand over my bare breasts, giving it just the lightest of squeezes until I moan into his mouth, needing more. I feel his hand sliding lower, all the way to my panties, tracing lazy circles over the damp, useless lace and I can't help rocking my hips into his touch.

Right on the edge. Right on the precipice of my orgasm but before I can reach that heaven, Matteo pushes up, hooking both of his index fingers into my panties and sliding them off, leaving me completely bare to his eyes and all air wooshes out of me as his eyes roam my body.

I'm not an oblivious idiot, I know there are new stretch marks across my stomach and hips, along with a few extra pounds here and there and my stomach is a far cry from flat.

"I don't look the same as the last time you saw me naked," I confess, feeling the need to pull one of these blankets over my body.

"You're right," Matteo says, lifting his eyes to mine. "You're even better now."

I lay there, gaping at the man while opening and closing my mouth, trying to find the right words to say but all that comes out is, "You're either insane, blind or a liar."

"Actually, all three," he says, shucking his shorts off to the side, leaving him only in very tight boxer briefs, and I choke on a whimper trying to climb its way out of my pussy.

Jesus Christ, this man is a work of art and he's on his hands and knees, crawling over my trembling body.

"I was a liar, telling myself I don't need to be stuck to one woman for the rest of my life." Matteo lands a kiss to the tips of my toes, crawling up higher as my heart beats out of my chest. "I am very, completely, utterly blind to all other women around me." His hot, wet lips land on my inner thigh. "And last but not least, I will forever be insane for you." A kiss on my stomach. "For your body." A kiss just underneath my breasts. "For your heart." His mouth wraps around my nipple, and I moan. "For your every breath and moan, my sunshine with claws."

"Matteo." His name is a plea on my lips.

"Shh, I'll give you everything you'll ever need." And he does just that, sucking my hard nipple into his mouth, drawing out my milk as he groans around me while his other hand has a possessive hold on my pussy, cupping it as the heel of his hand rubs against my sensitive clit.

My fingernails dig into his hair, shoulders, sheets around me and anything else I can reach while he ravishes my breasts. Sucking, licking, biting and it all drives me to the brink of my sanity, but once again before I can tip over into the climax land, Matteo stops, and I whine in protest, however it's short lived because the next second I feel his mouth on my pussy. And my eyes fly open.

"Matteo, we can't." I try to stop him, but he hooks his arms around my thighs, pressing his mouth closer to my core.

"But we can. I looked it up."

"You looked up when you can eat my pussy?"

"Yep, exactly like that."

I drop my head back to the bed. "Why am I not surprised?"

"Because you already know how crazy I am for you and if my cock can't have the pleasure of sinking into you yet, then my tongue sure as fuck will," he says and using the two of his fingers he spreads me open, baring me to himself and without breaking contact with my eyes he draws the tip of his tongue over my clit.

I jump, my whole body getting jolted from that one swipe as Matteo sends out a loud groan. "Fuck, I missed your pussy. And it just as sweet as I remember." With me still spread open he gives it another long lick, flattening his tongue over me. "Should I stop?"

I lift my head up a tad, just enough to send a death glare his way. "Don't you fucking dare," I grit through my teeth, and he sends me a smirk.

"No, I won't fucking dare to cross my fierce sunshine." But he doesn't put his mouth back on me. No, he decides to fry my brain completely because he leans back slightly, sticks out his tongue with a bead of his saliva at the tip, and I watch, mesmerized, as it rolls off his tongue and drops on my pussy. The extra wetness sliding down my slit and he brings the pad of his thumb to my clit, massaging his saliva into me, and spits some more.

Fuck...why is that so hot?

I think I'm going to combust. My tits aching for him, the milk flowing out and onto the sheets while my stomach clenches from his ministrations on my pussy. Just one more touch and I will come so hard, I can feel it simmering right there on the edge.

"Look at you covered in my spit," he says with awe, his eyes locked in on my pussy with his finger there and his mouth slightly agape from the sight. "I can't wait to cover you in my cum. How gorgeous you will look with it seeping from your every hole."

Unconsciously, I arch my back, needing more of him. Needing him to feel what he is doing to me.

"Give it to me," I tell him, and his eyes fly up to mine, those brown pools full of wild, dangerous fire.

"You want my cum, baby?" He cups my pussy hard and I press myself into his hold, panting.

"Yes, yes, yes," I chant, not recognizing my own voice.

I've never been this bold in the bedroom. Never voiced what I wanted or needed, simply taking what was given to me. And it wasn't much, usually.

But with Matteo, I feel so free. I feel sexy and empowered. Wanted.

Without warning, Matteo flips us over with me on top, wrapping his strong arm around my waist he pushes me up until my breasts are leveled with his mouth and wraps his lips around one, sucking hard and I feel a whole new wave of milk incoming, spraying through the other nipple. I bring my own hand to that breast, cupping it and direct it to his mouth.

"Don't let a single drop go to waste, baby." Matteo pops off the other nipple, his eyes trained on mine in undiluted lust as he takes my hand off and licks it, lapping at any milk that already escaped.

I feel my hips rocking, grinding into his hard cock that is right underneath my needy pussy as I watch him with parted lips.

"I won't," he promises and draws that nipple into his mouth, greedily sucking it as his hands travel down to my hips that can't stop moving and he squeezes my ass, pressing me harder into him. Helping me get off as he feeds on me. Matteo still has his briefs on, and I'm not even sure if I can be doing this, but I'm way past sane thinking.

God...his fucking cock feels so good and it's not even inside yet.

As if driven by mad lust, both of us start moving harder, faster and just as Matteo sinks his teeth into my nipple, I explode, coming all over his covered cock.

I'm still shaking and quivering on top of him when he pops off my tits.

"Now that I've had my main course..." Without a warning he flips me again, but this time upside down, until my pussy is over his mouth while mine is a breath away from his cock.

Oh my God, I am about to do a sixty-nine for the first time in my life.

Matteo slaps his hands to my ass cheeks, grabbing two handfuls and spreading me open. "I'm ready for my dessert. And to feed you yours," he adds, right before sinking his tongue into my pussy.

"Fuck, your cum tastes as sweet as those damn lychees." What? What lychees? But Matteo doesn't elaborate, oh no, he just casually drags his tongue over to my asshole, and I let out a long, guttural moan, slapping my hands to his thighs. "What are you waiting for, Zoe?" Matteo asks in between eating me out.

"W-what?"

Slap.

I yelp, feeling my right ass cheek sting and a mortifying realization washes over me. I liked it.

"I said, what are you waiting for, Zoe? You wanted my cum, baby? Then take my cock into that smart mouth and suck. Lick off all of your juices that soaked through my boxers when you rubbed your greedy little pussy over me."

"Oh my God," I groan, breathing heavy but shallow. I slide his underwear off and wrap my hand around his shaft, loving how he feels in my hand. How hard and heavy he is. How good he must taste. I lick my lips in anticipation and without wasting another second, I take him as deep as I can, moaning around his huge cock as the tiny slip of his precum coats my tongue and I suck it off him hard. Tasting me and him together.

Matteo's hips jerk up, his fingers digging into my ass hard enough to leave imprints on my skin. "Slow down, baby." His voice is strained but I have no intensions of doing so.

No, I need him to feel what I feel. Need him to lose it like I do for him. So, I move my lips around him fast, licking the underside of his cock with my tongue.

A second later, my left side feels the same sting as the right one because Matteo landed another slap, but instead of serving as a stop signal, it drives me even crazier. "What a bad little beastie I've got here. I told you to slow down," Matteo groans, slapping me again, and this time I moan at that sting and grind my pussy over him, in need of his mouth on me.

"Fuck, of course you liked that. You like getting slapped on this ass, while my cock is deep down your throat, don't you?" I bobble my head over him and he lands a series of slaps across my ass cheeks, painting them red. I feel my arousal dripping down his chin and that only spurs me on.

Popping off his cock, I bend lower, licking over his heavy balls and Matteo lets out a string of curses, so I wrap my mouth around his balls and suck on them.

"FUCK ME!" he roars. "Now, you've done it! Hold the fuck on, baby," he says, pistoning his hips and thrusting hard into my mouth as sticks his tongue into my pussy so far I see stars.

Both of us sucking, licking and biting each other like we are two hungry wild animals in desperate need of each other. I take his impossibly hard cock as deep as I can, saliva pulling around his shaft, at the same time as Matteo swipes his finger over my wetness and pushes it past my tight ring of muscle, deep into my ass and I feel the air whoosh out of me.

No one has ever touched me there and I always thought it to be dirty. Disgusting. But as Matteo works his finger in and out of my ass while his mouth ravishes my pussy I fly off, exploding over him. Drowning him in my climax.

My own orgasm making me suck his cock even harder, needing that extra contact and that does him in. I feel his hot cum, painting the back of my throat and I eagerly drink every drop of it, swallowing it and knowing with my every fiber that this is it.

Matteo is *it* for me.

I could deny it until I'm blue in my face, but the truth is, there was never any real argument there. He has been filling in that missing part of me ever since we've met, and I know I won't be able to live without him anymore like I wouldn't be able to live without my essential organs.

He's essential to me.

I slide off him but before I can get away Matteo hauls me back over him, laying me on top of his chest. "That's it, Beastie. That's fucking it. I'm never letting you go now."

"Please don't."

Matteo: So we're friends now, right?

Jacob: Of course we are man. The friendship deal was sealed the second you agreed to a dick piercing.

Alec: You are practically a part of the family now.

Matteo: Okay, good. Because I need some advice.

Jacob: Oh oh I loveeeee giving advice.

Alec: He does.

Alec: And that was a warning, Matty.

Jacob: Shut up! Where would you be without my VERY helpful help?

Jacob: That's right, nowhere.

Alec: I am pretty sure when you ask a question, you are not also supposed to answer it too.

Jacob: When have I ever done what I was supposed to?

Alec: Truer words were never spoken.

Matteo: Okay, not that I'm being needy right now, but can we circle it back to me?

Alec: He's totally being needy.

Jacob: Yep. But we love it.

Jacob: Give it to us! What can we do for you, our young and very much in love friend? We will share our unlimited wisdom with you.

Luke: Why am I in this group chat?

Matteo: You are the voice of reason.

Luke: Damn it, I was going to exit the chat but now I can't.

Alec: My man, Matty, you have the magic touch. Look at my big brother going all mushy on you.

Luke: Alec?

Alec: Yeah, big bro?

Luke: Shut up.

Alec: Shutting up in 3, 2, 1...

Luke: You are a clown.

Alec: At least I'm cute.

Luke: Keep telling yourself that.

Matteo: GUYS!!!

Jacob: I would like to go on record that I was the only one being a good friend here and actually waiting for Matteo to say what he needs to say. Shame on you, Colson brothers.

Luke: Bite me, Viking.

Jacob: You wouldn't be able to handle my jealous Joy.

Alec: Matty, I'm sorry for getting sidetracked. It's all Luke's fault though.

Jacob: Matteo? Hellooooo?

TAME THE BEAST

Alec: Why isn't he responding?

Luke: Because he finally realized you both suck.

> **Matteo:** Shh, I'm getting my advice from the girls instead.

Jacob: Ahhhhhh, no you didn't!!!

Alec: I'm questioning where your loyalties lay, Matty. This is breaking the bro code at its finest.

> **Matteo:** Desperate times, desperate measures and all that. I need to know when I can finally ask Zoe to marry me without her freaking out and you three are of no help.

Jacob: Why are you waiting to ask her? My man, with these girls you gotta put it all out there as soon as possible. Get in touch with your emotions, be vulnerable and shit. Lock it down.

> **Matteo:** Well, Joy just told me to take it slow.

Jacob: Pshhh, and that is why you DON'T ask the girls for advice. Take it slow...who says that? That's the worst advice ever!

Jacob: Please don't tell Joy I said that.

Luke: Joy asked me to tell you that she's going to kill you.

Jacob: Who included the grinch in this chat?

Jacob: Jesus Christ, she's coming for me, if I don't reply in an hour, send help.

Alec: Jacob is right. If you feel it, tell her! And if she freaks out you don't let her get away. She can freak out with you.

Luke: Was that the first smart thing I've ever heard you say, little brother?

Alec: What Luke is trying to say is that he agrees with his smarter, better looking younger brother.

Luke: Not even close to what I said. But I do agree.

31

Matteo

"I'm yours, no refunds." –Unknown

"Oof." I wince through my sleep, reaching toward my ribs that suddenly sting and feel like a stick or maybe Mellie's toy got stuck underneath them but it's not what my hand comes in contact with.

Nope, it's just the heel of my girl's foot, wedged firmly into my ribs. Still asleep, I feel a smile pull up on the corners of my mouth as I glide my hand over the soft skin of her foot.

She's adorable, pressing her feet into me. I like to think it's because she likes me so much she can't stand to be apart from me, even in sleep.

After our not-so-sweet-and-romantic night up in the loft, Zoe took my hand and silently led me to her bedroom. No words were needed. Not when she said the most important ones earlier.

Zoe is falling for me. Falling. And I'll be here to catch her and never let go.

Within seconds we were both out, exhausted from earlier but it seems my dick is well rested already because just the feel of her next to me is enough to get him gearing up.

Slowly, I wrap my hand around her ankle and just make the barest of moves to get it out from underneath my rib when a very clear and very menacing, "Motherfucker," pierces the air.

My eyes snap open as if I wasn't half asleep and I just lay there, frozen, for a good five seconds before slowly turning my head toward Zoe, who is sleeping soundly, her hair a mess, her mouth parted, and the cutest little snoring sounds come out from her.

I furrow my eyebrows. I must've dreamed it.

Shaking my head, I try to pull her foot away from me once again. I just wrap my hand around her when Zoe's fist comes out of nowhere, punching me right in my gut and I open my mouth in a silent scream at the same time as, "Die motherfucker," comes out of her mouth and that foot that was wedged into my ribs digs in farther and harder.

"What the fuck?" I whisper-shout. Now both my stomach and side are in agony and the sun isn't even up yet.

Without moving a single muscle, I tilt my head over to Zoe, who, once again, is sleeping like a baby and not a secret MMA fighter with bullying tendencies. That I guess my dick enjoys because the fucker only gets harder and harder.

You know what? All of a sudden, that ugly couch with bricks for a cushion seems like the softest cloud. I start to get up to move there and catch some z's before Mel wakes up, but Zoe apparently has other plans.

In one fluid move she twists on the bed, until her back is to me and sends her elbow into my chest, knocking the wind out of me. I gasp, letting out some more silent screams. I totally mean curses, as she hisses, "You can't catch me."

And I all but plea with the woman who not only do I *not* want to catch her, but I'd like to run the other way.

I roll over, trying to get away from this love of my life before she breaks my nose, but Zoe beats me to it, rolling over me and settling on my chest.

Don't move, Matteo. Don't even breathe.

"Help! I'm held hostage," I whisper-shout to no one at all, yet somehow my little sunshine hears me through her sleep and the next thing I know, her leg between my thighs moves, my eyes widening, but I'm too late.

Zoe knees me in my balls with all her might and I send her flying off me as I jump out of the bed, muttering silent curses, bent at my waist while barely holding tears at bay.

"What the heck, Matteo?" Zoe mutters, her voice groggy with sleep and my head snaps up to her half-opened eyes she's rubbing while frowning at me.

"What the heck?" I whisper-shout, my eyes bulging. "*What. The. Heck?*"

Zoe lifts up from the bed, her face paling as she takes me in. "Oh no, what did I do?" she whispers because somewhere in this room our baby is still asleep, having no clue her dad almost died just now.

"You just lost any chance of having kids with me."

"What?"

"Beastie, I think you forgot to mention a black belt that you must hold. You kicked my balls so hard; they'll be scared for life. Ain't no way they are making any fresh sperm for their assailant."

Zoe winces and bites her lip, but I still see the tiny smile there too.

"What are you smiling at, karate master?" I ask her, and she rolls her lips. Now, she's definitely holding in her laugh, and I groan.

Zoe gets on her knees and slowly shifts her way to me.

"Remember our very first talk at the bar? I might've mentioned I was a violent sleeper." She puckers her lips and winces cutely.

Now that I think about it, I do remember her saying something, but she wouldn't elaborate back then.

"Beastie." I level her with a look. "This is not violent. This is life threatening."

"I'm so sorry I kicked your ass in sleep, baby," she says quietly, planting a kiss on my closed lips but there is not a single trace of sympathy in her tone of voice. None. Zero.

"Could you maybe look a little more guilty for nearly killing me?" I pout.

"Sure," she whispers and gives me her best impression of puppy eyes. "That good enough for you?"

"You also called me names." I keep at it like the perpetual child I am.

"What did I call you?"

"*A motherfucker*," I mouth, and Zoe bursts out laughing, smacking her palm to her mouth to stop the sound from waking up Mel.

"Great." I swing my arms up. "And now she's laughing at me."

"I'm s-sorry. I'm sorry." She's wheezing, placing her hand on my crossed ones as she's still doubling over in her giggle fit. "But it's not considered calling you names when it's the truth."

"Oh, you're a funny one, aren't you?"

And there she goes laughing again, but the sound is music to my ears even when there is no sound. So, she can laugh at my expense any time.

Not that I'm going to tell her that. Yet. She still has some making up to do.

"Do you know where I can go to get a veteran of the war medal?"

"Um, when have you been to war?" Zoe asks as she wipes the tears from her eyes.

"With you. Just now. And I need it for the rest of my life. Might as well get some benefits for all this suffering." She can barely hold that smile of hers back.

"I have that medal for you."

"You do?"

"Mm-hmm," she says, sliding her hand down my chest, her nails slightly scraping down my flesh, and apparently my dick is not too bruised up because all of sudden he swells, getting hard for her just like that. "It includes *all* the benefits and life insurance."

"Does it now?"

"Mm-hmm. Good for you, you're already signed up," she says, looking into my eyes. "For life, Matteo."

Zoe reaches my cock and I suck in a sharp breath when her nails keep dragging over it. The little mix knows what he likes.

"He's still not sure if he forgives you," I tell her, but my hands are already on her body. Skimming over her perfect curves.

"Oh? Then maybe I should do a better job at apologizing," she says, pushing me back onto the bed.

"He says *definitely*." I lick my lips, watching her little fingers hook into my underwear, dragging it down and doing just that.

Zoe apologizes until there is no more cum left in my body.

And when she's done with that, she feeds me her sweet milk until my cock is up and ready for round two of apologies.

But what she doesn't know yet is that all it takes for me to forgive her is her simple existence. Zoe could cut off my hand and legs, burn my bar to the ground and call me every colorful name she knows, and I'd still be looking at her as if she's the most precious thing in the world.

Because I don't love her with my eyes. I love her with my soul.

Violent tendencies and all.

32

Never Have I Ever

Matteo: Never have I ever got kicked in my sleep.
Zoe: Stop complaining, you baby. I remember you being quite happy with the sincere apologies from the manager.
Matteo: Why do you think I keep coming back every night to your establishment?

33

Zoe

"Never love anyone who treats you like you're ordinary."
—Oscar Wilde

This past week I have felt like I've been living in some sort of a dream. The kind where you're dreading to hear that inevitable sound of your alarm clock waking you up. Only so far, not only have I not been woken up, but I fall in deeper and deeper.

And even all those reasons I had made up in my mind about why we can't be no longer seems important.

So what if he's younger? He shows more maturity than all of my prior—older—boyfriends put together. Not to mention his love and care for Mellie has erased all my doubts about that long time ago.

So what if he's never been in a relationship before me? He knows what he wants, unlike all the men I've dated before. And somehow that is me and my baby girl.

So what if every woman around town throws him flirtatious looks? He only has eyes for me. And he proves it every day. And night.

That man is insatiable, and I am just as crazy for him. I'm pretty sure he has a calendar where he marks days until my OBGYN appointment at six weeks where I should be cleared for sexual activities. Not that it has stopped him before.

He's been bringing me orgasms like candies on Halloween night. In large quantities that put you into a sugar—orgasm—coma. Not that I mind. Not one little bit.

But it's not just about sex. No, it's about homemade breakfasts every morning and walks on the beach. It's about him taking Mellie at night so I can sleep. It's about foot rubs and cracking jokes to make me laugh. Chasing me through the house like a rabid dog, waiting to sink his teeth into my body. And I mean that literally.

It's about sitting at the bar, watching him work his magic and be in his element. It's about him calling to sing to Mellie before bed if he had to stay out to close the bar that night. And endless love messages to me at all hours of the day. Sometimes I wake up with him next to me in bed yet there is a new message on my phone that he sent in the middle of the night. Last one read:

I miss you in my sleep, so I had to wake up in the middle of the night to get my fill of you, Beastie. Sorry if my touches woke you up.

And while I wake up to sweet words, Matteo wakes up with a new bruise and yet he still comes to our bed every night.

That's what it's all about.

It's also about living at the moment. Something I never knew before he introduced chaos into my life.

So what if I fell in love with him? It was inevitable.

The roar of Matteo's bike snaps me from my daydreaming on the porch where Mellie is hanging out on her baby swing.

No, we're not sitting out here waiting for his return from wherever he went two hours ago. Absolutely not.

Oh, fine, we totally are, but it's all Mel's fault. She wanted her favorite human back so I was just keeping her company.

Fine, I wanted my man back too.

Matteo parks next to my car, those thick thighs of his hugging his iron horse right before he slides off, taking off his helmet and his long hair spills free.

That man is every woman's walking wet dream. I swear.

"Mmm." A soft whimper comes from me at the sight. I really, *really* love his hair. I love it when he treads his fingers through it, pulling it into a messy low bun like he's doing right now. I love it *even more* when *my* fingers slip through that messy bun, pulling and tugging on it until it's all loose again.

Something about that action just does it for me and I shift on the couch, trying to relief some of the pressure in my core. But it's a lost cause because he spots us right away, flashing us his signature Matteo-grin and hurries our way, carrying a large bag in his hands.

As soon as he reaches us, he bends over, kissing Mellie's forehead and the girl melts sight there and then for him, smiling at Matteo like he's hung the moon and all the stars for her alone. "You missed me, my little watermelon?" he coos at her in a ridiculous baby voice that somehow my pussy responds to as well.

I need help.

"I missed you more!" he proclaims dramatically, and she gives him those in-love eyes. I love how much time and attention he gives her. Matteo makes Mellie his priority and that right there is what makes my heartbeat faster for this man.

After another minute of one-way conversation with my daughter, Matteo shifts his attention to me, and doubles over, clutching at his chest.

Right away panic sets into my bones and I rush to him, my hands on his face pulling him up to see what happened. "Matteo! Matteo baby, what's wrong? What hurts? What do you need?"

"An oxygen tank," he rasps out, trying to gulp fresh air and I'm becoming downright frantic.

"Why? Are you having an allergic reaction?"

"No, you just take my breath away," he wheezes out, and I cluck my tongue.

You've got to be fucking kidding me! I'm about to scream a bloody murder when, in a flash, he pulls up, hauling me against his body and his lips sink into mine.

"Every." Bite. "Damn." Bite. "Time." He doesn't let me speak because he keeps kissing me, soothing the stings he just made, and I moan despite myself as his hand travels lower, down the column of my neck where he can feel the wild beating of my pulse.

"Hey, beautiful mama," he says oh-so-casually.

"I'm going to kill you," I tell him, but the bastard only grins and winds his arms around my waist, picking me up and kissing me breathless.

"I missed you so much."

"You saw me two hours ago," I tell him, feeling a soft smile on my face but inside my stomach is performing somersaults.

"Mm-hmm." He kisses me again. "Two hours too long without you, Beastie. But I'm serious about that O2 tank."

Yeah, I had no chance of not falling in love with Matteo. Zero.

"Tell me you didn't forget me while I was gone? Because I spent each second away from you thinking about all the ways I will kiss your sweet body later."

See? This is what I'm talking about.

"Feeling clingy, are we?" I tease him, and he huffs.

"You bet I am." He nips at my lip. "Now tell me quickly before I check myself." Yet he doesn't wait for me to say anything and slips his hand into my leggings, moving toward my pussy and I yelp, slapping his hand away.

"Matteo," I hiss. "We're outside!"

"And?"

"Anyone can see us."

"Good for them." He smirks, pushing back toward my pussy. "Maybe they will learn a thing or two."

"Matteo!" I bulge my eyes at him, squeaking.

"What?" He mimics my tone. "I need to check if your sweet little pussy didn't forget me," he whispers into my ear as his finger swipes over my wetness, and I shiver in his arms.

"Matteo, you're unforgettable," I whisper back, my eyes now hooded, voice husky and that ache in my core a full-blown inferno.

"Yeah?" He smiles teasingly and rubs my clit as I shudder. "Good," he adds in a serious tone and his finger disappears from my pants, setting me back down on my wobbly feet.

Did he just…

"Matteo!" I whisper-hiss.

"Yeah, Beastie?" He smiles at me with the look of an angel boy, full of innocence and good intentions and not like he just brought me to an almost orgasm and left me hanging.

"I hate you," I grumble, giving him the evil eye.

"Sure, you do." He winks and proceeds to take out stuff from the huge bag he brought. The bastard is seriously not going to finish what he started. "Come look what I got for our girl."

When I don't make a move toward him, he smiles, rolling his lips and strolls toward me, gripping me by the waistline of my leggings and pulling me in as I stumble into his—per usual—nearly naked chest. "Come look what I got for our girl and then I'll take care of your girl," he purrs into my ear, and I dart for the bag with a little too much enthusiasm.

Matteo chuckles in the back and comes up behind me as I look through the million and one outfit he bought for Mellie.

"Oh my God, Matteo! Why are there so many clothes in here?"

He shrugs. "They were all so cute, I couldn't decide on just a few. So I got everything I liked."

Apparently, he liked the whole store. I look over the clothes quickly, noting that all of them are either in her size now or the next few up. He knows what size she wears. He knows how fast she grows and got her stuff that will be good for her in a month.

My heat melts once again for him and I am about to mount the guy right here and now—doctor approval be damned—when I catch sight of what it *says* on the onesies.

"Matteo, why does that onesie say, *Margarita me, baby*?" I frown, looking to the other one. "Oh, this one's even better," I say, heavy on that sarcasm. "*Daddy and I have one thing in common, we both love mommy's milk*. Have you lost your mind? She's not wearing that!"

"What? It's the truth!"

"Matteo!"

"Fine, fine. We can keep that one for in-house wearing," he pouts. "Look at this one." Matteo picks up what seems like a cute, simple pink piece. That is until he flips it over and I see the back.

Don't touch my watermelons is written on the butt area, and Matteo is wiggling his eyebrows at me. I run my tongue over my teeth and look at him. "You need help, Matteo. I swear."

"Admit it, you love these." He grins wide. "I got a whole bunch more!" Diving back into the bag, he pulls out what I have no doubt are more ridiculous pieces. "Jacob showed me this cool website—"

"I'm gonna stop you right there." I put up my hand. "The second the name *Jacob* left your mouth; no further explanation is needed."

"He's the best."

"Aha."

Damn it, Hope was right. We should have never allowed them all to bond like this.

"Can you keep your duck on a leash?" I say as soon as my friend picks up her phone, her beautiful face filling the screen.

"Who? Francesca? She doesn't wonder off," Joy says, thinking I'm talking about actual live duck they have as a pet.

Mm-hmm. You heard that right.

"No, the one who impregnated you." Joy sighs.

"What'd he do this time?" she asks, already knowing it's something ridiculous. In true Jacob fashion.

"He has bad influence on Matteo." I twist my face as Joy snorts.

"Let me guess. You now own a live crocodile because they get mistreated in the Zoos?"

"What?" I shriek. "I hope not!"

"Shame. I thought I could be off the hook if you guys already got one. Then it can't be that bad."

"You have a weird scale of bad, Joy."

"Have you met my husband? Weird is his middle name. I'm only surviving over here."

"Well, thanks to Jacob, Mellie now has a hundred onesies with inappropriate sayings on them."

"And?" Joy lifts her eyebrow at me, clearly unimpressed. "Zoe, I've been living in shirts that say *My wife's boobs are better than yours*,

Duck duck baby mama and so on, as you are well aware. So, if I can take it, so can Mellie."

I chuckle because I do know all about the clothes Joy and Jacob wear to work every day. And let's not forget the hugging socks.

"But since we are talking about bad influence..." Joy trails off, giving me *the eye*.

"What?"

"Not sure who is messing up who here. Just last night, your Matteo showed up with Mellie strapped to his front in that baby carrier, while he was holding a huge sign that said, *Private property, keep your hands off these cheeks*."

I can't help the snicker that comes out and roll my lips to prevent laughing full-on.

Matteo has been doing ridiculous things like that. He has about ten different signs he walks around with, while holding Mel. Ranging from innocent *My baby girl is better than yours* to *Don't even think about dating my daughter*. My personal favorite is the one he made for the Fantastic Four and his mom in particular: *If you steal my baby, I'll bite you. Grandmas included*.

"So, guess who made a fucking sign this morning?" Joy continues.

"Um, I'll take a wild guess."

"Bingo." She snaps her fingers at me. "As if the ridiculous shirts, hugging socks and a rubber duck collection that screams 'I am a secret maniac' wasn't enough for me." Joy sighs but there is also that dreamy look on her face.

My grumpy friend wouldn't change it for the world.

"Speaking of your puppy, where is he? Why isn't he interrupting our conversation yet?" she asks, looking around the little screen for him.

This has been another new norm around here now. The first time Joy and I FaceTimed, Matteo came crashing into the room where I was sitting and planted himself right next to me. When I asked what he was doing there, he simply said he can't be apart from me for that long.

I was on the phone for six minutes and forty-four seconds, insert eye roll...and ever since then, he's taken to doing that every time.

And always chipping in with his own comments here and there. Sometimes, he would just lay down next to me or with his head on my belly, asking with those puppy eyes for me to run my fingers though his hair.

Other times he would be next to me with Mellie, playing with her. But the point was to be with me. That's all that mattered and maybe I should've found that weird or clingy, but the truth is, I don't. I love how much he needs me, wants me.

Because I need him just as much.

But today he's not home. A few of the employees at Love and Peace got sick and Willa couldn't handle the bar on her own, so Matteo was forced to go to work.

God, it took me a solid hour of convincing him that we will not forget him and that I'll call every half hour on the dot so he could see Mellie and if she's awake, talk to her.

"He had to go to work," I tell Joy.

"And he actually went?" she asks, her eyebrows touching the hairline.

See, everyone is very well-versed in Matteo's obsession with Mellie and me by now.

"Yeah. He did."

"You don't sound too enthusiastic about that." Joy looks at me with suspicion.

"I am."

She laughs. "Yeah, that came out very convincing with that scowl on your face and growling tone."

I fall face forward to the table, sending out a frustrated groan. "He flipping ruined me! I feel like a part of me is missing when he's gone. I'm being irrational and clingy and jealous." My head snaps up. "Do you have any idea how many girls throw themselves at him over there?"

"How many?" Is that a freaking smile on her face?

I narrow my eyes at my soon-to-be ex friend. "Too many. They just all sit there, batting their eyes at him while their nice, not-mom tits spill out of their barely-there tops." And then I lose all control over myself when my voice turns high-pitch and fake, mimicking them. "*Ohhh, Matteo, I missed you, my pussy missed you too. Ohhh, Matteo, can you work me like that shaker? Ohhh, Matteo, I am so desperate for you, can I open my legs up for you right on this bar top?*"

I could keep going on and on if I didn't get distracted by Joy's booming laugh.

The bitch is literally twisted at her seat, laughing so hard she has to wipe the tears from her eyes.

"Well, I'm so glad someone finds my misery hilarious," I grumble, and it takes her a good minute to calm down.

"Jesus, Zoe, you are so far gone for that stray of yours."

"Tell me something I don't know."

"Go get ready," she tells me, still smiling.

"For what?"

"For going out."

"Why would we go out?"

"To stake your claim." Joy lifts one corner of her lips in a devious smile. "So, you better dress to kill."

"Who? Matteo?"

"Oh no, there isn't a cell in that boy's body that doesn't know he's yours."

"Then who am I going to kill?"

"The delusional competition."

I twist my lips, considering her plan and I like it. A lot. "I guess we're going out." We hang up and I look over to my daughter.

"Hey, baby girl," I coo to Mellie, picking her up from her bouncer and kissing that sweet, chubby cheek. "Do you want to go see Matteo?" Mellie gives me a big smile. "Of course, you do. See, all the girls are crazy for him."

I run through a quick shower while Mel hangs out in her bouncer next to me. It's getting pretty chilly in the evenings now so I pull on my favorite jeans that cling to my ass like second skin with a black long sleave that does the same, and dips nice and low in the cleavage area. I fix my blonde waves and apply red stain on my lips. Last but not least, I put on my red heels.

Joy did say dress to kill, right?

Satisfied with my look, I go through the huge pile of clothes Matteo got Mel, looking for the one I need. Because I'm not the only one who is staking her claim tonight.

An hour later, I walk up to LPs with Mellie in her stroller, where Joy and Jacob are standing, waiting for us. And bickering. But knowing these two that's most likely foreplay for them.

"I told you, you didn't have to come," Joy tells him and Jacob just huffs in response, folding his arms.

"Yeah, right. Like I'd ever let you go to *this* bar without me. Hey, Zoe." He redirects his attention to us, smiling wide at Mel. "Plus, someone needs to watch my angel of a niece when Matteo sees his girl in that getup and drags her into the hallway." He winks at me, and I feel my cheeks warm up.

God, I do hope so.

"Now, that's what I was talking about." Joy gives me an appraising gaze and smiles a little wickedly. "Yeah, Jackie, we are definitely going to be on babysitting duty tonight."

"Stop it, you two." I roll my eyes at them.

"I will gladly watch my goddaughter tonight." Alec's voice startles me from behind, and when I turn, I see him and Hope coming toward us.

"What are you guys doing here?" I ask them.

"Jacob told us about the plan. So, we came ready."

Both Joy and I narrow our eyes at the said blabbermouth. "What?" he squeaks. "There is power in numbers."

"You got that right, Viking," Fanny says as she too, comes around the corner, cracking her neck, followed by Nina and Jenny.

"Please tell me you didn't call the whole Love Hive here?" Joy grits out, shooting daggers at her husband.

"Of course not. Just a few trusted people."

"So, what's the plan? Do we get to trash talk?" Nina asks, looking way too excited about the prospect. "Willa already said she will be using her special cocktails on the bimbos tonight."

"I call dibs on body force," Fanny pipes out. "I've been meaning to try out this new kick, but Nerds refuses to let me practice on him," she pouts.

I still question how in the world my sensible father ended up with Fanny of all people.

"Oooo, I love trash talking! And I need to practice on someone other than Nina," Jenny exclaims, clapping her hands together. "Can I do it? Please, please, please?"

"Moooom," Joy and Hope groan at the same time, and then Joy turns to her husband. "Just a few trusted people, yeah? There is nothing trustworthy about them. Those three are preschoolers on crack and now you're on a whole new babysitting duty." She smacks his chest.

"Grace just texted that they can't make it. Something about Luke finishing another one of her romance novels." Hope reads out a text message, and Joy mutters, "Thank God for small miracles." While glaring at Jacob. "Who else did you text?"

"No one, I swear." He lifts his hands up in surrender.

"Please kindly text her that we will not be showing up with ice packs and Advil again," Joy responds. "She needs to get on our schedule after Zoe."

"Oh my God, Joy!" I groan. "I will not be needing that tonight."

"I happen to disagree." Nina winks at me. "You look stunning."

"Can I just say how happy I am that our plan has once again worked out," Jenny adds with tears in her eyes, and I want to question what plan they're talking about, but Mellie starts fussing, pulling my attention from the crazy women.

I swear my daughter can feel when Matteo is close by and is getting impatient with waiting for so long.

"Okay, just so we're clear..." I turn to face the circus. "There is no plan. There will be no trash talking and definitely no body force," I point to them.

"Oh, but she's fine with Willa's cocktails," Fanny grumbles under her nose.

"Duh, that's her mother-in-law." Jenny elbows her.

"Hey, I am practically her stepmother! Where is my special treatment? Just one kick?" She looks to me half pleading, half with an unveiled threat.

"Jacob." I look heavenward. "Thank your lucky stars that you're married to my best friend and happen to be my daughter's uncle, otherwise I'd unleash Fanny on you right about now for doing this."

"I just wanted to help!"

"Baby, next time before you *want to do anything*, please talk to me first, mmkay?" Joy says. "I'm the brains in this family."

"And what am I for?"

"Your hair and dick."

"That's all you need from me?" He sounds affronted and it's quite the picture to see this huge Viking guy with tattoos pouting.

"Fine. Your sparkling personality as well."

"Okay, change of plans." I clap my hands together. "You're all going home."

"Kidding me? I'm not missing the cat fights." Fanny pushes her way past me then hollers, "Plus, I promised your dad I'd play your bodyguard."

"God, this just keeps getting better and better."

"Well, if she gets to go, so do we," Nina says, grabbing Jenny's arm and they disappear into the bar.

"Okay, no offence, but for once, we are not in the eye of the shitstorm and I am not missing this show," Alec adds and slips past me with Hope in tow who is throwing me an apologetic look.

"That will be twenty-five cents!" I yell after him, inhaling and exhaling deeply. "I hate you." I shake my head at Jacob but before he opens his mouth to respond, Alec's head pops back out.

"Hey, um, about that claim." He clears his throat when we all stare at him. "You better get in here." Alec disappears back inside.

What does that mean? What is going on inside there? I find my pulse beating wildly in my veins, that heart of mine galloping in my chest as my worst-case scenarios play out like a movie and before I can think twice, I storm inside.

"Now, aren't you happy I brought backup, Wildflower?" I hear Jacob say but the sound is distant in my foggy brain.

Funny, before this guy crashed into my life, making himself a nice and cozy spot in there, I would never entertain a single murderous thought about another woman. I would simply walk away, nursing my yet again broken heart.

However, as soon as I step inside LPs and my eyes lock in on that skank's hand on my man's arm, there are no murderous thoughts in my head. Oh, no, they are now plans set in motion.

34

Matteo

"Never lie, steal, cheat or drink. But if you must lie, lie in the arms of the one you love. If you must steal, steal away from bad company. If you must cheat, cheat death. And if you must drink, drink in the moments that take your breath away." – Alex Hitchens, Hitch

"Linsey, for the last fucking time, I. Am. Not. Interested." Jesus, I don't know how many times I have repeated that sentence tonight.

It was like all hell broke loose when I came to work by myself tonight, and I think the whole of Loverly Cave female population has descended into LPs.

Everywhere I look, there are eyes on me, eyeing me like a piece of delicious candy, as if they've been on a diet for years. Was it always this annoying? How I didn't notice this before is beyond me.

No, I haven't because I lived for this shit. I thought this was as good as it got. The holy grail.

Well, I was an idiot. A bloody fool.

But worst of them all is Linsey. The same good-ole Linsey.

And I have tried to be nice. I have tried to be polite just wanting to get this shift over with so I could go home to my girls as soon as possible, but she is making it fucking impossible and I am one second from blowing up.

I noticed Fanny, Nina and Jenny walking in here earlier, going straight to my mom and you'd think they help me with *this*, seeing as they have been so invested in my relationship with Zoe…but noooo. The four of them are just standing there, watching my misery with amused faces.

Well, apart from Fanny. That scary grandma just looks like a child in timeout but still no help from her.

You all just watch me the next time you want some time with my daughter. That payback will be sweet as honey.

"Matty baby, come on, let's go have some fun. You must be so tired from being stuck in that house with crazy Zoe and her wailing baby. I get it, you were so sweet to help her when she has no oneeeee, but it's enough already."

My spine shoots up at the nasal sounds coming from her fucking mouth. Head snapping to her face, I try to count to ten and then ten more because she did not just say that.

She did *not* just call *my* Zoe crazy and *my* daughter a wailing baby.

I lower my face to hers, so the words don't have to travel too far to hit that pea-sized brain. "You will never say that again." My tone is low and threatening. "You will get your ass out of this chair this second and if I ever see you here again, I will call the town meeting and have you banished from Loverly Cave forever."

I am fuming with anger, my nostrils flaring as I try to rein myself in when the bitch lets out a high-pitched laugh. "Oh, Matty baby, you just forgot about the fun side of life. But I'm here to remind you." She bites her lip and the next thing I know her claws are fisted in my shirt, dragging me toward her mouth.

That's it. I'll have to hit a girl. Fuck!

It all happens too fast. One second, I'm raising my hands to push Linsey away and the next, a wave of sunshine hits me and a hand wraps around the fool's wrist, making her yelp and let go of my shirt.

"Excuse me." I look up to find a very angry—and so fucking hot—Zoe standing in front of us, Linsey's wrist going white with how hard she is grabbing it, and razor-sharp panic sets in the bottom of my stomach.

She's always beautiful. The most beautiful woman in any room, but tonight? Fuck, tonight she's pulled out all the cards I didn't even know existed. Those red lips, mesmerizing me and calling out for me to wipe that lipstick off with my mouth and my cock. Her shirt, clinging so fucking tight to her perfect curves, and I want to gouge everyone's eyes out for catching a single glimpse of what belongs to me. I won't even let my eyes to dart lower to her ass in those jeans because I know how good she looks in them.

God, please don't let her think I had anything to do with this. We just got to a good place. She just started to let me in, and I might lose it all because of the lifestyle I led before.

I look into Zoe's eyes, trying to come up with ideas how I'll be groveling my way back into her good graces, but she's still fixated on Linsey, who at least has enough brain cells to look terrified. I've never seen Zoe this furious.

Fuck.

"Beastie, there is nothing going on here. I don't want her, I swear. I tried to push her away. I was telling her to leave me alone the whole evening." The words just rush out of me in mad urgency. Needing her to know I would never do anything to threaten our family.

Because that's what we are.

"Look, I even buttoned my shirt today, see?" I point to my shirt that usually would always be half-way open, showcasing my skin and tattoos and the chain my father passed on to me. But now it seems wrong to have anyone else see me like that. It feels dirty to have their eyes on me.

"Good boy." Zoe throws me a quick glance, and I won't even mention what that praise just did to me. All I have to say is I'm about to stick out my tongue, rub against her leg and bark to be scratched behind my ears. And then she turns her lethal eyes back to Linsey and my jaw hits the ground.

"It seems you're lost. Can I help you find something on my boyfriend's body?" she says slowly, never wavering her gaze from the handsy-Nancy. "Because everything here belongs to me, and I don't appreciate you touching any of it. In fact, I might be pretty mad about it."

Fuck, again, but did Zoe just claim me as her boyfriend in front of the whole bar? Did that just happen?

Because my dick really likes that idea. He *really* likes it.

Linsey looks like she wants to say something but at that same moment the sweetest sound comes from my little girl whom I didn't even notice with all this shitshow. Mellie is chilling in her stroller right by Zoe and then my eyes snatch to the onesie she is wearing. It's the custom one I got her the other day.

One I didn't think Zoe would willingly put on her.

One that says, *My name is Mellie Loverson and don't you forget it*.

Is this Christmas or something? Did I miss the memo?

But I don't have time to think about the screwed-up calendar. I am jumping over the bar, pulling Zoe out of her stare down with Linsey and kissing her.

God, do I kiss her.

My fingers are lost in her blonde waves, my other hand holding on tight to her waist just above her sweet ass that I can't help but slide my hands into the back pockets of her jeans, and squeeze as well. Our lips are fused together and the whole world disappears as she kisses me back, murmuring "Mine" into my mouth, and I respond, "Yours."

"Matty baby?" Lindsey annoying voice sounds somewhere in the background. "But what about us?"

"Jesus, girl, have some self-respect, no?" Joy sighs. "But if that's not an option, we have Fanny over here who can help you find your way out."

"Now can I kick her?" Fanny's all-too-eager voice breaks our spell, and Zoe looks me over, rolling her eyes.

"No."

"Buzzkill," Fanny mutters, and Zoe turns her gaze back to mine.

"Shh, Fanny," comes from my mom. "Settle down. It's not every day my son makes me the happiest mother on Earth.

"Shesh, thanks mom," I throw out.

"Shh, Matty. Focus on your girls, not me," she hisses back, making me smile. But I do just that.

"Boyfriend, huh?" I smile, bending over to give Mel a kiss.

"Have any objections?" Zoe lifts her eyebrow.

"Do I look like an idiot?" I grin, moving back to Zoe and lean in for another kiss, my hands now cupping that beautiful face of hers. "You put that onesie on Mellie," I say in a hushed tone, afraid that maybe she didn't mean it the way my heart wants it too.

"I did," Zoe answers without giving me more.

"And you just claimed me."

"I did."

"What does that mean?"

"And here I thought you said you weren't an idiot." She smirks, and my heart flies out of my chest.

"I have many questions." And I do. I have many many questions that I have buried deep inside since the day I met her, but I was always too scared to ask them. Or maybe scared to hear the answers myself.

"And I will give you the chance to ask them." I open my mouth to start the questioning when she adds, "Later. After everyone here knows that Matteo Loverson is off the market."

Later tonight, a new sign was added to my collection. It says, "*This stud belongs to Zoe Holsted—future Loverson—keep away. Owner bites.*"

35
Never Have I Ever

Matteo: Never have I ever slept with my friend's ex.
Matteo: Why does your face look like that?
Zoe: I'm trying to decide if sleeping with him while *he's dating my friend counts.*
Matteo chokes on his own saliva.
Matteo: What???
Zoe: So, about those answers you wanted...

36

Matteo

"Love has nothing to do with what you are expecting to get—only with what you are expecting to give—which is everything." —Katharine Hepburn

Joy and Jacob wanted to take Mellie for a sleepover, but I refused. There is no way I was spending a whole night without our little watermelon, especially while she's wearing that shirt. So instead, Jacob offered to take over bartending and I took that offer faster than he could finish his sentence.

As much as I love my bar and love my job, tonight I wanted to be anywhere but there.

Zoe spent the walk home in silence, even when I asked if she was okay wearing those sexy-as-fuck heels, she simply nodded and kept walking, surrounded by the eerie silence of the night with only crushing waves from the ocean and the fall winds brushing against us.

Mel fell asleep on the way, so when we finally got home, I put her in her little cot in our room, kissing the top of her head and went in search of my fierce woman.

Zoe was sitting on the front porch, her feet free from those heels and tucked beneath her butt. I leaned against the pillar, watching her while a whole movie seemed to be playing out in her head.

"Talk to me or I'll start cracking jokes," I say, breaking the stifling silence.

"How about a joke then?"

"How did an Italian man die?"

"Um, how?"

"He pasta-way. Get it? Like pasta and way. Pastaway."

Zoe looks at me like she is trying to decide if I am the dumb or dumber from that movie but then throws her head back, laughing. "God, Matteo, that was awful."

"I know." I twist my lips. "Now put me out of my misery. Or the next one is going to be about a fish."

"I don't know, a fish one doesn't sound so bad."

"Zoe!"

"I lost it, okay? I lost it tonight when I saw her touch you. I never knew I even had it in me! I saw you two together and the next thing I knew I was planning her funeral! I don't do that, Matteo! I never have!" Zoe is whisper-yelling.

"So, what *do you do*?"

"Nothing. I walk away."

"But you didn't today."

"No. Because you made me lose it."

"How?" I keep probing, keep digging into her half-truths.

"I don't know how!" Zoe throws her hands up. "You are just...you." She waves those hands at me as if that is supposed to explain it all. "You turned my world upside down. Made me fall in love with you. I couldn't even spend a few hours away from you, for Pete's sake. I'm that pathetic!"

I shut her up, grabbing her and hauling her into my arms. My eyes searching hers.

"When did you know?"

"What?"

"When did you know that you're no longer falling, but fell all the way into the deep end? When did you know?" I ask, searching her eyes.

Zoe swallows hard, tears coating her eyes, "From day-fucking-one." She hits my chest with her small fists. "I fell in love with my one-night stand like an idiot. Dumb fool. Who does that?"

"Jesus Christ, shut up, woman," I interrupt her, my breathing rugged and cup her face in my palms and as she still throws her punches at me, I kiss her.

Not hard and rough like we always are. No, I kiss Zoe with every ounce of love I have for her. And those punches grow lighter and lighter until her hands fall limp over my chest, and she kisses me back.

I pull away from her slightly, whispering, "Me. I did that too. So, I guess we are two dumb peas-in-a-pod."

"Matteo, it's too soon! This whole time I was convincing myself that I was *slowly* falling for you, but there's nothing slow about this train wreck! I need time, I need to make a plan, not go on killing sprees anytime someone looks at you!"

I grin mischievously. "I happen to love speed. And your blood thirst."

"Stop that." She smacks my chest again and I decide to lay it all for her right here and now.

"Why wait, Sunshine? Why waste time walking around each other, playing at these dating games when we both know where this will end?"

"And where will it end, Matteo?"

"With you being my wife and that little girl our first daughter because I need more. Because it will never be enough with you. Because I love you more than life itself."

Zoe sucks in a sharp, shuddering breath. "This was not a part of my plan."

I lean my forehead against hers.

"Plans fail, Zoe. But my love for you never will." Zoe is searching my eyes for the truth, not knowing that I'd never lie to her. "Go ahead, ask me how I know for certain."

"H-how do you know that for certain?"

"Because when I told you I was in love with you, I wasn't joking. I wasn't talking about a mere crush or infatuation. I wasn't talking about the kind of love that loves with only eyes or words. No. Love like that never interested me. And the real deal? The one my parents shared? That one was out of the question because it had the ability to crush your soul completely. But when I saw you give birth to our daughter I realized there was nothing to crush because it already belonged to you." I jab my finger into my chest. "I love you with every promise I make to you. I love you with every smile or tear. I live for you. And I will never tire of reminding you of that."

"But you never wanted this." The tears are rolling down her cheeks without holding back.

"No, I never wanted it with *anyone else*." I wipe the tears with my thumbs. "But the second you walked into that bar; I knew you were not anyone else. You are one of a kind. My kind."

"God, you say all the right things."

I chuckle. "Nope, I say all the true things."

I keep going up until my hand glides over her full tits that have been taunting me since she showed up to LPs. "How about another truth?"

I squeeze her breast through her shirt and bra and Zoe whimpers, biting her lower lip and whispering a breathy, "Mm-hmm."

"I'm starving." I grip her shirt and rip it off her tits in one rough shove until her gorgeous tits spill free, little drops of milk already seeping out of her razer-sharp nipples and my mouth waters.

Zoe yelps, her hands flying to the back of my neck where she laces her fingers through my hair, tugging on the loose bun as she thrusts her tits into my face.

I bring the pad of my thumb to her nipple, grazing it slowly, spreading her milk over it. "All that possessiveness of yours made me so fucking hungry. Will you feed me? Will you feed my mouth and my cock?"

"Y-yes," she breathes out. "Yes, please. It's yours. All yours."

I push Zoe against the pillar and lower my mouth to her tits, sucking it one at a time and milking every drop from them. My cock grows impossibly harder with every drop I take.

She's delicious. So fucking delicious, I can't stop. Can't make my mouth leave her nipples. Can't get enough of her. All I can do is suck and nibble and draw my tongue over them, driving Zoe as delirious as I am.

"All mine," I growl. "I love you Zoe."

"Show me how much." She pulls on my hair, setting it free from the tie.

I slide my arms under her thighs, lifting her from the ground and she wraps them around my waist right away while our lips fuse together. I can't make it far. I need her too much, so I drop to the couch she has out here.

More. I need more. I always need more of her.

Her tits are out, and I make quick work of her jeans, along with her panties and then chuck mine away. "Look at you," I groan. "Look at how fucking beautiful you are." I wrap my hand around my leaking cock, giving it a few hard strokes.

Zoe's eyes are transfixed on my motions, her mouth parted and eyes hooded.

Fuck...could she be any hotter?

Yeah, she could. With my seed spilled over that delicious body.

"Grab your tits for me, Beastie, and hold them nice and snug for me," I instruct her.

"Why?"

"So I can fuck them and then paint them with my cum."

Zoe swallows hard. "Matteo, we are outside." She seems to only now grasp it.

"Yeah, so?"

"Someone can see us."

"We have been over this before, Beastie." I lick my lips in anticipation. "Let them. And there is no way I can make it inside right now. I need to fuck you so badly; I will die right here and now."

Zoe bites her lip, contemplating something in her head for a fraction of a second before she does as I asked—like the good girl she is—and grabs her tits for me.

My head falls back at the sight, but only for a moment, before I'm crawling over her, my legs on either side of her body as I climb all the way to her face, gliding my cock over her lips.

"Stick your tongue out, Beastie, and get him nice and wet for your tits." And without breaking eye contact she does just that. Her hot and soft tongue licking me up like her favorite lollipop and all too soon I must pull away before I come.

Zoe lets out a cute little protest, making me chuckle but in a breath I'm already sliding in between her mouthwatering tits.

"Fuuuuuck," I groan. "Fuck, that feels so fucking good." The feel of her soft flesh gliding against my hard cock feels like silk and pure ecstasy.

Zoe whimpers, her thighs clenching below, and I lean back, moving my free hand to her needy pussy.

"Jesus Christ, does getting your tits fucked make you so wet?" She's soaked. More so than ever and shudders at my mere touch to her clit.

This woman is going to be the death of me. My heaven and hell wrapped in one.

Zoe squeezes her tits harder, making it even more pleasurable to me as I stroke her clit faster and faster until she's all but shaking and panting underneath me.

"M-Matteo," she rasps out.

"Yeah, baby, that's right, fall apart around my fingers. Come!" And she does. She comes so beautifully, arching underneath me as I have her trapped between my legs and moaning shamelessly for all to hear.

Fuck. I'm done for it.

I pull out from between her and with just a few jerks, thick ropes of my cum decorate her tits, coating her perky nipples while her milk oozes out of them and my mouth waters.

Zoe watches me carefully and then bites her lip. "Well, now be a good boy and clean up your mess," she tells me, stealing my nonexistent breath. And without a second thought, while my dick is still twitching with the remains of my climax, I slide down and wrap my mouth around that nipple. Tasting my cum mixed with her milk.

Fuck. Fuck, fuck, fuck. I need more...

"Matteo!" Zoe cries out as I suck and lick every drop of *us* and my spent cock hardens once again.

"You were made for me, Zoe Holsted."

"I was. And you were made for me."

"I was."

And we spend the rest of the night showing how much we love each other with our mouths, but a few days from now? After that damned appointment?

I will fuck her so hard, so long, she will forget her name. And I will forget mine.

37

Zoe

"Actions speak louder than DNA." -Unknown

I feel my arm hit the mattress beside me with a thump. Empty. That's not right, usually there's a warm cushion for my blows.

My head snaps up, my eyes still bleary from sleep but see the empty side where Matteo always sleeps well enough.

I drag my hand over it. Cold. So, he hasn't been sleeping here for some time. Rolling over to my back, I scrub my face with my hands. Well, I guess he finally had enough of my bed-time karate, not that I blame him, but so much for, *"I can take it, Beastie. Do your worst, Beastie, I'm still sleeping here. I'm not leaving you."*

Wimp.

Where did he sleep then? The couch?

Frowning, I get up and make my way into the living room, but the space is empty, and his broad frame is not hanging off the sides of that brick disguised as sitting material.

I really should get a new one.

I take the stairs to the loft, thinking he probably went up here, to our make-shift sex bed as Matteo calls it. But he's not there either.

This is so weird. Where could he have gone so early in the morning? Both of us fell asleep as soon as our heads hit the pillows, tired from the day before as we spent it setting up Mellie's room.

We decided—well, I decided, and Matteo pouted about it the whole time—that it was time for her to start sleeping in her own room and spent the whole day in there. First, Matteo insisted he needs to draw watermelons on the walls. Go figure. Then we built her crib, moved the changing table and her stuff from my room in there and ended up going to Fifi's Goods to get a new dresser for her because apparently, according to that overbearing papa bear, the old one didn't fit with the vibe.

God forbid anything be out of place for his little Mellie.

Just thinking about how much Matteo loves and cares for my girl makes me all giddy on the inside. And throbbing.

Where is that man when I need him?

Sighing, I make my way back down and decide to take a peek into Mel's room. I was worried my little girl wouldn't take it well, sleeping on her own and expected to be up with her for half the night, but Mellie slept like a champ. I didn't hear one noise coming from across the hall.

Carefully, I prop the door open only to swing it open all the way when I find the missing man, instead of my daughter in the tiny crib.

What in the world is he doing in there? And where is my daughter then? I stride toward it, fully intending to shake Matteo awake but I can only blink when I see this hulking man wearing only a set of neon orange boxers and that silver chain of his, with long hair sticking through the crib bars. His beard a mess as he seemed to try and keep it from poking her soft skin while his strong, tattooed arm is curled up protectively around a tiny bundle that is my daughter, who is wearing that ridiculous onesie about them both loving my milk that I certainly didn't put on her last night.

The sight takes my breath away.

He barely fits in there and looks absolutely ridiculous, yet this is the most adorable thing I've ever seen. And now we know that crib was worth the money I spent on it, because somehow it didn't break under his weight.

Careful not to wake them, I back out of the room with a smile and run for my phone. I need to frame this for eternity.

Once I'm done, I smile softly and just stay there, watching them together. I don't know what I did to deserve this man, for him to want me and my daughter. To deem us enough, but I know I'm not letting go of this gift.

Even if he escaped from me in the middle of the night.

Gently, I run my fingers through his hair and Matteo stirs away, letting out a small moan from my touch.

"Shhh," I murmur softly, and Matteo pries his eyes open, giving me a smile of his own to match mine.

Full of love and adoration.

"Beastie," he whispers, his voice coarse from sleep and tries to move, but only winces when he does so. "Ouch."

"Yeah, running away from your bed and sleeping in a tiny crib will do that to you," I whisper, keeping my voice low and quiet.

"I didn't run away," he whispers back.

"Mm-hmm, sure. If you couldn't take my superior fighter skills anymore, you should've just said so."

"Bestie, I can take you on any day or night. Especially night." He smirks, shooting me a sultry look that looks particularly devastating in the morning light. "But my little watermelon needed me, so I climbed in with her."

"Needed you?"

"Mm-hmm. She woke up around midnight, crying so sadly. Feeling all betrayed that we moved her in here all by herself." Sure, she did—can you feel how far my eyes have rolled? "So, I stayed to keep her company. And when I came to give her the bottle, so not to wake you, she clung to me with her little fingers and wouldn't let go"

"Strange, I didn't hear a single noise come from the room."

"Strange indeed." He puckers his lips. "Now, help me get out of here."

After at least five minutes of careful maneuvering not to wake Mel, Matteo is out, although I really should have left him to deal with this himself. That little clingy liar.

Matteo was still stretching and wincing when he goes to take a shower and I make my way to the kitchen.

"We should go back to Fifi's today," he says, walking out of the bathroom in a towel alone and I can't even pretend my eyes are not devouring all that flesh.

"Why?" I lift my cup to take a sip of my coffee.

"We need to get a bigger bed for Mellie."

"No, we don't." There goes that eye roll again.

"I won't be able to walk if I keep sleeping in there."

I click my tongue, "Here's a thought...don't sleep in there."

"I don't like that thought," he grumbles. "Maybe we can just move her back into our room? You know, for her comfort?"

This man...

"Just admit she wasn't crying at all, and you were a needy little papa bear, sneaking into her crib," I say with a teasing smile.

"I have no idea what you are talking about." And there he goes, puckering his lips again.

A second later Mellie lets out a wail loud enough to wake Hope and Alec in the neighboring cottage. *Yeah, I didn't hear her at night, right...*

Before I can even blink, Matteo is already sprinting her way, that towel getting loose and falling off and I am greeted with his fine—very fine—ass.

"I'll get her!" he shouts, running into our room and a second later hopping out of there while still pulling his underwear on. "Papa is coming, my little watermelon. You realized I was gone and woke up, yeah?"

At this point, I'm laughing so hard I have to grip the counter from falling over.

I'm heading to them, with every intention to give Matteo a hard time, when a knock on my front door startles me.

It's six-thirty-seven AM, who could be coming here that early? Frowning, I stride over and open the door without first checking the peep hole. Because in Loverly Cave you just let everyone in.

But I should have checked. *Damn it*, I should have checked it because when that door swings open, I find the last person I expected—and that is saying something as you'd think it would be Mellie's sperm donor...but no.

My mother. Sorry, I mean Kelly because she stopped being my mom a long while ago. Kelly Holsted is on my doorstep, wearing her favorite—and quite frankly, permanent—pinched face expression.

"Well? Are you going to let me in, or have you lost your manners completely since you moved out?" It's only at hearing her voice I realize I've been just standing here, planted to the ground with only my eyes blinking as if they could somehow erase the picture in front of me.

I clear my throat and lower my eyes to the floor as I step aside and softly murmur, "Yes, of course. Sorry."

Thirty seconds. Thirty seconds is all it takes for her to derail me. And ruin the most perfect morning.

With a little huff of annoyance, she strolls inside, and I shut the door behind us, still completely lost at what in the world she's doing here or how she found me at all. But before I can think of asking her that, she says, "Imagine my surprise when I show up to your apartment and the new tenant says he has no clue who I am looking for." She clicks her tongue. "How dare you move without telling me?"

The only thing I can do is blink. Kelly hasn't bothered with me since dad packed us up and left. Sure, there was that one lunch together. As in the one after I became a doctor, and she deemed me important enough to meet me.

But that lasted all of one time, because she learned that I dedicated my life to being Dr. Joy Levine's assistant and that, apparently, was a disgrace. So, I've never heard from her again. I don't even know how she knew where I lived in Chicago.

Probably went up to a random apartment. Yep. That sounds plausible.

"Did you have to choose this middle of nowhere town? It stinks here." She wrinkles her nose.

"Kelly, what are you doing here?" I finally brave myself to ask.

"I came to see my granddaughter, of course."

I suck in a sharp breath. "How do you know about her?"

"I went looking for you and a very handsome doctor at your university told me you were pregnant when you quit and that I might find you in Loverly Cave town."

Another sharp breath.

Justin. There is no one else who could have given her that information. He's the only one who knew about my pregnancy and must've connected the dots between me and Joy to figure out that I was here.

"That's just so you, to go get knocked up by some random guy and then crawl into this hole to hideout. You couldn't even get married first," she huffs some more.

I'm still lost for words when Matteo emerges from the hallway with Mel in his arms. The guy is still only wearing his underwear and his hair is loose because Mellie seems to enjoy pulling on it nowadays, so he leaves it down for her.

"Dear God, who is that?" Kelly asks with horror and not the usual admiration every red-blooded female gives my boyfriend. Well, I have suspected her to be a vampire a long time ago.

"Dear God, who are you?" Matteo matches her tone before I can introduce them.

"Well, I never..." Kelly huffs. "I am Zoe's mother."

"Oh, thank God," he exhales dramatically. "For a second there I was afraid I was being rude to someone important."

I don't think I've ever seen her at a loss for words. I guess there's a first for everything.

Don't smile. Don't smile. Don't fucking smile, Zoe. But it's a lost battle. Especially when Matteo comes over and wraps his free hand around my waist, looking Kelly over with one eyebrow raised.

Matteo knows about my history with the woman. Over the time we've been together I have told him everything and it's safe to say he hated her even more than I did.

"I wasn't aware you were coming. Don't you know it's rude to show up at someone's house at this hour without at least a call?" Matteo keeps going, stealing the words from my mouth.

Kelly seems to finally pull herself together and narrows her eyes to him. "Who do you think you are? Speaking to me this way! And I came to see my granddaughter."

"Ha." He makes a sardonic sound then nods to me. "She really thinks I will let her come near my daughter. Funny woman."

Kelly turns her gaze at me. "Of course, you had a baby with this…this riffraff. That child is probably no good either. I don't know why I even bothered coming to save her from your incapable parenting." She looks us over. "Look at you! You didn't even bother to get your weight under control after pregnancy. I should have never let you leave with Kevin. He always did enable your laziness."

Matteo grows stiff beside me, his skin hot to touch and then an almost feral growl comes from him, but he doesn't say anything.

Years of not seeing each other and that's what she has to say.

I didn't realize I had given up hope for a normal relationship with her until this moment. Until I feel Matteo pulling me closer, as if landing me his strength and shields from her venom, allowing me to deal with her. To say my peace. I didn't realize I no longer needed her approval or love until the words she spewed made no difference to me.

"You know, Kelly, it is none of your damn business who I had this baby with. It's none of your business what my weight is. And it's definitely none of your business how we parent our daughter."

Never. I have never talked back to her. I have never stood up for myself and the stricken look on her face is living proof of that.

"I think that door is calling your name." Matteo points to the exit. "What a waste of a trip."

Indeed.

Kelly opens her mouth to undoubtedly say something ugly but the voices from outside interrupt her.

"I'm just going to talk to her, Nerds. Relax your buttocks." The sounds travel from outside and a moment later Fanny kicks the door open, striding inside in all her neon green track suit glory.

"I know how you talk to people, Fanny. That waitress at the diner is still terrified to look at me anytime we are there," my dad says to her, but his eyes are set on Kelly. "And just what the hell are you doing here?"

Why am I not even surprised that they somehow already knew she was here?

"Last I checked, she's my daughter," Kelly snarls back.

"Last I checked, you are no one to her," Matteo adds.

"And last I checked, you didn't care about her as long as you got your money," my dad says, and we all turn to look at him.

"What money?" I ask, my eyes narrowed and dad's shoulders sag as if the weight he's been carrying all this time finally took its toll on him. But weight for what?

"Start talking, Nerds."

"That was the only way she let me take you away back then." His eyes lift to mine. "She was your blood-related parent, and no court would have given me parental rights over her. So, I struck a deal, promising to send monthly payments if she signed the custody papers."

I don't think I heard that right. That can't be right, right? I knew she never thought I was good enough to be her daughter, but this? And my dad, this kind-hearted person whom I didn't share a shred of blood with did whatever it took to get me out.

"How long?" is all I can ask.

"Until you turned eighteen." He looks away.

"Dad—"

"I would do it again and again," he cuts me off. "There is nothing I wouldn't do for my daughter. I'm just sorry I didn't take her threats seriously this time."

"What are you talking about?"

"She called last week, somehow figuring out you had a baby and saw it as another opportunity for easy cash, right Kelly?" But she doesn't respond, only pursing her lips together and dad sighs heavily. "I should have just paid before she made this unwelcome visit."

My eyes ping pong between them and the look on my mother's face says it all. She did, in fact, come here just for that and my mouth goes dry.

"Damn it, Nerds. You are so hot right now." Fanny sighs, looking at him like kid at an ice cream. Good for you, Dad, but I might be sick right now. Especially after this news.

"You all are so fucking weird!" Kelly shouts, and Matteo cuts a cold look her way.

"That will be twenty-five cents," he says and walks up to her, his palm up.

"What?" She blinks at him.

"Twenty-five cents. We don't swear in this house."

"I'm not paying anything—"

"Twenty. Five. Cents," Matteo repeats with a low, threatening voice, and I nearly trip over my own feet when my mother scrambles for her purse, finding the damn quarter and places it in his waiting palm.

"Happy?"

"Not just yet," he says. "Tell us why you are here."

"I already told you. I'm here to see—"

"Cut the crap," Dad cuts her off. "Not one soul will believe you came to see your granddaughter. Just admit I'm right and you ran out of money."

Kelly purses her lips and that right there is answer enough for all of us.

"Now I'm happy," Matteo says, then adds, "She's all yours, Fanny."

"Finally." Fanny claps her hands. "Let's go, intruder, it's time to pay up." She grabs onto Kelly's arms and start dragging the sputtering woman out the door.

My dad sighs. "I better go because the officer told me last week there is no more bail available for Fanny." And follows them with a small wave

Okay then...

I'm still stunned at the morning events when Matteo's warm hand slides across my waist. "You okay?"

"I think so." I frown to myself. "Honestly, I'm not even sure what happened here. Did she really come here to scheme some more money out of Dad after he's paid her so much already? Why show up at our house then? It's just...a lot."

"Will it make you feel better if I admit it was me who needed to be with Mel at night?"

"Marginally, but only because that wasn't a secret to me."

"Then name your price. What can I do to put a smile on that beautiful face?" Matteo grazes my cheek with the back of his hand.

Little does he know, there is nothing he *needs* to do. Just being here with me, loving and caring for us is so much more than enough. I'm not upset over Kelly's visit or the fact that dad had to pay my way out.

A couple of months ago, I would be a wreck. A mess of tears on the floor at the revelation, but Matteo have thought me so much about myself. It's a lot to process but it's not painful.

However, I'll never turn down his offer...

My lips curl up. "Well...I can think of a few things after Mel goes down for her nap..."

A few hours after the morning mess, Matteo had to go to the bar. His new menu is about to be launched and I couldn't be more proud of him. He's worked so hard to perfect each drink. He also created a new appetizers menu to go with each drink for the best experience and I've definitely enjoyed helping him with that one.

Matteo is so much more than I originally thought of him. So much more than just a guy looking for a good time. And he's all mine.

Well, mine and...Mellie's. Maybe even more hers since this is the fifth voice message he's sent her—because God forbid she forgets him—since he left an hour ago. This one telling her a story about a purple lemon.

Yep, this man creates stories on the go for his daughter.

> **Me:** Why is it always that only Mellie gets these pictures and voice memos, hmm? Aren't you worried I will forget you?

> **Matteo:** Aww, are you feeling left out, Beastie? Don't worry, I've got a little something for you too. I wanted to give it to you later, but my needy girl obviously needs it now *wink face* There is a box in the closet in the loft. Open it.

No, I'm not embarrassed how fast I ran up there, but that doesn't mean my cheeks didn't grow as pink as they could when I did find that box.

Texting won't do. I need to call the bastard.

"Matteo! What the hell is this?"

"This is you putting twenty-five cents in the swear jar."

"Stop it. You know what I mean."

"Oh, so you mean the little toy I left for you?"

"Little?" I squeak. "There is nothing *little* about this," I whisper-shout, as if someone will overhear me and know that my boyfriend left a massive dildo as a gift for me!

"Why, thank you, Beastie." He sounds too pleased with himself. "You are really good for my ego. And my cock."

"What does your cock have to do with anything here? There is only this rubber one."

"Hmm, you see no resemblance? They promised it would be the perfect match."

My jaw drops and I keep whispering. "Matteo, you mean to tell me this is a replica of your cock?" Well, that last part is all squeaky and definitely not whispered.

"Sure is."

"Jesus Christ." I slap my hand to my face. "He got me his dick in a rubber form."

"Well, I didn't want you to forget me," he says smugly. "But I can send you voice messages instead."

"Shut up," I grumble but there is a smile on my face.

This man...I swear.

38

Zoe

"You can learn many things from children. How much patience you have, for instance." – Franklin P. Jones

"Good morning, Zoe and..." The doctor trails off, casting a glance at the sexy man by my side.

My boyfriend. For some reason, that word doesn't really fit because Matteo is so much more than that but maybe I just need to get used to it.

"Matteo." He extends his hand toward her with his dazzling smile that doesn't fool me because the man has been nervously pacing this two-by-two room since we walked in, yet I watch my OB's cheeks pink up.

I almost snort to myself. *Typical*.

"Nice to meet you, Matteo." She clears her throat, tucking her hair behind her ear.

Oh, for fuck's sake. I must make some sort of sound because her eyes snap to mine and the blush deepens as she quickly looks away from him, logging into her computer while Matteo silently shakes with laughter.

Yeah, my jealousy is *so* funny. So *so* hilarious. That's okay, we'll see who will be laughing later.

"So, how have you been?" Dr. Lane asks me. "Any discomfort? Lingering pain?"

"No, nothing like that. It's been a pretty easy recovery."

"Okay, I will take a look, to make sure you have healed properly."

"Please do." Matteo's desperate impatience breaks through and the doctor is back to blushing.

"Give me just one moment to gather what I need." She turns around, taking out gloves and lifts my gown, probing around my pelvis. "How is your baby doing?"

"Oh, she's great. She's with her grandma right now," Matteo answers before I can, but at this point I am used to this. Used to him boasting about Mellie and her little accomplishments. And every time I hear it, my heart melts a little bit more for this man who never once treated her as anything less than his flesh and blood. "She's the smartest little girl on the planet. She smiles already and sticks to her schedule. And you should hear her burps—" I slap his stomach, sending a glare his way.

"Not the burps again, Matteo."

"What? They are impressive!"

The doctor chuckles. "I believe you. So, are you the father?" she asks not-so-shyly, and I give her *the eye* not-so-shyly.

Pretty sure she can't ask that, but her desperation for my man must be stronger than the ethical code.

Matteo, though, beams at her question and proudly says, "I sure am." And puffs his chest out a bit more.

"Oh, how wonderful," Dr. Lane responds but her face does this amazing impersonation of a sour lemon. "Okay, now for the vaginal checkup." She sits down and probes around. After a few seconds she gets up, chucking her gloves and says, "Everything looks great. Healed without any problems."

"That's it?" Matteo asks with a pitch to his voice. "That was the checkup?"

"Um, yes?" The doctor looks flustered.

"Beastie, I could have done that, and we would have avoided my near-death experience last night," he says in all seriousness, his hands on his waist and I roll my eyes at his dramatics.

"Oh no," Dr. Lane interrupts. "Are you okay, Matteo?"

"Oh, I'm fine now." He grins, remembering just how much resuscitation his dick received last night but then his face grows somber. "But it was very much touch and go there for a second."

Sure, it was…when his cum was covering every inch of me and he still wanted more.

"Jesus Christ. shut up, Matteo." I slap my hand to my face.

"Do you need a checkup? I can take a look at whatever was bothering you. It would be no problem for me at all," she offers so helpfully, and I click my tongue.

"I'm sure it wouldn't be," I say with zero amusement.

"Oh no, my girl here took care of all my problems, but thanks, Doc," my suddenly clueless boyfriend replies, sending me a wink. "So does that mean she is cleared for sex?"

Poor Dr. Lane chokes on her own drool she was slobbering all over Matteo's feet, coughing profusely, she sends him a nod.

"Great." He claps his hands together and in a flash, he scoops me up in his arms. Half undressed, in a hospital gown and all. "Time to go, love."

"Matteo! I need to get dressed," I hiss at him.

"Ain't nobody got time for that, Beastie." Matteo throws me over his shoulder, grabs my stuff and using his hand to cover my exposed butt, hurries out the door. "Bye, Doc."

I might be throwing threats at him and describing in great detail how I'll be killing him later, but I'm also laughing the hardest I've ever laughed.

Thank God this crazy man is mine.

Love Hive:

Mellie'sdad: Attention! If you want to stay alive, stay off the roads for the next ten minutes.

Willoflove: What? Why? Matty is everything alright?

Willoflove: Why isn't he replying? Did something happen?

Toughtolove: Wasn't Zoe's six-week appointment today?

Peaceforall: It was! I just saw them leave the hospital! It was so romantic!

Ninasunshine: What was romantic? Why do I always miss the good stuff?

Peaceforall: Matteo threw her over his shoulder and ran out the door like his bottom was on fire.

Toughtolove: Ha! I'm sure it was. But more like the front area.

Willoflove: Did you have to plant that image in my mind?

CookieJ: Matteo, the traffic was rerouted.

Mellie'sdad: Mrs. J, I love you.

Joydon'tpissmeofflevine: I'm so gonna tell on you.

39

Zoe

"Whatever our souls are made of, his and mine are the same." – Emily Brontë

This might be the fastest car ride of my life because Matteo is flying through the suddenly empty streets when usually they are full of locals and tourists alike. His hands are gripping the steering wheel as if his life depends on it.

This kind of Matteo is my undoing. His raw desire for me is my kryptonite and my pussy throbs more and more with each second. When I go to slip my hand underneath the gown to touch myself Matteo barks out, "Don't even think about it."

"But I need it, baby," I whine, and he shoots me a look.

"Good. Keep your pussy nice and wet for me, cover your thighs with your juices that I will be licking off you the second we get home. But don't you dare touch her."

Usually, I would love to taunt him, but I know better than to tease my hungry beast. So, I bite down on my lip and pray he drives even faster.

The second he parks the car, my door is flung open, my body in his arms again as he carries me inside, no longer caring who I'm flashing with my near nudity around here. But now we're back in our loft, in our space.

Just him and I.

Our lips seal together as our hands tear at each other's clothes.

"I don't know where to start," Matteo mumbles into my mouth since he won't stop kissing me long enough to pull away and say the words.

His hands are everywhere, roaming over my body clad in that hideous hospital gown.

"Start anywhere, everywhere. Just...please," I beg him, and Matteo lowers me to the make-shift bed we have and trails kisses mixed with bites over my body.

His soft lips everywhere, just like I asked while my fingers treaded through his hair, over his broad shoulders, digging into his strong flesh.

Matteo brings his face up in between my tits, his hands holding me on the sides with his fingers brushing underneath my breasts and inhales the scent of my skin. Leaving a trail of goosebumps over it.

"God, you are so perfect. You are my air, Zoe." His breaths fans over my razor-sharp nipples, and my body arches in an invitation. "I love you," he whispers into my skin, and I clutch his hair stronger. "My mouth loves you. My cock loves you."

"I-I love you too. All of you. All of it." I'm panting.

"Tell me how much you want me to fuck you. How much you've thought about it."

"So very, very much," I whine. "Please." The ache between my legs is almost unbearable.

Matteo pulls himself up, sitting on his knees and brings the leaking tip of his huge cock to my pussy. "You are the first and only woman to have me bare. I won't stand to have anything in between us. Ever." He rubs himself over my entrance, making me delirious with every circle he makes, spreading his precum over my lips.

"Matteo!" I groan, clawing at his arms to come closer, deeper and he pushes inside. Just a little bit. Just the tip, yet both of us are breathing raggedly and Matteo's eyes are shut closed while he's murmuring curses about how tight I am and how I will be the end of him.

With just the tip in, I'm ready to come, my skin covered in a thin layer of sweat. I am ready to burst out of my skin for this man.

"You feel too good. I can't."

"Matteo, you better move. You better give me all of you."

"Marry me, Zoe Holstead," he says, sending me in a fit of giggles.

"I'll do anything, just fuck me, please."

Matteo snaps his eyes to mine. "I'm serious."

And he is, based on the look on his face, on the tremble in his voice. *Oh God*. He is.

"W-what?" All humor is gone from my face.

"Marry me, Beastie. Be my wife. Be mine."

"You cannot be seriously asking me that right now." I bulge my eyes at him. "The tip of your dick is inside me!" I point down, in case he forgot what we were doing over here.

"I think it's perfect timing." He smirks, pushing in just a bit further and my breath catches. I catch onto his forearms, but he stops again. "So?"

I narrow my eyes at the hot-as-sin man on top of me, "Are you using your cock as a bait to get me to say yes?"

"Sure am." He gives me another inch and my breath shudders. "Marry me, Zoe."

I shake my head, silent laughter escaping me as I bring my hands over my head. He's ridiculous, insane, crazy...but he's mine.

No, the boyfriend title never did feel right.

"And all these years, Hope thought the romance was dead. She just hadn't met my fiancé."

This time it's Matteo who sucks in a sharp breath right before a beaming smile stretches across his lips. "Fiancé? Is that a yes, Beastie?" He hovers over me.

"I guess it is. It's not like I can get rid of you anyway, so might as well have the perks of the marriage, like splitting the bills and chores. Oh, and taxes!" I can barely keep my smile at bay at his narrowed eyes. It's too easy to tease him.

"That's why you want to marry me? For tax deductions?"

"Mm-hmm." I nod, rolling my lips.

"I'll show you tax deductions." His nostrils flare a second before he dips his head and bites on my nipple. Hard.

"Matteo!" I scream but he keeps biting. "No, no! Not just for taxes. I love you, baby! Stop biting me!"

"Yeah? Then why?"

Without a hint of fear or hesitation, I place my hand over his bearded cheek and look right into those dark, warm eyes. "Because I want to wake up next to you every morning. I want to raise our daughter together and deal with her teenager tantrums together. God knows I won't be able to handle that on my own."

We share the same smile, knowing how right I am about that.

"I want to feel your warmth around me. Because I never knew love like ours. Never felt as accepted for who I was—flaws and all. Because I want to be with you every step of the way as you build your career and serve as your muse until the end of time. Want to see your handsome face full of wrinkles and your hair gray. I want to be here for all of it because I can't imagine doing it with anyone else. Can't imagine being anybody else's wife. Just yours, Matteo."

"So, not just for taxes?"

I laugh loud and hard, tears of joy slipping past my lashes. "No. Not just for taxes." I brush my fingers over his cheek again and find them wet, covered with his own tears.

"Baby..." I whisper my hand to his lips, kissing every finger as his eyes bore into mine.

"I didn't believe him," he seems to say to himself.

"Who?"

"Don't move," Matteo tells, slipping out of me and running down the stairs buck naked before I can comprehend what just happened.

"Matteo! Where did you go? Are you crazy? Get back here right this second! We are in the middle of sex, for Pete's sake!" I cry out, lifting up into a sitting position and glaring at the stairs, willing him just to show his face right now.

A few seconds later, Matteo appears, carrying something in his hand but I'm on a war path right now, so I don't even care what his excuse is.

"I am definitely reconsidering this whole marriage thing," I say as he approaches the bed, climbing on top of it again.

"Oh yeah?"

"Yeah. Totally. Who does this? How hard is it just to give me your cock like a good boy?" Matteo is right beside me, lifting my hand back to his mouth and then wraps his hand over mine but once again, my every ounce of blood is in my neglected vagina so I can't comprehend what he's doing. "And here I thought you were the one eager to do this part. Running out of the hospital like that. Who does this?" I cry out again, but he is just sitting there, holding my hand in his and smiling like a child in Target's toy section.

"What are you smiling at?" I say in a low, snarky voice.

Matteo bites his lip, those eyes glistening as he lowers them to my left hand and my rant stops just like that. Along with my heart.

There is a ring on my finger. A beautiful, intricate ring with a gold band covered in delicate swirls and engravings and a large, oval moonstone on top of it.

"I didn't believe there would ever be a day in my life I wanted to see this ring on anyone's finger." He lifts his eyes up to mine. "Until I saw you in the delivery room with tiny Mellie on your chest."

"Matteo," I breathe out, lifting it to see it better. "It's so beautiful."

"It was my mother's. Dad made it himself and told me that one day, when I meet the one who knocks the wind out of my chest, setting the world right, this ring will belong to her. I wasn't going to wait another minute to slip it on your finger," he says and cups my face he kisses me.

First, gently with tenderness, but that's never been us, and it turns raw and feral in seconds with Matteo climbing over me, his thick, hard cock resting in between my legs as my hips buck, looking for that connection to him. Now more than ever.

Matteo's hands reach out to mine, entwining our fingers together as his lips lower, devouring my neck. Sucking and biting on it and his cock pushes inside me.

Hard. Fast. All the way to the hilt.

Sheathing himself into my tight pussy that screams in a tiny protest mixed with pleasure. It's been so long since I've felt him. Since the best night of my life. The one I was keeping in my mind as a fevered dream without a single thought of it becoming my future.

"God, you are so fucking tight," he groans, holding himself inside me.

This. This connection between us. It's stronger than words. It's more than carnal needs.

It's *everything*.

"Move, Matteo. Please move. Fuck me. Love me. Own me." With a low growl, he does just that, pulling out nearly all the way and slamming back in while all I can do is moan and call out his name.

"What? That was enough romanticism for you? Does my fiancée want to be fucked like my own whore?"

"Yes, yes, yes," I chant and that sets him off.

Matteo flips us, with me on top of him and impales me on his cock again. "Oh, God," I whisper, feeling him up in my soul.

"I wanted to fuck you from the back. Wanted to see that ass as I stretch your pussy with my cock, but I thought this would be more romantic. Seeing as it's our engagement fuck."

"Aren't you the gentleman."

"Hold that thought." His hands squeeze firmly around my hips, to the point of pain that walks right on the edge of delirious pleasure. Using the hold on me he lifts me up and down, setting ruthless pace and fucking me hard from the bottom and all I can do is claw my fingers into his chest, holding tight.

"So, so good." My head falls back as I feel the first tendrils of my climax taking root.

Matteo's hands vanish from my hips as he lifts himself up, meeting me and wraps his mouth around my nipple, sucking the milk out greedily as he keeps fucking me and I feel his cock grow thicker, pushing against my walls. And then there's a sharp slap across my ass. The kind I will bear a mark from for days and I know I'm done for it.

There is no stopping it. I feel that wave crashing over me as it sets me, my whole world blurring when I come harder than I ever had and with a long grunt Matteo follows right after me.

Sweaty, panting and hot we fall to the bed, lying next to each other without talking for a few minutes.

"I just fucked my fiancée for the first time. This feels monumental," he says through harsh, labored breathing, and all I can do is just laugh.

"You are ridiculous." I shake my head at him, still catching my breath and then crawl atop his body, his cum still leaking out of me. Now coating his still hard cock. "But I wouldn't change a thing about you."

"Yeah?" His mouth curves up as his hand draws across my back.

"Yeah. I'm kind of crazy about your ridiculousness." I bend down, pressing a kiss to his waiting mouth.

"Okay, I know I should be saying something sweet right now, but my brain is glitching." He gives me this cute, wild stare and then whisper-yells. "There is both of our cum all over my cock and it's so fucking hot it's driving me insane. So store that thought, we will get back to it."

With another giggle I'm on my back, living out my every fantasy and dream. Again and again because my man is insatiable.

And so am I.

This is it. This is my forever.

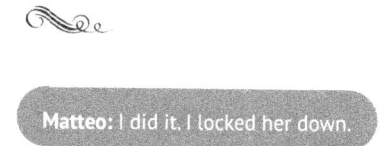

Matteo: I did it. I locked her down.

Alec: I will need you to elaborate because Hope and I just finished ACOMAF, and words like "I locked her down" are a bit of a trigger these days.

Luke: What the fuck is ACOMAF?

Alec: A Court of Mist and Fury. It's the one after ACOTAR.

Luke: What the fuck is ACOTAR?

Alec: Have you been living in a cave? How do you not know this? It's only the most essential book in the world of books.

Luke: You better pray my wife didn't hear that. Because you just became her mortal enemy.

Alec: Go ahead, ask Gracie what she thinks about ACOTAR. We are buddy-reading.

After two minutes...

Luke: Who the fuck is Rhys and why is my wife obsessed with him? And stop buddy anything with my wife.

Alec: Not gonna lie, I have a major man-crush on the guy.

Jacob: Is everyone just going to ignore Matty's statement?

Matteo: All good. I already texted my other friends. The real ones, you know.

Alec: Did he just question our friendship?

Jacob: He totally did.

Luke: I still do...a year later.

Alec: Matty, meet us at my tattoo shop in ten minutes! We will show you real friendship.

Matteo: Why does that sound like a threat?

Luke adds Joy and Hope to the chat.

Hope: Alec Colson, I swear to God, if you come home with another name tattooed on your ass, you are sleeping on the porch.

Joy: Well, that answers the question why my husband just ran out the door like his ass was on fire.

Hope: Why aren't you pissed about this?

Joy: Honey, the man kept me up whole night, arguing why we should get a crocodile. An ass tattoo is a blessing at this point.

Joy: You hear that Jacob? Ass tattoo equals no crocodiles as pets.

Jacob: Damn it. See what sacrifices I make for you Matty! That's real friendship.

Joy: Yet you still don't know that Matteo proposed last night.

Hope: Solid burn.

Luke: Forget those idiots and come over! We will celebrate!

Joy: Don't you dare! I need that ass tattoo!

Hope: If Matteo shows up with Alec's name tattooed on his butt, don't be surprised.

Zoe: What?

Joy: And Jacob's.

Zoe: I am so lost right now.

Hope: Oh no, you are just in Loverly Cave.

40

Epilogue

Two Years Later...

Zoe

"Never have I ever thought I'd find my husband in the bed with another woman!" I lean against the doorframe to our room.

"What can I say, I couldn't say no to all these ladies." Matteo grins, waggling his eyebrows.

"Papa, dis too." Mellie shakes yet another naked Barbie and throws it on the bed, and my crazy husband hoards them all.

There must be close to twenty dolls between them.

"What is this?" I point to the harem. "I thought you were putting her to sleep."

"I was. I am. But Mellie felt bad about all of her dollies sleeping alone and we brought them in."

"Uh-huh." I nod slowly. "I wonder who she learned that line from."

Matteo puffs out his chest. "From the best of the best, right, Watermelon?" He kisses her forehead, stroking her blonde curls away from her little face and tucks her under our covers. "And who's the best of the best?"

"Papa!" she exclaims loudly, throwing her little arms up.

"That's my girl." He kisses her again.

"And is there a reason your girl and the rest of the naked harem are not in her room?"

"Mellie loves our bed better, don't you?" he asks her, and she nods her head eagerly while smiling sheepishly because she knows I don't allow this normally. But whenever Matteo doesn't have to be at the bar, he lets her do whatever she pleases.

"Now, give Mommy the puppy eyes I taught you, so she doesn't kick us out," he whispers to her, and Mellie—like the good student of his she is—sits up, sticking her lower lip out in the cutest pout ever as she claps her little hands together in a pleading manner.

"Peesee, Mommy."

I shake my head with a silent laughter and stroll toward them.

"Well, how can I say no to this cutie?" I kiss her nose and she giggles. "I'll just make your daddy pay for it later," I say, throwing him a look.

He just licks his lips and mouths, "*Punish me, Beastie.*"

This man...I swear.

There is never a dull moment with him. Not from the day I met him or any single day since.

The last two years have been the happiest I've ever had. After Matteo proposed, we got married the following week because who needs plans, right? But I didn't mind, in fact, I was just in as much rush as he was to start our lives as a family.

Shortly after—as in the next day—he asked if he could adopt Mellie legally and there wasn't even a moment of hesitation before I said yes. She's been his daughter since the day she was born and these two have been as thick as thieves since then as well. Or more like she has him wrapped around her little finger.

Hence Matteo indulging her every wish, including sleeping with twenty naked barbies.

"What are you gonna do when this one is here?" I point to my swollen belly with our baby boy growing inside. "You better start getting used to Mellie sleeping in her own room." And I do say that for his sake because he's the unreasonable one when it comes to our daughter.

Mellie loves her room and has no issues sleeping in there.

"Nah." Matteo shakes his head. "We'll just get a bigger bed to fit us all."

I sigh. "Of course we will."

Matteo grins, pulling me in until I fall into his chest with a yelp and Mellie squeaks with excitement, thinking it's play time instead of bedtime. She climbs out from underneath the covers and starts jumping around too.

"Me too, Papa. Me too!" She throws herself at him and I duck out of the way just in time before he catches her, cradling and tickling her.

"Me too, me too," he mimics her playfully as she squirms, laughing.

This. This right here is what I've always wanted for my daughter. Since the day I read those test results, I wanted her to have it all.

But she has something so much better. *We* have something so much better.

A family. A real, loving, fun, understanding family with a man who not only loves us but gives us his all every day, every hour and minute.

I feel my eyes stinging with emotion and Matteo is right there, wiping away the stray tear with his thumb. "What is it, Beastie? Did we hurt you?"

"No." I shake my head with a teary smile on my face. "You made me the happiest woman on earth."

"In that case, never have I ever been happy to see tears," he says, swiping them from my cheeks and my shoulders shake with silent laughs.

"I thought we were done with that game a long time ago."

"None of it was ever a game to me, Zoe. It was just me getting to know the love of my life a little better."

THE END.

Afterword

Wellllll, another happy couple of Loverly Cave concluded their journey.

(Don't Worry, there are more to come ;)

Ah, what can I say? Zoe and especially Matteo stole my heart! I loved writing this book so much. I truly enjoyed every second of it. It was everything I wanted to have in a feel-good story, and I really hope those feelings were conveyed. Yes, there was no real angst here and I hope that didn't disappoint you guys.

Also, can I take a moment to say that some of the tropes (*kinks*) in this book took me by complete surprise and never have I ever thought that I would be so into them. With that being said, please expect more reverse age gap stories and definitely more of those *kinks ;)* in the future.

Thank you for taking yet another chance on my books. And if you have enjoyed it, I would really appreciate it if you could leave your review. It tremendously helps me as an indie author.

Acknowledgements

First and foremost, thank you to each and every one of you for you for picking up this book! It means more than you know to me that you guys enjoy what I write and my crazy silly town.

To my Beta team, a huge thank you to the best beta team a girl could have! Annie, Yana, Nat, Cat, Kaz, Tameka, your input, comments, suggestions and love for my stories are what keeps me going. Without you all my books would not be the same! I don't know what I have done to deserve you!

To my seester, Lemmy and her baby Luna PR, honestly, I'd be lost without you! There are no other words. Thank you for going above and beyond for me. For making my release day special and the journey to it, easy. There is no one else I'd rather have in my corner!

Mo, if you think I could possibly forget you here, nope! THANK YOU, for giving me the best freaking inspiration and letting me use it in my book! Zoe would not be the same without it. * Cough, cough * Violent sleeping ;)

To Caroline at Love and Edits, thank you for working your magic on my books and catching all those mistakes I throw around like Halloween candy. You are the best!

Thank you, my amazing ARC team, for once again believing in my story and giving it a try!

Also by

Race Me series:
Race Me Never
Race Me New
Race Me Now
Race Me ...
Race Me ...

***

The Demons of New York series:
My Broken Demon
My Shameless Angel
My Heartless Soul

***

Loverly Cave series:
The Romance is Dead
Meet My Wife
Running to my Soulmate
Tame the Beast
Book 5
Book 6

About the author

Daisy Thorn enjoyed living in her fictional world since she could understand what dreaming meant, until one day, she decided to put all those dreams on paper. However, she can't pick one lane and keeps swerving between romantic comedy and dark romance. It keeps things interesting in her head.

Daisy is obsessed with four things in this life: Her daughters, Harry Potter, Reading and Peanut M&Ms.

Weird fact about Daisy: she doesn't drink coffee. Crazy author!

***For more fun facts visit www.daisythorn.com

With Love & Always Yours,

Daisy Thorn